A WITCH, HER CAT AND THE SHIP WRECKERS.
A tale of a Scarborough Witch, her Cat, Ship Wreckers and highwaymen.

By Graham A. Rhodes

First published 2016
Internet Kindle Edition 2016

Templar Publishing Scarborough N. Yorkshire
Copyright G. A. Rhodes 2016

Conditions of Sale.

Also available in the Agnes the Scarborough Witch series -

A Witch, Her Cat and a Pirate:
A story of a Scarborough witch, her cat and John Paul Jones

A Witch, Her Cat, and the Devil Dogs.
A story of a Scarborough witch and bad things occurring on the North Yorkshire Moors

Dedication

This is the second book of Agnes. It would have been impossible without the help and encouragement of the following people –

Yvonne, Jesse, Frankie & Heather (& Granddad), Richard, Chris, The Badgers Of Bohemia, Jo, Tubbs & Missy, Ellie, Emma, Lucy, Magenta, Anna (Whose gig at the SJT Started all this off) & all at Cellars, Dennis & Dave, Ysanne in the hope that one day it will turn up in her bookshop. Oh and my long time Dutch friend Jan van der Vlies whose name I have borrowed. Get this in the Dutch curriculum my friend.

Many of the streets and places mentioned in this book still exist in Scarborough's old town and up on the moors. They are well worth visiting. Once again I have taken the liberty of using the names of old Scarborough fishing families. I hope they don't mind their ancestors appearing here. However the names and characters are all fictitious and should not be confused with anyone living or dead.

Graham Rhodes, Scarborough 2016.

List of Characters

Agnes 21st & 18th Centuries

Our hero, an elderly lady who, as far as she knows is over three hundred years old. She has no memory of who she is or where she came from. She lives in the same cottage in the Old Town of Scarborough in both centuries. She is either a wize woman or a witch, depending on who is telling the story. She is also a rather excellent computer hacker.

Marmaduke 21st & 18th Centuries

Marmaduke lives with Agnes in her cottage. In the twenty first he is an old, grumpy, one eared, one eyed, sardine addicted cat. In the 18th century he is a one eyed one eared six foot high ex-highwayman with very dangerous habits.

Andrew Marks 18th Century

The proprietor of the Chandlery situated on Scarborough's 17thcentury harbourside. Andrew is the eyes and ears of the small port. Nothing comes or goes in or out the port without him knowing about it, either legal or illegal.

The Garrison Commander 18th Century

The military commander of the Garrison based at Scarborough's Castle. Posted to Scarborough for a mistake he made during the American War of

Independence he is very definitely a soldier of the old school.

Lieutenant Smalls
A young military man and the right hand man of the Garrison Commander. An intelligent and thoughtful officer who could go far.

Sergeant Lewis
A regular army sergeant, ambitious and always on the look-out for a free breakfast.

Whitby John
Ex-fisherman and landlord of The Three Mariners Agnes favourite public house.

Salmon Martin
A fisherman and regular of the Three Mariners.

Andrew Stott
Fisherman

Jim Pullin
Fisherman
Baccy Lad
A young lad eager to please and helper at the Three Mariners

Dancing Jack
A highwayman with a secret.

Ex-Colonel Thomas Reynard
A jolly bad sort.

Grimes
The Colonels right hand man, also a very bad sort.

The Colonel With No Name
Military Intelligence

Dammit Johnson
Just unlucky.

Three Builders
They think they are builders Agnes discoverers
otherwise

A WITCH, HER CAT AND THE SHIP WRECKERS.

Chapter One

The night was as black as pitch. The wind roared out of the north causing the waves to rise higher and higher, crashing over the deck of the small ship that was trying to make a run towards the nearest safe harbour. On the deck the helmsman was valiantly struggling to keep the ship on course. The rain poured off the brim of his hat and ran into his eyes, but despite not being able to see and his eyes stinging with the salt water, he knew if he took one hand from the steering wheel to wipe his face his other arm, as strong as it was, was not strong enough to hold the wheel steady and prevent it from spinning out of control. He shook his head to try to rid himself of the water.

Next to him the ships' captain steadied himself by gripping the rail in front of him with both hands, silently cursing himself for trying to outrun the storm. A new sound rose above that of the storm.

He looked anxiously up into the night, trying to see through the driving rain and the sea spray. He couldn't see anything but heard the manic flapping and tearing of one of the top sails. As he turned his head to rid the spray from his face he thought he could make out a small pin point of light flickering in the distance. At first he thought he was seeing things. He tried to rise his eye glass but the wind was too strong for him to let go of his grip on the rail, let alone lift his telescope up to his face.

Words were useless, swept away by the noise of the wind and the lashing rain. He nudged the helmsman and nodded towards the tiny point of light that kept appearing and disappearing in the driving clouds of rain and sea spray. The helmsman looked in the direction that the captain had nodded, saw the light and, with a mighty heave of the wheel he felt the grinding and the groans of the ships timbers as the three masted ketch struggled to turn against the wind and the tide. The Captain squinted into the storm and the darkness trying to make out the position of the light.

"Must be the light at Scarborough Castle!" he shouted, but his words were taken and lost in the noise of the storm. His mind raced. According to his calculations he had figured Scarborough harbour and safety to be over an hour away. There again, he heard himself argue, the storm and the wind had probably blown them further south at a greater speed than he first estimated.

He was still running his rough calculations through his head when the noise of the storm was drowned out by another, newer sound. A heart stopping sound of grating and crashing, of grinding and splintering. Suddenly the ship gave a violent lurch upwards and he found himself falling backwards. As he fell his last sight was that of his helmsman being suddenly thrown sideways and disappearing over the side of the ship leaving the wheel to spin crazily out of control. There was another great crash as the ship reared up even higher, tearing itself apart on a reef of jagged rocks that shouldn't be there.

Chapter Two

As the wind and rain battered at her window Agnes held her cup of tea tight to her chest and murmured in annoyance at her television as the picture broke up, froze and pixilated itself. She turned to the cat sat curled up in the chair beside her.

"The storms dislodged the aerial. That's another thing to put on the list!"

The cat ignored her.

"I suppose I'll have to get someone in to fix it if only for the look of things!"

That annoyed Agnes. She knew full well that with her powers she could fix the aerial in any number of creative ways. She could easily get onto her roof. All she had to do was take the mind and body of a seagull, and there was certainly no shortage of them. However once up there a seagull couldn't adjust the aerial. Seagulls have no hands and aerial adjustment was definitely a two handed job. She toyed with the idea of once she was on the roof reverting to her normal form, but sighed as she realised the consequences of a neighbour suddenly seeing a little old lady perched on the apex of her own roof. That wouldn't do. She didn't want another visit from the woman from Social Services. As it was they already had compiled a large file dedicated just to her. She knew, she'd read it. Out of curiosity, after the last visit she had sat at her scrying bowl and watched as her social worker "Call me Maddy, everyone does!" sit at her desk and make notes in the file. It was easy to read over her shoulder. What wasn't easy was reading what people had written about her. It seemed that someone, somewhere had made the suggestion that she be put on some "at risk" register, for no other reason than she was an elderly woman living by herself. She had laughed at that.

If only they knew how old she really was. There again she didn't really know herself. She had lost both interest and count after she had passed three hundred. Just before she broke the spell of her scrying bowl she cast a small spell and sent it off into the water. She would like to have been around the next day when her file would be found with all the pages blank. There again, as nice a thought as it was, she didn't really need a cheap laugh. She was beyond that. Actually she wasn't. Even a three hundred year old witch needs a laugh now and again. Anyway it wasn't a laugh, it was more of a guffaw.

Back to the problem of the aerial. She looked at the television set and, with a brief movement of her hand and fingers, the image on the screen unfroze, flickered and sprang back into life. She hadn't even made it back to her chair before there was a blinding flash followed by a loud bang that it made the cat leap from its prone position in the chair to suddenly find itself hanging by its claws from the top of the curtains, before the flash had faded away. Agnes blinked as she realised that her house had been struck by lightning!

It must have been the magic aerial she had created.
It must have attracted the electrical storm. Making
sure that nothing was actually burning she stamped
into the kitchen, waved her hand and magicked up
herself a steaming mug of hot, strong and very black
coffee. There was a muted ripping, tearing sort of
noise coming from the living room and she turned
just in time to see the cat falling in slow motion, its
claws ripping the curtains as it fell back onto the
sofa. As it arrived on the cushion it looked angrily
back towards the kitchen. Agnes hid a smile and
drank her coffee.

The following morning Agnes had to put up with
visit after visit from anxious neighbours asking her,
in very concerned voices, all about the lightening
strike and enquiring about her health. Oh it was
good to see them. They were, generally speaking,
kind and caring folk. But they did get in the way,
and hindered her in getting things sorted out. She
could hardly magic her chimneystack back together
again when the entire street had seen its bricks and

shattered chimneypots spread all over the cobbles. What wasn't on the pavement was through her own roof. No there was no possible way out of this, she would have to call in the builders. That would certainly complicate matters.

It was lunchtime before the woman from the council arrived. Evidently after two and a half cups of tea, Agnes gathered that someone, somewhere in the council offices had made a suggestion that whilst her house was being repaired Agnes should consider the option of self-referral into a local care home.

Ten minutes later the social worker found herself back in the street holding a jar of home-made jam in one hand and a jar of home-made chutney in the other and wondering why anyone back at the office could think that the elderly woman she had just seen was incapable of looking after herself.

Agnes had hardly shut her front door when the builders arrived. Agnes blinked as she opened the door. In her own mind she had assumed that finding a builder who could actually start the job would take a couple of days at the very least. Finding a builder that could start the job immediately would probably take a deal longer. The one she assumed was in charge explained. It turned out they were the friend of a friend of a neighbour who they owed a favour to and that they had some spare time between jobs, and well, a favour is a favour and as they only lived a few streets away. Agnes nodded in submission. They could begin the work straight away.

It took a little while for Agnes to realise just why the builders had so much spare time between jobs. It was simply that they were not very good builders.

After the morning she had experienced Agnes felt like she needed a drink, and one a lot stronger than tea of coffee. As she headed towards the cellar doors she suddenly realised she hadn't warned the builders about the cat. Neither had she warned the cat about the builders. Oh well she thought, they'll be a nice surprise for each other. She shut the cellar door behind her. Halfway down the stairs she suddenly turned towards the wall and walked straight through it.

Almost as quickly as she disappeared she reappeared, only now she was dressed in clothes belonging to another century, the eighteenth century to be précis, which by happy coincidence was exactly the time and year she and her house were now in. She walked out of her cellar, through her eighteenth century living room, out of her front door and into the maze of tiny streets and alleyways that made up the Old Town of eighteenth century Scarborough.

As soon as she was in the street she realised she had escaped from one storm damaged cottage to another. By the broken slates and smashed bit of brick covering the cobbled street she realised the previous nights storm hadn't just occurred in the twenty first century. A mighty storm had also battered the town the same night almost three hundred years previously. She was pondering on the possibilities of coincidence and parallel universes when a small figure ran around the corner and almost knocked her over.

The young boy stopped in his tracks when he saw who he had just avoided.

"Now then young William, Where are you off to in such a hurry?"

The young lad looked up at Agnes with trepidation and a bit of a wobbly bottom lip. The last person anyone in the Old Town wanted to upset was Agnes, the local wize woman. Like most of the children in the Old Town he had been brought to respect Agnes, especially as he had been told many, many times that if he was naughty his parents would go see Agnes and ask her to turn him into a frog. She wouldn't of course but she had no problems in being held in respect. After all there wasn't a family in the entire Old Town that hadn't benefitted from her wisdom, her knowledge of herbs and potions, and in very special circumstances, a little wriggle of her fingers to create a spell that made their hard lives just that little bit easier.

He held her penetrating gaze. "Mi Dad told me to get to the Customs House as quick as I could. There's a wreck on the rocks just of Hayburnwyke!"

Agnes wondered how the news had spread so quickly. It was only mid-morning, but then a shipwreck would be a major event up and down the coast and bad news travels fast. Mind you Hayburnwyke was only five or six miles up the coast. An hour's ride on a decent horse. She reached into her pocket and pulled out a small and battered bag of sweets. She shook the bag in the direction of the young boy. He looked at the bag with deep suspicion.

"They are sweets!" Agnes remarked.

The boy stretched out his hand and felt inside the bag. His fingers found something hard and round. They closed around it and he pulled out a large bull's eye. His eyes grew even wider. Down the shop near the harbour those sweets cost the best part of a halfpenny, each! He stood looking at the treasure.

"Go on, take it, and you'd better be off to deliver your message!"

The boy suddenly remembered about the urgency of the message he carried. He popped the sweet into his mouth. Muttered a thank you and continued on his way down the street. As soon as he thought Agnes had turned round he broke out into a run again.

"And watch where you're going!" Agnes shouted after him. She had abandoned her idea of a walk. Instead she returned to her cottage, walked straight through the living room, into the kitchen and straight out into her own back yard. A shipwreck up the coast deserved her attention.

There was a slight shimmering in the air and a seagull suddenly appeared. No one in the Old Town paid any attention to yet another seagull rising up into the air.

Chapter Three

It took about fifteen minutes for Agnes to fly up the coast. As she crossed the North Bay she could make out the distant headland. Hayburnwyke itself was at the centre of the next small bay. She flew higher, increasing her range of vision. Then she saw it. A large three masted ship had broken its back on the rocks that stretched out from under the headland at the far end of the bay. As she approached she could make out the broken timbers and wreckage, the broken masts and tangles of ropes and rigging and sail that swirling around in the water, caught in the turning tide. In an hour or so it would be high tide once again and what remained of the wreck would be washed out to sea. As she approached the site she could make out a group of men moving along the small rocky beach. Some were carefully moving among the rocks pulling at ropes, dragging broken timbers behind them.

Agnes's first thought was sabotage. At the far end of the beach she could see that someone had dragged four bodies out of the water and laid them out in a small grim row under the small cliff at the centre of the bay. She gave a slight shudder as she realised it must be the bodies of the members of the stricken ships' crew. She landed in a wood that covered the top of the cliff. There was another slight shimmering of the air and suddenly the figure of an elderly woman appeared at the top of the path that led down to the rocky beach.

As she emerged from the woodland and stepped onto the open beach a figure dressed in rough clothes and wearing a huge pair of sea boots approached her. Agnes recognised him; it was Andrew Stott a fisherman who ran a small ketch out of Scarborough Harbour.

As they neared each other he gave a grunt "Might have known you would show up sooner or later!" he said.

Agnes smiled. "You know me Andrew; I like to keep a weather eye on what's going on!"

Andrew pulled at his whiskers with his hand. "Aye. You're always there, I'll give you that. Especially when there's bad news."

Agnes' smile didn't move. "Usually that's when people need my help the most!"

Andrew moved to wipe his nose with the sleeve of his old and battered pullover. As he began the movement he suddenly noticed the look on Agnes' face and thought better, he dropped his arm self consciously down by his side.

"I once told you off for doing that when you were a nipper!" She said.

His face, made ruddy by the weather, went even redder. "I know I remember!"

A thought crossed his mind. That telling off must have been over thirty years ago now, and he still remembered it. It also crossed his mind that, despite him growing thirty years older, Agnes hadn't aged at all. In fact she hadn't changed at all, he even suspected she was wearing the same clothing.

Agnes could sense the direction in which Andrews thoughts were travelling. Well it was no use in having a sixth sense without using it. She also made full use of her seventh and eighth senses as well when he needed to. She wriggled her little finger slightly and suddenly, without Andrew even realising it she changed to subject and all thoughts of her age left Andrews mind as quickly as they arrived.

"So what do you think happened?" She nodded towards the wreckage of the ship that was slowly being battered and broken up by the waves pounding the rocks.

Andrew turned "Looks like it ran onto them rocks at the end of Black Nab. Must have lost its direction in last night's storm."

He shook his head. "Should never have been that close to the shore. By the way I hope you checked your roof this morning. From what I hear everyone was busy first thing picking up their roof tiles from the middle of the road. I heard your chimney was a bit wonky."

Agnes nodded towards the shipwreck. "At least no one in town was hurt by the storm."

Andrew followed her gaze. "Aye, we've only found four of the crew. I have a feeling there's another two bodies floating around out there somewhere."

Agnes raised an eyebrow and Andrew scratched his beard. "I figure a ship that size would have at least six crew members. Maybe more...but I hope not!"

Agnes changed the subject "What was she carrying?"

"Well we found her cargo of timber, and a few kegs of butter, but I've a feeling there was a lot more on board than just those. I found a couple of kegs of gin floating among the wreckage. There was room on that ship for a devil of a lot more."

Agnes nodded. "Who was here first?"

"As far as I can make things out, us! Five of us. Me, Jim Pullin, Salmon John, Old Mathew Goodie and Peter Mainprize. We saw it as soon as we passed yon headland. We'd left the harbour just afore high tide. We were aiming for them fishing grounds just to the north of here. This time of year there's a good few cod to be caught off them rocks."

Agnes looked out to the sea. "Where are...."

Andrew nodded northwards. "We beached up the other side of the headland. Safer landing there. Tide was low so we walked round the nab. Better keep an eye on it though. Another hour and we'll be in danger of getting cut off."

Agnes was thinking. "When you arrived was the beach deserted?"

Andrew nodded. "Apart from the bodies, yes."

Agnes asked the obvious question. "So where did the cargo go?"

Andrew gave a shrug. Then he felt her stare boring into him. He looked down at his sea boots. "Well we might just have found a couple of kegs bobbing around out there. Be a shame and a waste to let them float away!"

Agnes gave a half smile. She knew full well that the proceeds from just one keg would feed and clothe a family like the Stott's for at least a couple of months.

"I'm not talking about flotsam!" Agnes said. "I'm talking about the rest of the cargo. Just how many kegs do you think she could have been carrying?"

Andrew turned and looked towards the remains of what had once been a small trading vessel.

"Maybe fifty at the most!" he replied.

"So where are they?" Agnes mused, more to herself than to anyone else.

Andrew cast an anxious look towards the sea. The tide was coming in and the sea was rising.

"We'll have to make a move soon." He said. Agnes gave him one of those looks. "How did young Tommy know about the wreck? I bumped, or rather he bumped into me in the Old Town. He said his dad had sent him to the Customs House to tell them about the wreck!"

Andrew sniffed. Aye that would be about right. When we saw what had happened Tommy's dad turned around to go back to Scarborough to let someone know what we'd found."

"That was decent of him!" Agnes remarked with a sniff.

Andrew gave another shrug and answered in what was very much like a whisper. "Aye well we promised him a share in whatever we could find!"

Agnes nodded in understanding. Suddenly a frown crossed Andrews's forehead. "Mind you, he said thoughtfully, "By rights and given a fair wind and a running tide he could only have got there in the last half hour at the very least." He looked at Agnes. "How did you get here so fast?"

Agnes gave him her sweetest butter wouldn't melt in her mouth sort of smile. "I jumped on my broomstick and flew here!"

Andrew wasn't impressed. "I wouldn't put it past you!" he said.

Agnes sighed. "You know full well Andrew; if I told you my secrets I'd have to turn you into a frog, or a salmon. That would be more fitting don't you think?"

She moved her fingers just a little bit, the air moved ever so slightly, and Andrew forgot he'd asked a question if the first place.

"Better get going! I take it you'll be making your own way back to the town?" Agnes nodded and Andrew turned and crunched his way across the pebbles and the shingle. As he approached the rocks where the wreck laid he put his fingers to his mouth and gave a shrill whistle. As the sound echoed around the cliffs, Agnes noticed four or five figures appear between the rocks. They all met by the base of the headland before disappearing into the next bay. As they stumbled among the rocks Agnes noted they were all struggling valiantly to walk among the rocks whilst holding what appeared to be a keg under each arm.

She watched whilst the men disappeared and walked along the beach keeping close to base of the small cliff. Somehow someone must have been here. Someone must have been here either during the night, or very early in the morning, just after the storm, and that, she realised with a little shiver down her spine, whoever was here must have expected a ship.

She gave the matter some thought as she walked among the pebbles and small rocks. Perhaps the ship was a smuggler itself, one that took one risk too many. Perhaps whoever was on the beach was expecting another ship. Perhaps... She shook her head. Too many perhaps and not enough facts. She looked seaward just in time to see the fishing boats rounding the headland, heading back towards Scarborough harbour. She knew that in the evening to come she would be able to buy a glass of cheap Dutch gin in every pub and tavern along the harbourside, and beyond.

It was an hour later when she found the first clue. The tide had come in and the wreck was shifting, sliding and breaking up as the waves tossed it further onto the rocks and dragged wooden spars and timbers away to float further and further off-shore. She had spent the last hour criss-crossing the beach and the rocks, looking for anything that shouldn't be there. She eventually found it in a small patch of long grass where the cliff suddenly dropped to the beach, making what seemed to be a small track that led through the woodland and back up towards the top of the cliff. It was a horse shoe. Not an old rusty one, but one that had been made recently. It was still shiny and didn't seem worn. She followed the track for a few yards and found some torn branches and a mess of foot and hoof prints. So somebody had been here. Now she had a fact.

The air around her shimmered and a gull rose into the air. It gave a couple of slow wing beats and glided up the small rift in the cliff following the small track as it weaved its way through the woodland below.

The path emerged at the top of the cliff and led across a field before joining a longer road that followed the line of the cliff top. Agnes knew if she travelled south she would pass through the village of Burniston before reaching Scarborough. If she travelled north she would come to the village mof Cloughton and the road leading across the moors to Whitby. Which way had the horses and men gone? You takes your choice.

There was another shimmer and suddenly at the junction of where the two roads met an elderly woman suddenly appeared. She stood looking up and down the larger road. Despite it now being deserted, looking at its pitted and muddy surface it was very apparent that a heavy morning's traffic had come and gone its way, across the surface was a network of footprints, hoof prints and cart tracks. Agnes concentrated her power, trying to tune into a trace of a feeling. Nothing! In actual fact, she told herself, she had very little to tune into, just thirty or forty kegs of Dutch Gin, and the men who carried them. It was impossible to make out any clue as to the who's, what's and how's. The trail ended here.

There was another shimmering of the air and a seagull rose into the air and flew towards Scarborough. Agnes made a point of landing in her own back yard. She thought that turning up at the harbour inside the next two hours would cause Andrew Stott to ask even more and harder questions. Questions that would be difficult to deflect. She walked into her kitchen, into her cellar, through the wall and returned to the twenty first century just in time to see a scaffolding pole crash through her living room window. It was late afternoon and the builders had started their work.

Chapter Four

The rest of Agnes's day passed in another flurry of
visits from neighbours, a glazier and a sudden and
complete absence of builders. That night she
planned to sleep in her bed in the eighteenth century
as she had very little faith in the security offered by
a tarpaulin stretched over the hole in her twenty first
century roof. This time she took her cat with her. As
they stepped through the wall the cat changed.
Instead of an angry ginger tom cat she was now
accompanied by a tall, muscular, angry, ginger
haired man with a fine set of whiskers, a ginger
beard, a missing ear and wearing a black eye patch
over one eye. He stared at Agnes with his one good
one.

"Would you be so kind as to explain just what is
going on?" he purred, stroking the back of his head
with his hand, pausing only to lick the back of his
hand before patting his hair into place.

Agnes stepped back and tried to ignore the cat like movements the man was making. She knew full well the transition took some time to occur. In fact sometimes where food was concerned the transitions didn't happen at all. Many times she'd pulled him up for drinking out of a saucer and, as to getting him to use a knife and fork, well she gave up on that years ago. She had contemplated using magic, but figured that, as a twenty first century cat who frequently went back through time to become a 18th century rogue, ruffian and ex-highwayman, he was probably too full of magic for hers to make any difference. Instead she made do with her special look. After all, that special look had been known to put fear into the hearts and minds of the bigger, tougher and rougher men she had occasioned across in her many years.

"There's been a shipwreck". She said.

Marmaduke stopped stroking the back of his head. "I was actually talking about those three jesters that claim to be builders!" he replied.

Although she was beginning to have doubts herself about the ability of the builders she wasn't about to admit it. "They are fixing the roof." She said, more defensively than she intended.

Marmaduke raised an eyebrow. "Is that why they put that big metal rod through our front window?"

"It was an accident!" she countered.

"It was stupidity." Marmaduke replied.

She didn't really have an answer to that so she marched into the kitchen. Marmaduke followed and rummaged in the cupboard emerging with two tins of sardines.

"Toast?" Agnes asked.

Marmaduke let out a small cat like growl.

"No toast!" Agnes answered her own question.

She tried to ignore the way he hooked the small tomato sauce covered fish out of the tin with his long finger nail as she told him the story of her morning and what she had discovered at Hayburnwyke.

Finally after he had licked each of his fingers clean he sat back in the chair.

"You're probably right! Someone knew that ship was expected. That means there are only three possibilities. One...." he held his finger up and got distracted by a bit of sardine that he'd somehow missed. Agnes waited patiently until the finger had been licked clean and then inspected just in case a trace had been missed,

"....is that it was a smuggling operation gone badly wrong. Or two...." he held up a second finger and looked at it closely. Agnes held her annoyance in check as the second finger received its close examination. Nothing was found so Marmaduke continued. "...it could be the work of wreckers!"

Agnes nodded.

"Or three, it's a huge coincidence that men with horses, and I presume some sort of transport large enough to carry thirty kegs of gin off the beach, just happened to be there at the same time that a large ship carrying gin wrecked itself on the very rocks they were standing on!" he let out another cat like growl. "I won't be putting any of my money on the third option!"

Agnes filled the kettle and placed it on the unlit stove. She wriggled her fingers and a jet of steam blew out of its spout. She rummaged in her pocket and pulled out two very twenty first century teabags. No matter how hard she tried, no matter what herbs, lotions and potions she used she was resigned to the fact that she could never magic up a cup of tea as good as the one produced from a little white bag by a man called Tetley.

They sat in silence deep in thought as they drank their tea. Agnes was using her favourite mug that proclaimed she was "The World's Best Granny!" Ignoring protocol as usual, Marmaduke sipped his from his saucer.

"Smugglers or wreckers?" She finally said.

Marmaduke looked up from his saucer. "The only way to know for sure is to find out who did it."

Agnes looked up. "Well any news of contraband gin is bound to get around. The folk in the Three Mariners would be the first to know."

Marmaduke shook his head. "No it won't work like that. Thirty kegs is far too much to get rid of locally. Word of that amount of gin around would soon reach the ears of the excise men. No, that contraband is heading inland. It'll go to a prearranged meeting place and be split up into smaller loads of six or seven kegs. It will be in York, or Malton, or Thirsk, maybe as far as Leeds in a matter of days. Moving a shipment of thirty kegs in secret takes some organisation, both in the getting and getting rid of." He paused and then added, "There's no one around here with those sorts of connections."

Agnes topped her cup up with some hot water and retrieved a tea bag from its place on the draining board and dunked it in her mug a couple of times. She took a gulp.

"Well there's not a lot we can do. We can't examine every cart between here and wherever. Whoever it was came and went and are now long gone."

"Anything for a quiet life" remarked Marmaduke as he tried and failed to lick behind his left ear.

The next couple of weeks went quietly. Well as quietly as it can be with three builders attempting to do a job that day by day was proving far too difficult for them. Fearful that they would never get to finish the job Agnes took to inspecting their day's work every evening after they had gone home and added a little tweak of magic here and there. A special type of magic that secured loose bolts, re-cemented crooked brickwork, and strengthened the new roof beams, which even to her untrained eye were nowhere near strong enough to hold the roof up without her intervention. Of course Agnes would never call what she used magic. In her mind they were just little tricks. Little tweaks to reality. She never understood how, but there again, she had been doing it for so long now that she had given up on reasoning the whys and wherefores. Many years ago she figured that to go down that line of self questioning would eventually drive her mad. So she stopped thinking about it, accepted it, and just did it. Oddly enough the more she didn't think about it the stronger her powers seemed to become.

Indeed for a "wise woman" there was a lot she didn't know. For a start she didn't understand where she herself came from. Try as she might she could never remember her mother or father, or where she was born. Try as she may she could never remember being a child. Her memories were always of herself as an elderly woman with some strong powers over reality. She had given worrying about that years ago as well.

Every couple of days Agnes would slip back to the eighteenth century and spend long evenings sat in her special chair by the fireside in the bar room of The Three Mariners. Sitting there sipping her glass of gin, she would tune into the various conversations ebbing and flowing all around her. She discovered the latest price of coal, that a seal had been seen at the harbour mouth. That whale oil had nearly double in price, that Mrs Mainprize was expecting again. Just the rounds of local daily gossip, night after night. Still at least it got her away from the builders who now after "repairing the roof" were now attempting and failing to reconstruct her chimney stack. Twice now innocent passing tourists had nearly been killed by bricks falling from the roof.

As the conversations of the eighteenth century drifted around her Agnes took a final gulp of gin, winced and contemplated whether she should finish the chimney herself and stare at the builders long and hard enough so they would believe they had successfully completed the job themselves.

Desperate situations called for desperate solutions. Marmaduke hadn't helped. Back in his twenty first century cat form he had taken to hiding in dark corners and jumping out at the unsuspecting builders with all claws outstretched.

That added to the delays by destroying what little concentration they had. It proved a very difficult task to hammer a nail into a piece of wood whilst keeping one eye open for the ginger menace.

Chapter Five

The man gave a silent curse as his foot slipped on the wet seaweed and he flailed his free arm to keep his balance and prevent himself from falling backwards into the rockpool. The night was moonless and so dark that he was unable to see where he was treading. He stumbled on towards a line of large, jagged rocks that stretched out into the sea. He couldn't see them but knew they were there. He'd practised the scramble among the rocks during daylight hours and had counted the paces between each obstruction. He knew he was almost there.

Over the sound of the wind he could hear the distant whinnying of the horses hidden along with their riders under a cliff, taking cover in a small wood that swept down from the land to reach the end of a small shingle beach. It had taken him days to find such a track leading onto such an inlet. At last he came to a large rock that stood higher than the rest.

He checked the wind. It was strong, but not blowing a gale, yet. He felt along the surface of the rock until his hand slid over the edge. He moved his hand down feeling along the side that faced seaward until he found it. The small alcove that he had cut out of the rock that provided a safe niche from the wind. His hand felt the band of metal that he had used to secure the lantern into position the previous day. He squatted down behind the rock, protected from the wind and pulled out his tinder box and struck a spark. The spark lit the kindling and he used a small piece of tarred rope to transfer the flame from the tinder to the wick inside the lantern. He waited a couple of minutes to make sure the flame held and the lantern remained lit before lowering the lantern glass. With a final glance out into the darkness where the incoming tide was rising, he turned and felt and stumbled his way back across the bay to join his fellow wreckers and their horses.

Chapter Six

Agnes was sitting in her usual seat in the Three
Mariners when word reached her. Another small
trading vessel had run aground on rocks to the north
of Hayburnwyke. She quickly gathered all the news
that had reached Scarborough. Evidently the wreck
had happened two days ago but the news had only
just filtered through. It had been a calm dark night
with a high running tide. Rumour had it that the ship
was heading to Hull when it hit the hidden reef
somewhere just south of Black Nab. The incident
had been attended to by crew put together by the
Robin Hoods Bay fishermen. It was said that there
were no survivors and by the time the rescuers had
arrived the ship had already broken up on the rocks
losing both its crew and its cargo. Agnes made
enquiries as to what the cargo was.

"Not even sure what ship it was!" Came the answer.

"They keep their cards close to their chest do those lot up at The Bay!" another voice said.

Agnes got up and left the inn. She knew exactly who would know what ship was missing and where "lost" cargos might reappear, and it wasn't the harbourmaster. It was Andrew Marks, the man who ran a ships chandlery business on the harbourside. Nothing moved along the Yorkshire Coast without him knowing about it. Rumour had it that he ran one of the largest smuggling operations in the North East, but everyone knows that rumour and fact are two very different things. However if Andrew didn't run the operation himself, he certainly knew the men who did.

Andrew sighed when he saw Agnes walk into his shop. When she saw him he quickly moved his head in the direction of his office. Whatever she wanted Andrew wanted their conversation to be private. Agnes disquieted him. He knew her, he knew her reputation and he knew that she knew more about his business dealings than anyone other than himself should know. It further annoyed him that, once in his office she sat in his favourite leather backed chair.

"What can I do for you today Agnes?" he asked.

"Well good afternoon to you too. With the exception of my roof I'm fine. Thank you for asking!"

Andrew felt himself redden. She had only been on the premises for less than five minutes and she had him on the wrong foot already. This was going to be a long meeting.

"Stop looking so worried!" Agnes said and smiled. It was the kind of smile that just made him worry even more. "I'm not after complaining, nor am I going to ask anything about a certain shipment of silk that happens to be languishing in your store room."

"How the devil do you know about that?" The words were out before Andrew realised he had spoken aloud.

Agnes kept smiling "I know most of what's going on!" she replied.

Andrew pulled his jacket down and considered sitting on the desk. Then he thought better of it and sat in the second best office chair.

"But not everything, otherwise you wouldn't be here" he said.

"True!"

There was a silence that Andrew eventually broke. "Well then, how can I help you?"

"I'm after making enquiries about the ship that went down a couple of days ago now. Up Robin Hood Bay way."

Andrew nodded and Agnes continued.

"I was after knowing the name of the ship and the cargo she was carrying."

Andrew gave a little grunt. "Handled by the rescuers up in the Bay. No survivors, no idea of the cargo or the name for that matter, probably washed away, unless that lot from the Bay got it first."

"You'd know if a cargo suddenly appeared?"

Andrew shook his head. "Not if they took it up Whitby way. It takes me all my time to keep a track of cargoes coming in and out of here. Let them lot up there look after themselves, they usually do."

Agnes looked at him closer. It didn't make Andrew feel any better. "So there's no ship due in port that hasn't turned up yet?"

"If you are asking if some merchant is anxiously walking up and down the harbourside wringing his hands asking after a missing ship and cargo, no!"

Agnes raised an eyebrow. In any conversation she usually reserved the position of sarcasm for herself.

Andrew noticed the eyebrow and read it as the subtle warning it held. "No, nothing that was due is overdue. Mind you a lot of shipping turns up unannounced, despite the Customs and Excise men."

Agnes changed tack. "And you don't know anything about how a cargo of gin magicked its way from that wreck over at Hayburnwyke?"

Andrew snorted. "You mean that gin that suddenly turned up in every hotel and inn and hostelry between here and Filey?"

Agnes smiled again. "Oh I know about that. I know where that came from. Legitimate salvage I believe!"

Again Andrew noticed the direction Agnes was heading for and deftly avoided it. "Nothing wrong in legitimate salvage. It's just they undercut every supplier around!"

Agnes's eyes narrowed. "You mean you...."

Andrew cut her off. "I mean thanks to "legitimate salvage" I still have five kegs of Dutch gin in the cellars. Five kegs I can't sell."

Agnes tutted. "You mean you can't get rid of them at a decent profit. You will. Be patient. There were only seven or eight kegs. They'll soon run out and you'll be able to sell at you're normal price. Business will soon be back to normal!"

"I know that. It's just that I'm a bit uncomfortable holding it for any great length of time." He looked around and lowered his voice. "You never know when the Excise men will drop by!"

Agnes understood. She nodded. "Well it was but a hope."

Suddenly a penny at the back of Andrews head dropped. Agnes wouldn't come to him asking questions for nothing, for no good reason. She must know something about something that he didn't know. That worried him. Agnes might be good with her herbal cures and her advice but she definitely could be bad for his business.

"May I be as bold as to ask why you are interested in that wreck and its gin?"

Agnes sat back in his chair and gave him one of her special looks. "I don't suppose then you have any idea where a cargo of between twenty or thirty kegs of gin could have disappeared to?"

Andrew shook his head. "I heard of the missing cargo from Andrew Stotts own lips. Believe me Agnes, if I knew of the whereabouts of that amount of gin I would be a very rich man."

"How much is it worth?"

"It's not the value of the gin. Didn't you know the Excise Office has put out a reward for information?"

"So they know about it and are investigating the wreck?"

Andrew sniffed. "They know because the ship's owners also want to know what happened to their cargo and the ship's owners have friends in high places who ask awkward questions. By rights when Andrew arrived on the scene he should have seen the sea awash with kegs of gin. There were only about a dozen. They didn't think it worth their while contesting Andrews salvage claim, and by investigation, if you mean have the Excise got around to offering a reward and printing handbills yes. If you mean has anyone actually left their building and gone to the site of the wreck and looked around, no."

"So the ship wasn't on an illicit smuggling run and just got unlucky?"

Andrew looked shocked at her suggestion. "Good Lord no. It was a legitimate coastal trader working between Newcastle and Hull. Mainly carrying timber, some coal, and anything else the owners could cram into its hold."

"Why was it carrying so much gin?" Agnes asked

Andrew sighed again "Agnes, it was a merchant ship. People buy and sell and between the two there's usually transport involved."

Agnes gave a little snort. Andrew was beginning to become sarcastic again. Another raised eyebrow was enough to make him realise his mistake. He opened his mouth to speak but Agnes stopped him by raising her hand.

"My question, the thing that niggles at the back of my mind is, just did how a lot of horses and men just happen to be in the same place at exactly the same time as the ship runs aground."

The chandler scratched the back of his head. Then Agnes could almost hear the penny drop.

"Wreckers!" he said.

Agnes nodded. The chat had helped clarify her own and Marmaduke's conclusions.

"Wreckers!" she replied.

By the end of their "little chat" Andrew had agreed to ask as many fishermen and deck hands he could find to spread the word. Beware of strange lights and if anyone sees anything, a keg of the finest Dutch Gin would be their's for the telling.

Chapter Seven

Later that night as Agnes and Marmaduke sat in
their eighteenth century living room avoiding the
chaos created by their twenty first century builders,
it began to rain and Agnes realised she had done
nothing about her damaged eighteenth century roof.
She looked across the room to where Marmaduke
was sitting preening his whiskers and beard with his
fingers. She sat back and wriggled her fingers.
Above her head roof tiles slowly and quietly
rearranged themselves and bricks shuffled
themselves back into the familiar shape of her
chimney stack.

"I think you need to go to Robin Hoods Bay" she
suddenly said.

Marmaduke gave a small start and looked behind
him to see if anyone else had come into the room
without him noticing them. They hadn't.

"Why:" he finally asked. Given the circumstances it was a fair question. Agnes began her explanation by repeating the conversation of earlier with Andrew Mark.

"What I want to know is the name of the ship, what cargo she was carrying and if any of its cargo ever showed up."

Marmaduke shook his head. "You're better at getting information out of people. You just have to look at them and they tell you their life story."

"Ah, in normal circumstances yes. But we're talking about Robin Hoods Bay!"

Marmaduke just looked puzzled. Agnes explained further.

"Robin Hood's Bay is small, very small. It's a very tight knitted community. An elderly lady suddenly turning up asking awkward questions about shipwrecks and missing cargos would create more questions than answers."

Marmaduke thought it through for a few minutes. "Do I get to ride a horse?" he asked suddenly.

"No self respecting highwayman could be seen without one!" she replied.

It took the best part of the following morning for Agnes to locate a horse and call in a favour from its owner. When Marmaduke saw it he realised it wasn't exactly the roaring thoroughbred he had imagined. He also realised the animal was familiar to him. The last time he had seen it the horse had been pulling a coal cart up and down Castlegate. He looked at Agnes. She shrugged.

"It's a horse!" she said.

Marmaduke climbed onto the beast and very quickly realised a major relocation of his sword was called for. Then he found that the reins kept catching on the handles of his two pistols. He pulled then out of their holsters and with an accusing look at Agnes, shoved one into his belt behind his back and the second down the inside of his jacket that was already concealing a bandolier equipped with ten finely honed and well balanced throwing knives.

 Dusk was dropping when he finally steered his horse down the steep hill that twisted and turned between the close set houses and finally reached the bottom of the village, where it met the sea. On the left he could see a small tavern. He got off his horse and led it towards the building.

The room fell silent as soon as he entered. The interior was dark however, as Marmaduke spent half of his life as a cat, the lack of light posed no problems for him. He simply looked around the room seeing groups of unfriendly faces looking back at him. Men in deep shadows. Gnarled hands gripping half empty, leather tankards. He walked up to what passed as a bar where the publican already had one hand reaching underneath for the stout wooden cudgel he kept there.

"Rum, a room and stabling for my horse?" He asked.

The man behind the bar found the cudgel and pulled it towards him. He knew this type. He knew trouble when he saw it standing across the bar from him.

"Don't do stabling!" He said. "Stabling's found at Laurel Inn up the hill!"

"Is there anyone who could take him there?" Marmaduke asked pleasantly making a coin appear miraculously between his fingers.

"Don't do rooms!" the barman stated.

Marmaduke stared back and narrowed his eyes. "Do you do rum?" he asked.

He was suddenly aware of a movement behind his back. He sidestepped and spun around kicking out his right leg. The resulting crunch was a satisfying sound. He moved another step to his right and his would be attacker hopped backwards his hands going down to hold his damaged knee.

Marmaduke became aware that everyone in the room had stood up. Two men were heading between himself and the door. Four were moving carefully towards him whilst the man behind the bar had pulled out his cudgel. Marmaduke sighed. Why did it always have to be like this? With a sudden blur of movement he leapt onto the bar and pulled out both his pistols. Suddenly the atmosphere in the room changed from one of inherent threat to one of panic. Some men froze where they stood, others tried to turn back. The man behind the bar took his hand away from his cudgel.

"There's no need for firearms!" he said.

Marmaduke didn't even look at him. Instead as he spoke he waved the two pistols in an arc making sure that everyone in the room was covered.

"There was no need to be so rude to a stranger whose only request was for a bed, a stable and some rum." He replied.

"We've got rum!" said the barman, but before Marmaduke could answer he noticed a man deep in the shadows trying to circle behind him. Without looking he moved his arm. The sound of the discharge deafened everyone in the room whilst the flash of the powder temporary blinded them.

Marmaduke took the opportunity to leap from the top of the bar and landed in front of the door facing into the room. He moved so quickly after the explosion that by the time their sight returned everyone was still staring at the empty space on the bar. He gained their attention by shouting in the direction of the man he had taken aim at.

"That put a hole in your hat. The next time it will be through a head!"

The occupants of the bar shuffled away from him. He continued. "Now whilst I have your attention you can help me out with a slight problem I have. I want to know about the recent wreck, the name of the ship and the cargo it was carrying!"

Everyone remained sullenly silent. Marmaduke dragged a nearby chair towards him, spun it around so it was in front of the door and sat on it. He shifted his jacket slightly hoping they would notice the bandolier and throwing knives strapped across his chest. Just to hammer the point home he replaced his discharged pistol into his belt took out a knife. He began tossing it casually in the air each time catching it by the handle and throwing it up again. The movement was hypnotic.

A voice spoke out of the darkness at the end of the bar. "You can't hold us here all night!"

Marmaduke peered into the darkness. He could see full well who had spoken but he allowed the speaker to think his was lost in the gloom. He was a small man wearing a large brass earring. When he saw Marmaduke's eyes staring towards him he shrank back and tried hiding behind the man in front of him.

"I've no intention of holding anyone against their will. All you have to do is to tell me what I want to know and I'll go on my way, and you can all go home."

A new voice came out of the gloom "it were nowt to do with us!"

Marmaduke continued tossing his small blade up and down. "Never said it was. But it was your boats that went to the wreck so someone round here must know something!"

A large man wearing a battered and worn pair of high sea boots and a greasy hand knitted pullover that was stained down the front with what looked like fish scales pushed himself forward.

"I was on one of the boats!"

Marmaduke turned his head to the direction of the speaker. "And...."

The man behind the bar suddenly found his voice. "Why should we tell you? We've no idea who you are!"

Marmaduke suddenly let the throwing knife go. All eyes followed the spinning blade as it flew across the room and embedded itself in the barman's baggy sleeve pinning his arm to the top of the bar. As it hit its target Marmaduke spoke again.

"You should tell me because I'm asking, and I have a pistol in my hand, and as to who I am, well let's just say I'm acting on behalf of an interested party, who in turn is very interested in the whereabouts of the ship's cargo."

As he spoke he slipped another throwing knife into his free hand.

"Bloody thing was empty when we got there!" The man wearing the sea boots said. Marmaduke looked up at him and the man continued. "By the time we got there it was well onto the rocks. The tide was on the turn and couldn't get too near for fear of running aground ourselves. A shore party was sent for but by the time they arrived on the scene the ship was awash and breaking up. The masts had gone already."

Marmaduke nodded. "And the cargo?"

The fisherman stroked his beard. "That was the odd thing. From what I could make out it was only carrying timber. At least that's the only stuff that was washed ashore."

"Aye but there must have been more than timber a'board!"

Marmaduke turned his head in the direction of the new voice. The speaker took a step back as Marmaduke met his gaze.

"Why do you say that?" he asked.

The man sounded flustered. "Well it stands to reason. No ship would make a voyage with just that timber. Not enough profit to make the journey worthwhile."

Marmaduke nodded. "So what do you reckon she was carrying?"

"Your guess is as good as mine, but whatever it was it had gone by the time we got there. Someone made a clean haul; the shore party didn't even find as much as a floating barrel."

Marmaduke smiled allowing everyone watching him to notice how his two canine teeth were slightly longer than usual and appeared worryingly like two very sharp fangs.

"So let me get this straight. You figure someone came and lifted the cargo before you even got there!"

His statement was met with a lot of nodding heads. Marmaduke stood up and pushed the chair away.

"Well that wasn't too difficult now was it? Perhaps in the future you could be a bit more friendly and accommodating to strangers."

With that final comment he quickly turned and went out of the door. He shut it behind him and looked for something to keep it shut. There wasn't anything so he jumped onto his horse and headed up the hill on the road leading out of the village. Behind him the men in the bar spilled out onto the street, jostling and pushing each other. Later that night they would argue among themselves as to why nobody did anything about the stranger, which then turned into a heated debate as to who the stranger could have been, and who he was working for, and finally the inevitable fist fight broke out when the argument switched to how they let what must have been a very valuable cargo be stolen from right under their noses.

Once Marmaduke reached the road leading across the moors he became aware of a white shape gliding alongside him. He slowed his horse down to a trot and held his arm out for the seagull to settle on. Once it had landed on his arm he stopped the horse, dismounted and allowed the gull to hop onto the ground the air shimmered and Agnes stood in front of him.

"A bit on the dramatic side, is that your idea of making discrete enquiries?"

He sniffed. "I got the answers though!"

Agnes nodded. "Well apart from the ships name!"

Marmaduke changed the subject. "Exactly like the ship wreck at Hayburnwyke though!"

Agnes nodded. "Oh yes. It was the work of wreckers. This time I have proof."

As she spoke she pulled a lantern out of.... well actually Marmaduke had no idea where she pulled the lantern from. One minute it wasn't there, the next Agnes was holding it up for his inspection. She continued. "They made a mistake. They left this behind!"

Marmaduke examined it. "Where was it?"

"Well, whilst you were terrorising the local fishermen I had a look at the site of the wreck. I found it near the wreckage. It was in a specially made niche carved out of the foremost rock on the reef. Anyone at sea would have seen its light and assumed they were near a village, or a harbour, or somewhere other than a reef of rocks!"

"So the ships were lured onto the rocks."

"Just as they did at Hayburnwyke. So who are they, and how do they know which ship to take?"

Marmaduke asked himself the same questions over and over to himself as he rode back to Scarborough. Above him a seagull wheeled and turned in the night sky as it followed him on the journey home.

Chapter Eight

They were back in the twenty first century. Agnes was standing in her bedroom, staring up through the hole in her ceiling, inspecting the half built chimney stack and shaking her head sadly.

Despite her secret adjustments the work still didn't match her expectations. It didn't need a building inspector to tell her that the rebuilt structure wouldn't stand a chance in a strong wind, let alone a storm. It did need the building inspector to point out that the bricks that had been used didn't match the character of the building and, as the property was a grade II listed building smack in the middle of a conservation area, the chimney would have to be taken down and rebuilt using the appropriate materials.

She turned towards the three builders who were all standing in the far corner guarded by a large ginger cat that grinned just enough to show two evil looking fangs. To add to the builders discomfort the cat kept extending ad retracting its claws. They looked very long and very sharp.

"It won't do! Knock it down and rebuild it, only this time use the right bricks." Agnes snorted.

One of the builders spoke. "Not too sure how we can get hold of those types of bricks Missus."

Agnes assumed the one who spoke was in charge. She gave him a look that would curdle milk. He took an involuntary step backwards only to realise be was already backed into a corner, in more ways than one.

"Get the right bricks!" Agnes said quietly.

The unfortunate builders took that as permission to leave and almost fell over themselves in their haste to escape out of the room. Marmaduke followed them downstairs growling softly, just to make sure they left the premises.

Later that night they were sat in their seventeenth century living room. Marmaduke was sprawled half in and half out of a comfortable chair in front of the open fire. Agnes was pottering about in her kitchen when she suddenly appeared at the door holding her large scrying bowl in front her. She walked across the room and carefully placed in on the table. She returned to the kitchen and returned with a large pitcher of water and a basket holding a selection of powders and herbs. Marmaduke opened his one good eye in her direction.

"If we are to find the person who's behind these attacks we need to look for them and as they seem to have managed to successfully cover their tracks in the physical world I'm going to try to find them in the non physical world!"

Marmaduke raised an eyebrow, a movement that caused his eye patch to move. "Meaning?"

"Meaning I'm going to use magic!" she said.

"Oh!" replied Marmaduke as he shuffled his body into a more comfortable position. It was going to be a long night.

For the next few hours Agnes hunched over the bowl, peering deep into the waters and the images it showed. Every so often she would stand upright, clear the image with a sweep of her hands before using them to rub her aching back. She would then sprinkle a few herbs and a pinch of powders into the water and repeat the process all over again.

Marmaduke woke with a start as Agnes place a hot cup of tea on the fireplace next to his seat. He rubbed his eye and tried to focus. He'd been in the middle of a dream where he was riding a horse, hunting giant rats. The dream confused him as he wasn't sure whether it was a human or a cat dream. He forced himself back into whatever present type of reality he found himself in.

"The same men!"! Agnes said as she settled into the second most comfortable chair. "It was the same men both times. They met near a beach, arriving in ones and twos. There were a lot of them, and they had a string of pack horses. In both cases they lit the lights and stood by watching as the ships ran aground and broke up. They watched as the crew drowned, any that actually survived the wreck were dragged out of the sea and had their throats cut. Then they were thrown back into the sea. Then as the tide turned they moved in and lifted the cargo. Mind you they knew exactly what they were looking for. Went straight for it. They had it off the ship and loaded onto the horses in under an hour." She paused and took a sip of her tea.

She was on a roll and Marmaduke knew better than to interrupt her with questions. He poured his tea into his saucer and began to lap it up. Agnes didn't even notice as she returned to her observations.

"There must have been at least a dozen men, and their horses, and strong pack horses as well. After they left the beach they separated, scattered into different directions. Mind you the majority of the cargo was on the pack horses. They left some tracks that headed inland. From what I could see they avoided the main roads and stuck to old tracks. I lost them as they entered Harwood Dale."

Marmaduke paused waiting for more. When he was sure there wasn't he spoke.

"So you reckon they are local?"

"I think some of them come from around here. Not Scarborough but them villages up the coast, Cloughton and Burniston and the places between here and Robin Hood Bay. She paused again then added, "But I think the leader and his top men don't come from here. I think it was them that took the contraband across the moors."

Marmaduke's whiskers bristled. "Saltersgate!" He said.

Agnes looked across the room at him. The fire had burned down and a log suddenly spat and spouted into life. Marmaduke gave a shrug.

"Anything smuggled along this coast that's destined for transportation inland goes through Saltersgate!"

Agnes nodded. Of course it would. She should have thought of that herself. Saltersgate was a small hostelry sat at the bottom of a hill on the main turnpike road that ran across the moors, linking Pickering with Whitby. There illicit goods were loaded and unloaded onto wagons and carts for redistribution to York and onwards towards the larger towns of the West Riding.

"I think we may have to have a closer look at Saltersgate." She said.

Marmaduke shook his head. I can't go in there. They don't take to strangers there, and actually I'm not a stranger to them. They're a tight bunch, they know every haulier, carter, waggoner and smuggling gang for miles around. If you go in there asking questions, well you won't come out. There's more than a few men disappeared over there, Revenue man as well. Those moors are big."

Agnes tutted to herself. Perhaps knowing where the goods were heading wasn't the right approach to finding the wreckers. She still had no idea how they knew which ships to attack or for that matter, when they should attack them.

"Perhaps we should be checking where the ships came from." Marmaduke said.

Agnes was surprised. She wasn't aware that she had spoken out aloud. Marmaduke continued.

"The first was a coastal trader working from Newcastle. Suppose we assume the second ship came from the same port?"

Agnes nodded. It made sense so there was no harm in following that idea. Marmaduke continued.

"If that's the case both ships would be logged complete with their ships manifest before it left the port. The person we need to speak to is the person who is getting that knowledge and passing it onto the wreckers!"

Agnes looked up at him. "You're getting very smart these days, for a cat!"

Marmaduke looked back at her with his one good eye.

"As a highwayman theft was my stock and trade. Smugglers, highwaymen, they are both the same. They all rob, they all steal. They all need their dealers, their contacts, someone to sell their stolen valuables onto. They also need information. They need to know what stagecoach to rob. Which one is carrying something worth robbing. They pay for that information. There isn't an inn or hostelry the length of the Great North Road that doesn't have an informer working for some gang or other. Sometimes there are two or three separate informers in the same inn, each one passing on information to a different gang, to the person who pays them.

Highwaymen don't work alone. They are just part of a chain. Smugglers and highwaymen men are the same, they do the same job, they rob. It's just that instead of getting shot by a highwayman the victims of smugglers end up getting drowned."

Agnes sat back and blinked. This was one of those rare times that Marmaduke had referred to his past. In fact it was so rare that that she actually couldn't remember the last time it had happened, and they had been together many, many years.

She ventured a question "Do you remember much of your past?"

He nodded. "Bits and pieces. But I read most of that in your history book of yours."

Briefly a look of vexation cross Agnes's face. "How did that get here? No telling what damage a twenty first century history book can do in the eighteenth century!"

Marmaduke smiled. "You brought it with you." He said and began to preen his whiskers with his hands to cover up the grin that was suddenly appearing on his face.

The next morning saw Agnes entering the chandlers shop once more. Once again the scenes from the previous week were replayed out. Agnes just couldn't help herself. She knew how annoyed Andrew Marks got when she sat in his best office chair. Although, as he resigned himself to sitting in the second best chair, Andrew did a good job of hiding his annoyance.

"How may I help you today?" he asked politely as one of his employees served them with coffee. Agnes sniffed the drink in her cup and a full roasted smell of fresh coffee assaulted her nostrils. She looked up at Andrew. "Dutch, if my nose doesn't deceive me."

"And all duty paid!" Andrew added.

Agnes smiled. "I never expected anything else from your fine emporium. I've come to ask a question. Who would have access to a shipping list, one that gives the details of both cargoes and departure times?"

Andrew thought for a minute. "Well Customs and Excise for a start. The harbourmaster for another. Then there's the ship owners."

"But they would only know what their own ships were carrying surely!"

Andrew shook his head, "Don't you believe it. A lot of the owners like to know the movements of their competitors. It pays them to know what's going where, and whose making a profit."

"So plenty of people could know and use that information?"

Andrew nodded. "Yes and that's not counting the dockers. They know the movements of every ship in and out of their harbour, and what it's carrying.

They should, after all they are the ones who load and unload it."

Agnes nodded her head. "I see the problem, especially in a large port."

Andrew sighed. "Let me show you. Come stand by this window."

Agnes got up and walked across to a large window that looked out over the harbour. Outside the dockside was alive with activity. A fishing boat was being unloaded and a basket of fresh fish was being lowered onto the harbourside where a group of men were waiting to empty the basket into some wooden boxes. Further down the dockside some boats were being tied up whilst others were just casting off. Men sat on capstans mending nets with huge needles, Women carried boxes of fish to trestle tables where they sliced and gutted each fish before throwing them into barrels. Along the dock side carters and their horses were busy delivering and collecting goods of all shapes and sizes. A group of off duty soldiers from the Castle garrison walked past on their way to The Dolphin, or The Beehive or some other hostelry. The scene reminded Agnes of a giant ant hill.

Andrew broke Agnes's thought. "You can be assured Agnes that just about everyone out there knows what ship is in and what ship is out of the port. They know what it is, or was carrying. They know the crew; they probably could even tell you the name of the ships cat. They have to. The harbour gives them their living, be it legally or illegally. Now imagine the scene in a bigger dock, say Hull, or Liverpool or London."

"Or Newcastle." Agnes added.

"Yes Newcastle. Why Newcastle in particular?" He asked turning from the window.

Agnes continued looking out at the scene below her. "I have a feeling that's where both the wrecked ships sailed from." She turned and was about to walk back to the best office leather chair. She stopped in surprise when she realised that Andrew had already taken it. She huffed her way across the office and settled into the second best office chair. As she sat down she thought she detected a smile drift across Andrews face. He began to speak.

"Anyone who really wanted to know anything could easily find out all the comings and goings. However getting the timing right would be the real problem. Given a strong wind you could get down here in the best part of a day or two. If the wind and tides are against you it could be three. Also different ships sail at different speeds, the size of the ship and the cargo she's carrying also make a difference. I think anyone wanting to make sure where a ship was would have to post lookouts down the coast, just to follow the ships progress."

Agnes blinked and blinked again. It was no wonder that Andrews business was doing well. It wasn't just down to his sometimes illicit dealings. The man actually ran his business with a very sharp brain.

On her way back home Agnes did some thinking. Surely she should have realised the importance of Saltersgate herself. Surely she should have known that everyone working in a dock would know what ship was going where. Surely she should have worked out the need for lookouts. Perhaps she really was getting old. Perhaps her mind wasn't as sharp as it once was. Mind you, she said to herself as she rounded the corner of Castlegate and walked down her own street, perhaps it's just that I can't be expected to think of everything! She entered her own house.

That evening she tempted fate and stayed the night in the twenty first century house. Despite the wrong brick the rest of her roof had passed inspection and her bedroom now had a fully functional ceiling. Anyway this night she wasn't planning on spending much time in her bedroom. Instead she was sat in her living room in front of a large computer screen on which images came and went. Web sites and documents opened and closed. The odd thing was that Agnes wasn't using either a mouse or keyboard. She was sat in her comfortable chair just seemingly flicking her fingers randomly at the screen. What was equally surprising to anyone who looked closely was that Agnes didn't even have a broadband connection.

Suddenly her printer sprang into life and a sheet of paper emerged, floated across the room, and settled on Agnes's lap. She picked it up and examined it closely. It was a map of the coastline between Newcastle and Scarborough. On it, marked in bright red, were the shipping lanes that down the coast. Marked in bright green were a number of outcrops and headlands and other bits of land that ships using the sea lanes would pass close to. There were a number of them but the ones that caught Agnes's eye most of all was the one nearest to where the wreckers had struck. It was called Ravenscar, a small hamlet with a cluster of houses and a large hall clustered atop a steep cliff at the southern end of the bay that held the village of Robin Hoods Bay.

Between the two were a series of alum works where miners and labourers broke up the mineral ready for ships to collect from a small jetty. She flicked her fingers at the computer again and an image of Ravenscar appeared on-screen. From the picture she could see that the cliff top held a commanding view of the entire bay and the sea beyond. From such a position someone could spot a ship a least an hour before it would pass. There would certainly be enough time for a signal to be given telling the wrecking gang it was time to gather. She checked the map again. Ravenscar was less than five miles from the sites of both the wrecks.

She examined the scene once more and then walked across the room to her scrying bowl, just to make sure. Technology was fine, but she still liked to back it up with her tried and tested magic. She sprinkled a powder across the surface of the water, passed her hand over its surface, and peered into its depths. Out of the water an image of Ravenscar cliffs emerged. It was dusk and the sun was just setting towards the west, behind her viewpoint. Stretching out in front of her she could see the wide vista of the sea. From here the horizon seemed miles away. It confirmed things in her mind. This had to be the place. There couldn't be anywhere else more suitable. She waved her hand across the water and another image appeared. This time the image was of the cliff top itself. She looked closely. Then she noticed a small track that ran alongside the side of the headland and seemed to disappear down the cliff. With a move of her hand she changed the viewpoint. From her new position she could see that the track turned into a narrow pathway that led down the headland, leading towards the beach a couple of hundred feet below. Just as the pathway turned a corner she noticed a small alcove carved out of the rock face. It was a perfect place for someone to watch the comings and goings along the coast without being seen themselves. In Agnes's mind there was now no doubt. She'd found the wreckers lookout post. It would have been from here that the signal would be sent that, in turn, would send a second signal onto a distant beach to light fires and lanterns that would entice ships onto the treacherous rocks and reefs, luring them to their destruction.

"And of course." she said to the empty room, "The man at Ravenscar would be told when to take up their position by a message, or signal, from further up the coast. That same message would tell them what ship to look out for. It's simple when you know what you're looking for!"

She waved her hand over the water and the images dissolved until only a bowl of water remained. Agnes sat back in her chair and moved her fingers at the computer screen. The images faded to be replaced by those of a computer game, Agnes spent the next two hours playing Football Manager in a vain attempt to lift her team out of Division One and into the Championship League.

Chapter Nine

The following day Agnes returned to the eighteenth century and walked into her yard. There was a shimmer and suddenly a seagull rose above the red tiled roofs and chimneypots. It circled over the town once before setting off north, keeping a parallel course to the cliff tops.

It took the best part of an hour for her to reach Ravenscar and its cliff top position. After regaining her human shape she soon found the small track that led down from the cliffs. Agnes noted it was a lot narrower that it appeared in her scrying bowl and that it would prove a difficult and challenging scrabble for anyone with a hint of vertigo.

She soon came across the little caved carved out of the solid rock. She entered it and sniffed. In the still air she could make out the faint aroma of stale tobacco and old alcohol. She examined the floor. It was stone and swept clean leaving no trace of any occupancy. She sat down on a carved ledge and looked out at the view. In front of her was the bay. In the near distance she could make out movement from the men labouring in the alum works. In the far distance the sun illuminated the red roofs of Robin Hoods Bay. The cliffs swept from the village in a great arc until they ended at a headland almost opposite her position. The she allowed her eyes to sweep the sea and the distant horizon. From where she sat she couldn't figure out just how many miles she could see, but she knew it was a great distance. Turning her head she realised she could see the horizon almost as far as Scarborough, although cliffs and headlands prevented her from seeing the actual castle headland. Out at sea she spotted a number of sails, boats going about their everyday business. Fishing boats, mainly sticking to the waters in the bay which, she assumed, were from Robin Hoods Bay. She watched the mid distance as some three masted coastal traders made their way north and south, up and down the coast. Finally in the far distance she could make out the sails of the larger ships, the big ocean going traders and cutters using the see routes that would carry them out into the North Sea and beyond.

All in all it was a spectacular view, but more importantly, it was perhaps the most perfect place to sit and observe the shipping lanes without drawing notice to you.

As she sat taking in the view she suddenly became aware of a sound. She held her breath and listened carefully. Someone was coming down the path. She looked around. There was certainly nowhere to hide. In an instant there was a shimmer in the air and, just as a figure appeared outside the entrance to the small cave, a rather large seagull waddled out and launched itself off the cliff side. As she took off she heard a curse and an exclamation of surprise emerge from the lips of the man on the narrow cliff path as he almost lost his balance. Another voice spoke. Agnes realised there were two men on the cliff path.

"Did you see that? Damn thing almost had me over then!" It was the man who had almost overbalanced who was speaking.

"Just hope they're not building a nest in there!" The second man observed.

"If they do I'll soon get rid of it." The first man replied. Both of them entered the small cave and Agnes landed on a small rock outcrop just above the entrance hoping to eavesdrop their conversation, but she was unlucky. The rock sill cut off sound from below and all she could hear was a low mumbling. She considered her position. She couldn't revert to human condition, the rock was too small to hold her weight. The air shimmered and the seagull disappeared. In its place a small mouse scurried off the rock and scrambled down the cliff face to the cave entrance where she hid herself in a large plant by the caves entrance. As she took up her position under the plant Agnes scanned the sky's above the bay. The last thing she needed right now was to attract the attention of a hawk, or an owl. The sky was clear of predators, just a few gulls lazily gliding in the airwaves above her head. She settled down and tried to adjust her hearing to the murmurs coming out of the cave. As far as she could hear there was no conversation. Just a series of grunts and soft curses mixed with the noise of bumps and clicks. Puzzled she took a risk, ventured out from under the plant and scurried into the cave finding a hiding place right at the back. The two men were too busy to notice the quick fleeting movement. She settled into her hiding place and watched as she realised the two men were busy in the process of erecting a large telescope. The instrument was so large that to use it required the erection of a wooden and brass tripod. It was this that was causing the two men problems. Somehow they had contrived to get the workings stuck and one of them was his hands and knees trying to adjust the height of its legs.

"Old Sam won't be happy if the thing has a wobble!"The man standing remarked.

"Old Sam can take it or leave it!" said the man on his knees in frustration.

Suddenly there was a loud click as a metal fixing finally clipped into place. The man got up from his knees and rubbed his hands.

"That's got it!"

"Good, about time. Let's get off. I'm not happy about that path. Soon as we're gone from here the better!"

"Better shove that bag over here!" The other remarked. "Don't want it to get damp and don't want the gulls to get hold of it. If the gulls ate Sam's snap and he was stuck up here a night and a day without his food and drink we'd never hear the end of things!"

Agnes was suddenly aware of a small hessian bag being tossed across the cave in her direction. It landed inches from her. As soon as the men left, and Agnes was sure they weren't coming back there was another shimmer in the air and an elderly woman stood at the back of the cave. In front of her was the telescope. Agnes stepped forward to examine it in detail. Whoever owned it had spent a lot of money. It was what would be come to be known in the twenty first century as a "high end model." It was solid brass fixed onto a tripod of highly polished oak, with expertly crafted brass fixtures and fittings set into it. Very expensive Agnes thought. Whoever owned it she figured that it wasn't either of the two men she'd seen, nor in all likelihood would it be Old Sam.

No wonder it was brought backwards and forwards on each occasion. To leave it here for any length of time would be to risk damaging it. Then a thought struck her. It had just been erected, so that meant that sometime in the next couple of days it would be used, and probably by Old Sam, whoever he was, especially as the men had left supplies for a day and a night. At last she felt she was getting somewhere. However if it was to be used it meant that the wreckers were going to take up their grizzly work again. It meant that another ship and its crew were not only in great danger of losing a valuable cargo, they were also in grave danger of losing their ship and their lives.

She needed to get back to Scarborough. However she just couldn't resist looking at the hessian bag and its contents. She opened it up and found a hunk of fresh bread, some cheese and an apple, alongside some sort of pie. She sniffed it. It was rabbit. There was also a small flask filled with a port wine. She smiled to herself and waved her hand over the bag. The bread turned stale, the cheese turned mouldy, the apple rotted, suddenly the pie smelt bad and the port wine turned to vinegar. She smiled to herself. "See how he enjoys those!" she thought. Sometimes she could be downright wicked.

Marmaduke was sitting in his twenty first century most favourite chair when Agnes swept in, picked him up, thrust him down the cellar stairs and into the secret door in the wall.

Once they were in the eighteenth century he began to brush himself down.

"That was a bit hasty!" he observed.

"We've very little time." Agnes replied as she led them back to the kitchen. She explained the situation as she made the tea.

"We need to know the name of the ship they are looking for." She said as she handed him a cup and saucer.

Marmaduke poured his tea into his saucer. Agnes pretended not to notice. "Why?" he asked.

"So someone can warn them." She replied. "We might just save someone's life."

Marmaduke nodded and looked up at her. "Perhaps it won't be necessary. The ship will be the one heading for the rocks! We won't be able to miss it!"

Agnes shook her head. "We need to warn them of the dangers. We need them to come inshore as far as possible. Then no further. They need to convince the wreckers that the ship has fallen into their trap and give us time to stop them in their tracks!"

Marmaduke carefully placed his saucer on the kitchen table. "Us?" he asked. "Just us two?"

Agnes smiled "No. I think we need to call in a few favours!"

Chapter Ten.

By her reckoning Agnes figured she had at least twenty four hours in which to get help and organise a group of men that could travel up the coast inside the next day. She also needed to know which ship the wreckers were targeting. She walked across to her scrying bowl. She needed all the help she could get.

Marmaduke stood by looking over her shoulder as Agnes swept image after image away with the sweep of her hand, adding more powders and herbs each time the image changed. At last she seemed to find the image she was looking for. She took a step back and nodded towards the bowl. Marmaduke looked closer. In the pool of water he could see the entrance to a large and very busy harbour. Boats and ships were entering and leaving, loading and unloading. Marmaduke was wondering how Agnes could tell one from the other when she pointed out a three masted vessel that was ploughing a heavy line through the harbour mouth, and headed in a southerly direction.

"That's it!" She said.

Marmaduke looked up from the scrying bowl. "How can you tell?"

Agnes stepped back from the bowl. "For one thing its size is similar to the other two ships that were wrecked. For a second thing, like the others it is carrying a valuable cargo. As well as some timber and coal it is also carrying two dozen kegs of fine Scotch whiskey and a dozen kegs of Dutch gin. That makes thirty six kegs in total. Enough to make them a handsome profit, and not too big a load that they won't be able to get it off the beach."

Marmaduke nodded and looked at Agnes "How do you know what its carrying?"

Agnes smiled "Research. I discovered that all the records of shipping in and out of Newcastle was saved and placed in an archive. Then a few years ago someone with a great deal of time on their hands digitised the records and put them on-line. All I needed to do was cross reference the records with today's date. Well that is today's eighteenth century date. I figured that the preparations in the Ravenscar cave were for sometime in the coming forty eight hours, so I ran a check on all the ships that left Newcastle on a date suitable to pass Ravenscar within that date. That was the ship that stood out." The Venture" meets all the criteria!" She flicked a finger and the printer sprang into life, printing out its details alongside a small illustration of the ship itself.

Marmaduke's eyes had glazed over as soon as Agnes mentioned the words "digitised" and on-line". He could cope with Agnes use of magic. To him that was the most magical thing in the world. However the use of twenty first century computers and the internet was a type of magic he just couldn't understand, nor did he want to. It was a step too far for an ex-highwayman and a cat.

Chapter Eleven

The meeting that Agnes called was held in the office of the Commander of the Castle Garrison. He sat at the head of the table in his full dress uniform. His fine set of grey side whiskers and moustache his gave him the appearance of a startled badger. He had experienced "working" alongside Agnes and Marmaduke before and had come to respect both their opinions and their powers. He knew full well that if Agnes called a meeting something was seriously wrong somewhere.

Also seated at the table was a very puzzled Andrew Marks who had been forced to leave his chandlery by a very insistent Marmaduke and as everyone in the Old Town new, when Marmaduke was insistent he gave a whole new and sinister dimension to the meaning of the word.

Despite the Commander sitting at the head of the table Agnes began. To emphasis her points she brought with her the scrying bowl and gave the Commander and the Chandler a viewing of selected images that underlined and backed up what she was saying.

When she had finished she sat back, "So that gentlemen is the problem before us. Sometime in the next twenty four hours or so a ship is going to be lured onto the rocks between here and Robin Hood's Bay. What are we going to do, indeed what can we do?"

The gentlemen in question sat back in their chairs. Neither of them said anything. Marmaduke hadn't looked in the scrying bowl. He'd see it before and remained in his chair picking his teeth with a very long finger nail.

A knock on the door only emphasised the silence. Without waiting for an answer the door opened and a soldier walked in carrying a silver tray with cups, saucers, and a large silver tea pot. He placed it in the centre of the table, took a step back and saluted.

"That all sir?" he asked hoping against he might be invited to stay.

"That will be all for now Lieutenant Smalls". The Commander barked. The Lieutenant marched back towards the door. As he placed his hand on the handle the Commander suddenly remembered who was in the room and what they had just seen. "Don't be far away!" he barked.

Suddenly he exploded with a very loud and very violent sneeze. Marmaduke looked across the table and shrugged. It wasn't his problem that the Commander was allergic to cats. Agnes filled in her pocket and pulled out a small cloth bag.

"Take this with your tea!" She said as she pushed it across the table.

The Commander picked up the bag, sniffed it, ripped it up and poured the contents into his tea. Before anyone could stop him he downed the cup in one large gulp. He winced as he replaced the cup in his saucer.

"My wrong!" said Agnes. "I meant sprinkle a pinch of it into your cup!"

The Commander looked towards her. "My dear Agnes. Trust me. If it takes a full sachet to rid me of the taste of this tea so be it." He looked balefully into his cup. "It's the best tea. I make sure of it. I order it specially. It's what they do with it that puzzles me. I can never understand how they can make it taste of a mixture of metal polish and gunpowder at the same time."

Across the table Andrew Marks kept his face as neutral as possible. He knew a local tea merchant that was making a nice profit repackaging a special tea and replacing it with a very much cheaper variety. Now Andrew realised who the merchant was making his profits from. He kept his silence. In his business knowledge was power. Well knowledge is useful in any business, but Andrew wasn't above using a bit of leverage. However people at the receiving end of this "leverage" tended to call it something else. Usually blackmail!

There was a sudden growl from the opposite end of the table. Marmaduke cleared his throat. "Can I remind everyone that time is passing!"

The Commander grunted. "And time and tide wait for no one eh?"

His words didn't get the laugh he expected.

From nowhere Agnes produced a large map and spread it across the table. "I've marked it up". She explained. "The lines on the sea represent the shipping lanes. The red dots the site of the two wrecks. The big blue dot is the lookout post at Ravenscar. All we need to do is to figure which reef the wreckers will use and we can surprise them in the act."

"What about the ship?" Asked Andrew

Agnes looked up from the map. "That's where you come in. I want you to pull in a few favours and find a couple of fast boats that can sail out and intercept "The Venture" before she rounds the headland here, above Robin Hoods Bay." She pointed at a spot on the map.

Andrew pulled a face. "It's a good days sailing, and you say we've only twenty four hours?"

Agnes looked him straight in the eyes and gave him one of her special looks.

Andrew suddenly nodded. "I think I know just the two. Henry Talbot and Old Peter. They have a couple of skiffs down there. Given a good wind and a trim sail they can outrun just about any boat along the coast. Well apart from the Excise cutter that is. That is fast!"

"Then if that's the fastest boat, that's the one we'll use!"

Andrew shook his head. "Agnes even your powers won't persuade the Excise men to lets us use their boat. They wouldn't even consider it!"

Agnes looked across the Garrison Commander. "You're army. Don't you outrank the Excise? Couldn't you commandeer their boat? Tell them there's some national emergency?"

The Commander shook his head, sneezed and straightened his moustache. "My dear lady. I represent the army. The army may I remind you is strictly land based. The only people able to commandeer an Excise cutter, belonging to the Crown, may I add, would be the Royal Navy, and as far as I'm aware there is no senior ranking naval officer within a twenty miles radius!"

He was abruptly cut off by Andrew. "Yes there is!" he said. All heads turned towards him.

"He is a First Lieutenant or something like that. He's on leave from somewhere down south. Here to visit his mother. Something like that. You'll know her Agnes, she lives just round the corner from you."

Agnes thought back. Come to think of it she had seen a man in a naval uniform walking down her street a couple of days ago.

"Well that's handy!" She said.

She turned to Andrew "Would the Excise Cutter be ready to sail?"

Andrew nodded. "It's always ready, always fully rigged."

"Right we'll use that!" She said.

"How do you....." Andrew was saying until Marmaduke cut him off. He looked at Agnes. "You've got a plan haven't you?"

Agnes just smiled and nodded as she turned to the Commander.

"You said you were land based. Well I think we'll be needing some of your soldiers."

The Commander looked down at the map. "Devil of a lot of coast to cover!"

Agnes nodded. "I've thought about that. If we station three groups of them at critical points along the way we should be able to surprise the gang. The first troop could swoop down followed by the second and third group. I've marked the possible positions on the map." She looked up at the Commander, and gave him one of her looks.

The Commander examined the map and harrumphed. "Could get some in positions. Hold a few more in reserve. Could also send a patrol along the coast road, just in case anyone gets past us. Trouble is co-ordination. How do we know when to hit the beach, or for that matter, how do we know where we hit it?"

Agnes looked at him. "That's why you'll have to act on my signal. When you see it head towards it. That's where the attack will be staged!"

The Commander pulled at his whiskers. "What sort of signal?"

Agnes shook her head. "I've no idea. However, you'll know it when you see it."

Marmaduke looked u at Agnes. "Do I take it that you intend finding them by yourself?"

Agnes shook her head. "No I mean we are going to find them. Then we'll signal the Commander here and he and his troops will take lots of prisoners!" She gave one of her sweet smiles that had the effect of making everyone else around the table look elsewhere.

"Andrew?"

Reluctantly Andrew turned towards her just in time for her to give him another special smile. "Just in case the Excise men don't prove helpful could you make sure you have a standby crew ready, never know we might need your contacts and their boats yet."

Without even realising it Andrew nodded his agreement.

Agnes stood up. "Well gentlemen, we know what we have to do. I suggest we make a start!"

Chapter Twelve

Marmaduke and Agnes parted company with Andrew at the end of their street. They watched as Andrew hurried down the rest of Castlegate and headed down a flight of stairs that led down a dark alley that, in turn, opened out on the foreshore, the harbour and his chandlery. Marmaduke sniffed the air. He could smell the aroma of freshly cured herrings drifting up from the smoke houses below, their smoke drifted up the hill and mingled with the smoke from the many fires and chimney pots. Agnes noticed his whiskers twitching.

"Come on let's find our Rear Admiral!" She said.

"I thought he was a First Lieutenant?" Marmaduke said, his mind still very much on herrings.

Agnes smiled "Oh he'll be a Rear Admiral by the time I've finished with him."

"How are you going to do that?" Marmaduke asked, the thoughts of herrings disappearing as the smell was replaced by a smell nowhere near as nice. He let go a small sneeze.

"The young man owes me a favour. I've just remembered who he is. He's Mrs Potter's lad. I brought him into the world."

The charm offensive began straight away. Instead of stopping at her own front door Agnes carried on down the street and turned right down a small alleyway branching off to the left. It was called Tuthill. Agnes walked down until she reached a small cottage where she stopped and knocked on the door. It was opened almost straight away by a woman of indeterminate age. She wore a shawl thrown over an old dress whose front was covered by an apron stained with fish blood and scales that said she worked at the nearby fish market.

As soon as the woman saw who was at her door she pulled it wide open and ushered them into a small but tidy living room. A small fire was burning in the open grate over which hung a metal hook. Without asking the woman hung a blackened kettle on the hook and swung it back over the open flame.

Without being asked Agnes sat down in the nearest chair. It was that sort of neighbourhood. There was no need to ask if a cup of tea or a chair was required. There was no need to ask to sit down. Once the door had been opened you were expected to make yourself at home.

"It's about your Peter." Agnes said.

A cloud crossed Mrs Potters face. "He's not been up to any trouble has he? He's only been home a few days. Been given shore leave as he's between ships at the moment."

A series of thoughts flashed across Agnes's mind. Of course he would be. Now the war with America had concluded with the colonists gaining their independence from England and the Crown the Royal Navy was undergoing a series of changes.

Some of the older ships were being decommissioned. Obviously someone at the Admiralty thought enough of the young First Lieutenant to keep him in the service. She smiled to herself. Perhaps the lad might end up a Rear Admiral after all.

"No he's not in any trouble. I just need his assistance in a little job I have to do."

The words "no he's not in any trouble" caused Mrs Potter to raise an eyebrow and immediately begin worrying. Everyone in the Old Town knew about Agnes and knew that any of her "little jobs" were anything but normal. After all she was the wize woman. She rarely needed anyone else's help, with the exception of the large one eared, one eyed, man with ginger hair who was currently standing by the side of her range watching the kettle boil and twitching his whiskers.

Despite herself Mrs Potter found her mouth asking the question that sprang to the forefront of her mind.

"You won't be asking him to do anything that involves...." She was going to use the word magic, but at the last moment thought better of it and changed track. "...involves doing anything that might be against the Admiralty Regulations."

Agnes smiled her most reassuring smile. "I'm sure the help I need will not be against any regulations!"

In fact she was sure that type of help she required wouldn't even have been thought of by whoever it was that made the rules and regulations. There again, she'd actually never read them so she didn't know for sure.

Marmaduke broke her chain of thought. "Where is the lad anyway?" he asked.

His mother looked up at the strange man standing in her living room. "He'll be down The Beehive. He has some mates working on the fishing. That's where they all meet up."

Agnes nodded, she would wait. What she wanted to talk about wasn't for everyone's ears, besides there was every reason to assume that the wreckers had their own spies operating in and around Scarborough. After all they seemed to have a network stretching from Newcastle to Ravenscar. No, she had to admit, they would have at least one man in Scarborough. She would have to be careful. She wondered whether Andrew Mark had worked that out yet. She nodded to Marmaduke who stepped across the road and lowered his head allowing her to whisper in his ear. When she had finished he stood up and with a small bow in the direction of Mrs Potts, walked out of the house.

Agnes looked at Mrs Potter "Just sending him off on an errand, something I forgot." She gave a little laugh, "I must be getting old!"

Mrs Potter didn't know whether to laugh or not.

Marmaduke strode down the alley, turned left, ran down a long flight of stone steps and was heading along the foreshore when he saw Mrs Potters son emerge from The Beehive and, with a slight stagger, head off in the opposite direction of home and his unexpected meeting with Agnes. As Marmaduke continued on his way towards the chandlery he spared a thought for the young naval officer. The poor lad had no idea just how completely his life would be altered.

The lad found that out for himself as soon as he entered his mother's house to find Agnes sat by the fireside chatting amiably with his mother.

"Peter!" said Agnes as soon as the young man stepped through the door.

The young man froze as his mother got out of her chair and signalled for her son to take her place. As he sat down she poured him a cup of tea and then put her shawl over her shoulders.

"Agnes would like a word. I'm just popping out for a loaf!" With that she walked out of her own front door and they heard her hurried footsteps disappearing down the alleyway.

"And how is the navy treating you Peter?" Agnes asked.

Peter sat still, not wishing to commit himself to anything. Despite being still a young man his years in the navy had taught him one thing above everything else. Never volunteer.

"There's no need to be afraid!" Agnes said sensing his hesitation. She gave him one of her "reassuring" smiles. The smile was even more alarming to the young man. Agnes wriggle a finger a little bit and the man visibly relaxed.

"Now..." She bean. "I'm going to tell you a story", and she narrated the story of the two wrecks, emphasising the fact that all crew had been lost. She continued by relating her theory concerning the wreckers and her plan to catch them.

Seated in the chair Peter listened. At various points in the narration he tried to speak, to ask questions, but for some reason his mouth just wouldn't move. Eventually Agnes stopped talking and Peter suddenly found his voice.

"And you want me to enlist the help of the Navy? I'm afraid I'm not that influential. Even if I submitted a report it would be days before anyone read it. Then another month as it would pass from one desk to another...."

Agnes cut him off. She knew how bureaucracy worked. She also knew that it would be exactly the same for the next three hundred years, and probably beyond.

"That's exactly why we need your help Peter." She smiled again. "I want you to commandeer the Excise Cutter!"

At first Agnes thought the young man would choke. Eventually she had to stand up and give his back a slap, as he tried to wipe the tea from his uniform trousers. When things calmed down he found his voice.

"How am I supposed to commandeer an Excise Cutter? The Navy has no jurisdiction over such things!"

Agnes smiled. She had prepared herself for such a question. She half closed her eyes and visualised her own front room and a very large book open on her lounge table.

"Under the current Kings Regulations a senior ranking Naval Officer may commandeer any vessel for assistance in the event of a National Emergency!"

The young naval office began spluttering again. "How do you know the Kings Regulations?" he asked.

Agnes looked him straight in the face. "Peter Potter, I know everything. I certainly knew enough to deliver you all red and screaming into this world."

Peter reddened. "But it's not a national emergency!" he spluttered.

Agnes paused just for a second. "It's a very ambiguous bit of legislation I must admit. As it doesn't actually describe what a National Emergency is I figure that it's open to interpretation. Some may say that a gang of wreckers disrupting shipping routes along the North East coast of England could be interpreted by some as a National Emergency."

The young man sighed. He had been to sea. He had seen battle, seen men die and ships sunk. He had lost men and friends. His greatest fear was being shipwrecked, being sunk. Being dragged under the water by tangles of wreckage, holding ones breath until, ones lungs burst. Feeling the water filling ones lungs, gasping for a breath that wasn't there.

"I take it you have a scheme in mind?" he found himself asking.

"More of a plan!" replied Agnes. "I want you and a squadron of men to march to the Excise Office. Then claim their cutter in the name of The King. Read them the appropriate orders, signed by a top Admiral of course, and stamped with a very official looking seal."

Peter sat, looking unconvinced. "Just two things. Where do the squadron of men come from and where do we get the orders from?"

Agnes smiled again. "Leave that to me. They will be there when you need them."

Peter nodded. He knew full well that when he needed them they would be there.

Later, after Agnes had left, when Peter thought about their conversation he suddenly realised something. It came as a bit of a shock. He realised that he had never been afraid of being shipwrecked. In all his time at sea he had never had a nightmare about drowning. Where had all that come from? A coal on the fire suddenly burst into life and Peter forgot everything about being shipwrecked and nightmares. Instead his mind switched to the very normal thoughts that ran along the lines of "What have I agreed to?" and "how am I going to do it?" and finally, "What will my mother say?"

As it happened his mother would have been very proud of him.

Agnes walked back to her house and busied herself criss-crossing across time between the eighteenth and twenty first century. It was night time when she finally made herself a drink in her eighteenth century kitchen. On the table in her living room was a near perfect forgery of an official looking Admiralty order complete with a signature of a very well known Rear Admiral and a Royal seal. It looked very, very real. Agnes was very proud of it. Especially as she had managed it with very little magic. All she'd done was to find a suitable document on the internet, print it out on a colour printer she didn't have. She did the same with the

Royal Seal. Once she'd laid the prints together she'd made a movement with her hands and suddenly the document was in front of her. She had been forced to alter the wording here and there, just enough to give an Excise Officer the impression that if he didn't obey it, his life would suddenly become very, very complicated.

She looked down on it and as she drank her coffee she gently ran her fingers over it. It sparkled where she touched it.

The front door opened and Marmaduke filled the doorway.

"What have you been up to?" She asked without turning around.

"I saw Andrew and told him about your worries. He said he had already thought about it. He's holding back putting the crew together until the last minute. Even then, if and when they have to sail, he won't say anything until they are out to sea."

Agnes turned towards him. "And then...."

Marmaduke sat down and stretched his body out. It rippled just like a cats. "I did the rounds of the harbourside. The Beehive, The Dolphin, The Dog and Duck, finished up in the Three Mariners, you know just keeping my ear to the ground."

Agnes looked him in the eye. "I take it your questioning was a deal more subtle then when you asked questions in Robin Hoods Bay?"

Marmaduke just sighed and began to scratch himself behind his ears. Agnes waited a full five minutes before she spoke. "Well?"

Marmaduke shook his head. "Nothing. Not even a whisper. Just the usual gossip. Bit of contraband here and there, mainly they are complaining about the weather, the lack of fish, the usual stuff."

Agnes looked up "What about the weather?"

"Oh you know how superstitious that lot are. They reckon there's been a red sky in the morning for the last two days. Means there's going to bad weather on the way."

Agnes nodded. "Just the right weather for the wreckers. Just the right night for a ship to flounder on the rocks!"

Later that night a seagull drifted across the face of the cliff at Ravenscar. It wasn't surprised to see a slight glow from a position below the edge of the cliff. The watcher was in place. She figured that it would happen tomorrow, probably in the evening. The gull rose on the growing wind, wheeled around and riding the air currents, headed down the coast, back towards Scarborough.

Chapter Thirteen

Early next morning, before his breakfast had arrived, the Commander of the Garrison was surprised to see Agnes sat in his chair next to the fireplace. He looked back at the closed door and then back at Agnes. He had no idea how she had entered his office.

"Damn it Agnes. I'm in the centre of a castle guarded by a garrison full of troopers all bearing arms. How did you...."

She cut him off with a wave of her hand.

"Still sleeping badly I see." She rummaged in her pocket and drew out a small hessian bag. "Sprinkle this in that glass of whiskey you keep by your bedside." She paused then added. "And don't use it all at once. There's enough in that bag to put you out for a week and just now I need you very much awake. It's going to be a long day, and an even longer night!"

The Commander said nothing. The only thought in his head was how the devil did Agnes know he kept a glass of whiskey at his bedside.

A sudden knock at the door heralded the arrival of the Commanders breakfast. The Commander barked out an order and his lieutenant entered the room followed by two troopers holding trays loaded down with silver plates and platters, covered trays of hot food, knives and forks, silver tea and coffee pots plus numerous other items deemed necessary for the Commander to have a successful and satisfying breakfast. After the soldiers had placed everything on the table they saluted and left. Agnes looked at the spread. There was bacon, eggs scrambled and fried, sausages, mushrooms, black and white pudding, kedgeree, fresh warm bread, coffee, tea, toast and a thick damson jam.

Agnes couldn't help herself from commenting. "You certainly know how to look after yourself!"

The commander harrumphed. "That's the army for you. Serve up a decent breakfast with all the trimmings, but you try asking for more gunpowder, or muskets, or anything remotely useful....anyway help yourself. There's always far too much for one person."

Agnes didn't need telling twice. She reached across the table, selected a large fresh bread roll, cut in two, placed three rashers of bacon inside it, placed the two halves back together again and began eating her sandwich. It was then she noticed her hosts face.

"Damn novel way of eating!" The Commander commented as he piled sausages, bacon and eggs onto his plate. Agnes tried to remember if Lord Sandwich had actually created his invention yet.

As they ate she told the Commander of the latest events he wiped his whiskers with a large white linen napkin and shouted out an order. Lieutenant

Smalls was inside the room instantly. The commander left the table and guided him to the opposite wall where he'd pinned Agnes's map. She listened as the Commander pointed to different Areas and gave the Lieutenant a series of orders. Finally the Lieutenant nodded, took a step backwards, saluted and left the room. The Commander looked back at Agnes.

"Patrols will be on their way within the hour, they will be in position by late afternoon."

"They may be in for a long wait! I have a feeling that the wreckers won't strike until darkness." Agnes remarked.

"Unless "The Venture" is early of course" The Commander said.

Agnes nodded. There was always that possibility. "I'd better get the Excise Cutter on its way then." She said.

The Commander raised an eyebrow. "How are you planning to achieve that?"

Agnes smiled. "With the help of some subterfuge, oh yes, and half a dozen of your men if I may. I'll only need them for an hour or so. Tell them to meet me outside the Chandlery in forty five minutes time."

The Commander was about to say something about his men and who was in charge of them, then he saw the look in Agnes's eye and thought better of it. "You won't be taking them to sea I trust?" he asked

Agnes shook her head. "No, I won't be making sailors of them."

The Commander opened the door and barked a series of orders to his Lieutenant. When he turned back to the room it was deserted. The only clue that someone else had been there was a half eaten bacon sandwich left on a silver plate.

By the time the orders had been given and a platoon of soldiers was being organised at the Castle Gatehouse Agnes was sitting in the small living room in the house at Tuthill. In front of her Peter was standing, feeling very self conscious in his full dress uniform, as Agnes gave him a very critical once over.

"You'll do" She said finally. She just managed to resist pulling out a handkerchief and wiping a small speck of soot from the side of his face.

"Right!" she said finally. "Let's go and meet your platoon!"

They walked out of the house, down Tuthill and towards the Chandlery where she could see six troopers already standing, leaning on the walls of the shop. They were being "entertained" by Marmaduke. She allowed herself a small tut. The last thing she needed as Marmaduke putting daft ideas in their heads. Marmaduke noticed her approach and quickly brought his story to an end.

The soldiers looked in the same direction. The first thing they noticed was a tall young man dressed in a full Naval uniform. They fell silent as they realised that despite the different military service, he still outranked them. Then they noticed the elderly woman walking at his side. To them the sight of Agnes was more worrying than the sight of a dozen Rear Admirals. They had all been involved in her past escapades and were all grateful that they had lived to tell the tale. As she looked them up and down they shuffled themselves into some sort of order.

She noticed the consternation on their faces. "All you need to do is to march behind our Lieutenant here, and look as if you mean it. There is, shall we say, a crisis brewing and with your help we will prevent it. Your job is to dissuade the men at the Excise House from saying no!"

She paused and gave them a final look. "Right gentlemen, if you would be as good as to line up and march behind our naval officer here, we'll get started."

The soldiers shuffled into a rough approximation of a formation. She nudged Peter and he began to march down the Foreshore. The soldiers followed him in a shambling excuse of a march. It didn't look good and both Agnes and Marmaduke realised it. There were a lot of words that could be used to describe the gait but whatever words were used the least descriptive was that they looked like an efficient fighting force. Marmaduke whispered in Agnes's ear. She gave a slight nod. Marmaduke stepped in front of the six troopers stopping them in their tracks. It was as much as they could do to stop themselves walking into each other. Marmaduke gave them his hard stare. Ordinarily one would expect a hard stare from a one eyed man to be only as half effective as a hard stare from a man with two eyes. With Marmaduke it was different. His one eyed stare was twice as effective, especially as the stare involved slightly parting his lips, revealing his teeth, that seemed to the soldiers as if he had suddenly grown two fangs. He moved his head signalling for them to move closer to him. Marmaduke never revealed what he actually said to them, but whatever it was it was very effective. Suddenly the six troopers lined up in formation, stamped their right feet, and began marching in a style that could only, under normal circumstances, be seen on the training and parade grounds in the best military academies. Suddenly they looked like a very efficient and very deadly military unit. Agnes nodded her head in approval as they marched down the road towards the Customs House.

Of course the sight of Marmaduke and Agnes marching down the Foreshore in the company of a Naval Officer in full dress uniform and six troopers from the garrison didn't go unnoticed by the fishermen, fishwives, dock workers and other harbour side inhabitants. As the group proceeded on their way more and more people downed their tools, stopped whatever they were doing and followed on behind, just in case they missed something! By the time they reached the Customs House there was a ragged crowd of almost a hundred people tagged on behind them. Agnes smiled. The more the merrier she thought.

When they reached the door of the Customs House the young Naval Officer played his part to perfection. He marched straight up to the door, pushed it open and addressed a rather startled Excise man who just happened to be standing behind it. Without pausing the Naval Officer barked an order and the six troopers behind him snapped to attention. The noise brought the office in charge out of his back office. He was followed by other curious Excise men who drifted in from other areas of the building. What with the troopers, the naval officer, and as many followers as could squeeze themselves into the building the front of the Customs House was packed with people. Agnes suddenly flexed her fingers and reality was altered slightly. Suddenly what the Excise men could see was a tall Naval

Rear Admiral in full dress uniform accompanied by a well drilled and very fierce looking platoon of Royal Marines. As they stood with their mouths open the Rear Admiral reached inside his tunic and pulled out Agnes's forged document and presented it the Officer in Charge. The man was so overawed that as he accepted the document he actually saluted.

The room fell strangely silent as the Excise man looked at the waxen seal. Despite the fact that he had never seen one before, he recognised a Royal Seal when he saw one. He carefully removed it and unfolded the document. As he read the contents his face turned white, then pink, then red and then back to white again. He looked up at the Rear Admiral.

"You are requesting to commandeer our Cutter?" he spluttered.

Peter shook his head. "I am not making any such request, however my orders state that The Royal Navy wishes to commandeer your cutter!"

The Excise man shook his head and stammered his reply "I don't have the authority... I'll have to put this to my senior officer."

Peter looked around the room before addressing the man. "Is he here?"

The Excise man shook his head. "He's down in Bridlington!"

Peter nodded an understanding. For a brief second the Excise man looked relieved. Then Peter spoke again.

"Does the document give mention to referring to a senior officer?"

The Excise man reread the document. He knew full well there was no such mention. He hoped on a second reading the words would miraculously appear. They didn't. He shook his head. Inside he was panicking; he wasn't used to making such decisions by himself.

Peter continued. "Well Sir, may I suggest that you jump to it. Immediately!"

He almost shouted the last word. It had the desired effect. The Excise officer suddenly galvanised into action. After all it was a Royal Warrant, and it was backed up by what seemed to be a very efficient military unit. Just looking at them made the Excise Officer worry about the future of his career. Unlike many people working on the harbour side the Excise Officer liked his job. He liked the authority, he liked the status, he liked chasing and arresting smugglers. Most of all he liked the wages. He didn't want to lose any of it.

Peter had now grown used to the idea of being a Rear Admiral and was thoroughly enjoying himself. He spoke again. "I will of course, require your men to crew the cutter. As you see my men are Marines. They are fighters not sailors."

The Excise was going to respond but his eye caught the sight of the Royal Seal again and he thought better of it. He turned to his men.

"Four of you. Take the Naval Party to the docks. Get ready to sail and take her wherever the Royal Navy demands."

He turned back to the Rear Admiral. "Sir I entreat you to take the utmost care of my ship and of my men. They are now under your command. In the meanwhile I will prepare both the appropriate paperwork and inform my superior officers of what has transpired."

Agnes picked up her ears at his last comment. She knew she would have to make sure that particular despatch would never leave Scarborough Town.

The large number of people crowding the doorway suddenly found themselves facing both the troopers and the excise men. They gave way as the party squeezed through the door. The crowd was a bit disappointed as most of them had expected a fracas at the very least. Some began to drift back to whatever they were doing when the party first passed by. Others hung on in the hope that trouble would break out on their way to the cutter. They too were disappointed.

From his position standing by the window in his office Andrew Mark watched the party march from the Customs House in the direction of the harbour and the cutter. As he had said it was primed, fully sailed and ready to leave. He remained watching as the party boarded the ship and the excise men made the preparations to sail. He noted that neither the six troopers Agnes or Marmaduke boarded. As the clipper cast its ropes and began its journey out of the harbour Andrew held a piece of paper in front of him. It was an anonymous note he had found slipped under the shop doorway sometime during the previous night. Andrew read the words on the paper once again. Written in a fine copperplate hand were the words "Foxy Tom".

As the cutter left the harbour mouth and began its speedy journey north, and the six troopers marched their way back to the Castle Garrison, Agnes examined the piece of paper. As Marmaduke leant on the office wall looking out of the window, scratching the back of his good ear with his fingertips, Agnes turned the bit of paper over and over examining both sides. Eventually she looked up at Andrew.

"I take it you're assuming it's a clue to our wrecker, and you've no idea who could have written it?"

Andrew shook his head "No one around here could write like that. I even compared the writing with my receipts and orders, just in case. I could identify it. I couldn't!"

Agnes nodded. "I assume it's not the name of a boat, probably someone's name. Ever heard of it before?"

Andrew shook his head again. "There's definitely no boat in the harbour of that name. I asked a few discrete questions here and there, nothing!"

Agnes thought to herself as Marmaduke began to pick his teeth with what Andrew though was a very long and very sharp fingernail.

"So, the writers not local then?" she said eventually.

Andrew dragged his attention from Marmaduke and his teeth cleaning and looked at the paper still in Agnes's hand. "As I said, I made a few discrete questions. If there was anyone operating a wrecking crew around here, no matter whatever his name, the people I asked would know."

Agnes looked him in the eye. "Would they be telling you the truth though?"

Andrew held her gaze and smiled. "Oh yes. They wouldn't lie. If ever I found that any of them lied they would be out of business before they knew what was happening."

Agnes nodded. There wasn't a roll of silk, a packet of tea, a keg of gin, a box of kippers, or anything else for that matter, that passed through the harbour that Andrew didn't know about, legal or illegal. She found herself wondering just how far his influence stretched, and who owed him those very large favours. She decided she didn't need to know, yet.

As she stood up she looked down at the piece of paper. "Do you mind if I take it with me?"

Andrew nodded and Agnes slipped the paper into her pocket.

She turned to Marmaduke. "Time to make sure the Commander has his troops on the move."

As she walked towards the office door she back turned to Andrew. "I'll be in touch."

Andrew and no doubt she would. He wasn't sure if that was a good or a bad thing.

They had reached the end of her street when Agnes suddenly turned towards her house. "You check on the soldiers. I want to take a closer look at this bit of paper. Marmaduke nodded and continued up the hill.

Chapter Fourteen

As Marmaduke arrived at the Castle Gatehouse a guard suddenly stepped forward to challenge him. He was a Sergeant. Behind him six troopers under his command stood in the shadows.

"Where do you think you're going?" The sergeant asked.

Marmaduke stopped and looked at the man. He was small, wiry, and very sure of himself.

Marmaduke smiled. "Commanders business." He stated.

The sergeant returned the smile. It was as cold as the steel sword that dangled at his side. "Ah well, you see this gatehouse is my business, and these stripes allow me to decided who goes on and out of the Castle."

He looked Marmaduke up and down making no secret of what he thought of undesirables like him!

This time Marmaduke didn't smile. He leant forward and spoke in a low growl that only the sergeant could hear. "I'm here to see the Commander. If you have a problem with that I suggest you keep it to yourself. Now this situation can go two ways. You can let me though and nothing will be said, or you can continue trying to impress your troopers over there and discover for yourself just what the third circle of hell looks like."

The sergeant was going to sneer something that he considered wit, but as he opened his mouth Marmaduke gave another smile, this time showing his fangs. The words dried in the sergeant's mouth especially as he noticed Marmaduke's hands. One was resting easily by his side, just next to the handle of a long wicked looking his sword. His other hand was dangling at the front of his jacket. It was slightly open showing the handles of a pair of pistols pushed into the top of his belt. However it wasn't the pistols that worried the sergeant. It was the man's hands, his finger nails to be precise. They looked long, sharp and vicious. More like claws than finger nails. He quickly realised that his attitude had got himself into a type of trouble he might not get himself out of. He had spent his entire army career keeping out of trouble, this wasn't the time nor place to change that. In an attempt to save face in front of his men he resorted to army bluster.

"Do you have a written order?" he asked.

Marmaduke said nothing.

The sergeant continued, seeing a way out of his situation. "My orders, from the Commander himself, are to stop anyone from entering without due orders and the appropriate paperwork."

Marmaduke was getting bored. He let out a deep growl. The sergeant took a step back, more in surprise than fear. He then became aware of a blur of movement in front of him and suddenly the business end of a pistol was half an inch from the end of his nose. Behind him Marmaduke heard the snap of half a dozen muskets all being raised and cocked.

Before the incident could escalate further another voice broke the tension. It was the voice of Lieutenant Smalls.

"Stand easy! Sergeant, let the man through. He attends to the Commanders business."

The Sergeant tried to keep face. He saluted smartly. "Sir, The man has no written orders. My orders distinctly state that entrance can only be guaranteed once the order have been seen and approved."

The Lieutenant sighed. He had dealt with Sergeant Lewis before, and lots of other Sergeants just like him, equally cocky, all thinking that three stripes on their arm gave them the power to interpret Army rules and regulations to their own advantage and to give them permission to bully everyone under them.

Give them a bit of power and it goes to their heads. An idea crossed his mind.

"Sergeant, accompany this gentleman to the Commanders Office. Once there stay there. Your orders are to stay as close to this gentleman as possible."

Marmaduke sighed. The last thing he needed was a nursemaid. Then he realised the subtlety of Lieutenant Smalls's actions.

"Lieutenant, do I take it that Sergeant Lewis has been transferred to my command?" he asked.

Lieutenant Smalls smiled. Marmaduke was quick on the uptake. Sergeant Lewis was about to spend the rest of the afternoon, and probably most of the night, learning a very valuable lesson. Never throw your weight around people who were a lot heavier than you, and never bring yourself to the attention of your superior officers.

The three men turned and marched through the gate and up through the Castle until they reached the Commanders office. They knocked and entered at the short sharp grunt of response. The Commander was sat at his desk in full uniform. He looked up as they entered the room.

"Ah Marmaduke, I take it Agnes is joining us?"

Marmaduke shook his head. "Not immediately. She has something else to attend to first."

He continued to narrate the events of the mornings work.

Cutter After he had finished the Commanders face turned a darker shade or red. "Good God man! You mean she actually succeeded in getting the Excise to part with their?"

Marmaduke nodded. "She's even got them to crew it. Under the command of a Rear Admiral of course!"

"Rear Admiral....?"   The Commanders blustered.

Marmaduke shrugged. "Our First Lieutenant Peter Potts got promoted this afternoon!"

The Commander harrumphed. "Not sure if I approve of promotion by trickery. Could undermine the whole military establishment, what? I mean anyone could end up in charge." He never noticed the slight smile that flitted across the lips of both his Lieutenant and his Sergeant.

The Commander suddenly paused and gave his moustache a tweak.

"Damned odd that though. I used to know a fellah called Foxy. Wasn't his real name of course. Let's see. It was at the Middlesbrough..., no it wasn't, it was at the York Barracks. Some years ago now. Seemed to remember the man was a Colonel or something. Ordinance, or supplies. A desk bound Johnny, bit of a pen pusher I seem to remember. It's been a long time. Memory isn't as sharp as it used to be."

He looked at the men standing in front of him. "Stands to reason. The older you get the more there is to remember. Fellah can't be expected to remember every Tom Dick and Harry they come across!"

Marmaduke's mind worked fast. If Foxy Tom had been a Colonel in supply he could have forged a number of connections over the years. He knew Agnes would appreciate the information as soon as possible. He was surprised when he realised Lieutenant Smalls thinking had been even quicker. He had already scribbled the information down, folded the paper and was handing the note to the Sergeant.

"Make sure your fastest runner delivers this immediately. If Agnes hasn't received it personally within the quarter someone will be on a charge!"

As the conversation had continued the Sergeant had become increasingly aware that he had become witness to something that was so way above his head it was in the clouds. He was glad to get out of the room. He snapped his best parade ground salute, stamped and marched out of the room.

The Commander raised an eyebrow "Who the devil was that?"

The Lieutenant smiled. "Sergeant Lewis Sir. He's on a training mission. I've seconded him to Marmaduke here for the remainder of his mission."

The Colonels eyebrow went even higher. "Good God man! What the devil has the poor man done to deserve that?"

Marmaduke felt slightly offended.

The Lieutenant ignored the question entirely. "Speaking of missions Sir?"

The Colonel harrumphed again. "The mission, yes, of course. All the platoons were dispatched this morning, I should think by now they are should be here, here, here and here!" he stabbed at the places on the map as he spoke. "They are heading here,

here, here, and here. They should be in their final positions before dusk. As you'll note, each position commands an area of coast that Agnes identified as a possible wreck site. You'll also note that each position is linked by either a road or a track allowing a line of communication between all of them. I've made sure that each platoon has a designated runner."

Marmaduke realised that the Commander had turned this into a military operation and was actually enjoying himself. After all, after an undistinguished career in the American Wars the only other battle he had had taken part in was the one at the Castle a year previously. The man was positively bursting for action.

"And now Gentlemen, the time has come for us to saddle up and get underway!"

His words dropped like stones down a deep, deep well.

"Us, Sir?" Enquired the Lieutenant.

The Commander harrumphed again. "Of course we ...."

He was cut off by the arrival of the Sergeant, who ignoring the Commander, marched straight up to the Lieutenant and saluted. "Message dispatched, Sir!" He stated louder than necessary.

The Commander noticed a hint of sarcasm in the Sergeants manner. You didn't get to command a whole host of troopers, sergeants, and lieutenants without being able to spot sarcasm from the lower ranks. He didn't like it one bit.

"As I was saying Sergeant, the four of us will ride out and liaise with the nearest position before taking up our own position here, right at the centre if the operations."

Marmaduke looked at the map. Strategically it was the right place. It was the place he would have chosen himself. He just didn't expect to be sharing it with the Commander of the Garrison. The Sergeant was even more horrified. He was about to go on a mission he knew nothing about in the company of his Lieutenant and his Commander, and even worse a hired mercenary who looked as if he would slit your throat as soon as look at you. He kept his face as expressionless as he could, but inwardly he was cursing his luck to high heaven.

Chapter Fifteen.

Meanwhile in the twentieth century Agnes started work on the bit of paper by scanning it into her computer and running a programme that claimed it could identify any make or type of Paper ever used. She hoped it lived up to its claims. Of course the manufacturers of the software would be startled to know their programme was being used on a computer that wasn't attached to the internet. It wasn't even plugged into the mains. It just responded to Agnes's moving hands and finger. She was waiting for the programme to do its work when a psychic bell rang at the back of Agnes perception. She tutted and hurried down her cellar steps, through the wall and answered her eighteenth century door. A soldier stood there holding a folded piece of paper. She couldn't help but notice that the man was not only sweating, and that he was very, very red in the face, but that he was so out of breath that he couldn't speak. He spluttered something between gasps of breath and handed her the note. She thanked him and, before shutting her door, advised him to walk back to the Castle and to take life a bit more slowly.

She returned to the twenty first century where she and unfolded the note and read the words scribbled by the Lieutenant.

The words made her think. A Colonel nicknamed "Foxy" at York barracks. Somewhere on-line there must be a list of soldiers that had been stationed at the barracks. She moved her finger and checked the screen. There was a new image on the screen. It held the image of her piece of paper and a block of information. The paper was from the mid 1700's. She knew that, she read on. It had been made by a paper manufacturer in Manchester. The company had a contract to supply the Army. She sat back and allowed herself a slight smile to herself. It was tenuous but it was a link. "Foxy Tom" was beginning to emerge from the shadows.

She moved her fingers once more and the computer sprang back into life. The screen filled with names and lists and ranks and dates, shifting and scrolling as the search progressed. After a few moments it settled and a short list of names appeared. She had asked for a search of men of rank serving at York barracks during the mid 1700's whose names had connotation to a fox. She had been very creative. She ran down the list and read out the names of General William Rufus, Colonel Reynard, another General by the hyphenated name of Lane-Fox. She smiled, the search had even added a Lieutenant General Hunt. She ran her eyes up the list once more and instinctively her eyes rested on the name of Colonel Reynard. She flicked her finger at the screen once again and the name in the screen glowed slightly as further information scrolled across the screen. She leant forward and read. She discovered that a certain Colonel Thomas Reynard had served in the Army stationed at York Barracks for eight years before he had been discharged for "dishonourable behaviour from a man of rank". Despite searching further she could find no further information about him once he had left the army. She ran check after check but nothing could be found, the man had simply disappeared from all records, military or otherwise. She sat back and checked that date. The Colonel had been discharged three years before the present date. Well that was to three years before the current date in the 18th century. She had a feeling she was getting nearer to finding Foxy Tom.

It was time to return. The sun was just beginning to set as a seagull rose from the Old Town and spiralled high into the sky before turning and flying north in the direction of the coming storm. As she gained height she could make out shipping sailing up and down the coast. She could see the fishing boats bobbing in the two Scarborough bays. In the distance she thought she could see the Excise

Cutter. She tried to look further north. Somewhere out there was "The Venture", sailing south with her precious and valuable cargo.

There was a sudden blur in the air and a seagull appeared alongside the Excise Cutter. No one on board paid any attention to yet another seagull. On board she could see the Excise men were busy at work trimming the sail, trying to get every last bit of speed out of the ship. Behind the helmsman she saw Peter, looking every inch the Rear Admiral she had promoted him to. He was standing by the ships rail scanning the seas ahead for a sign of "The Venture". She noticed he had pinned her small drawing of its shape onto the rail in front of him.

"Smart lad!" She thought, "Might even make a Rear Admiral one day."

Satisfied, the seagull disappeared in a blur only to reappear above the cliffs of Ravenscar. Even in her seagull form she felt her heart skip a beat. Below her in the darkness she could make out the figure of a man carefully making his way along the track that led down the cliff to the small cave carved out of the rock. She thought of him tucking into his supplies. She would have smirked, but it's a well known fact that seagulls can't smirk.

Chapter Sixteen.

The four platoons had left earlier that day. A mile behind them the Colonel, Lieutenant Smalls, the Sergeant and Marmaduke followed on. Marmaduke wasn't happy about the company. He preferred to wok by himself. His only consolation was that the army had provided him with a better horse. The route had been specifically chosen by the Commander. It circuitous to say the least, but, as he pointed out, running between hedgerows and along edges of woodlands it provided them with the as much cover as possible. The last thing the Commander wanted was his presence to be seen.

Looking at the surrounding countryside, Marmaduke was almost thrown off his horse when it reared up suddenly. He grabbed the reins and jerked its head to one side, bringing it to an abrupt halt. They had just rounded a corner and almost ran into a wagon slung across the road blocking any further way forward. Behind the wagon stood four men, all armed with shotguns. The Commander had managed to stop his horse but Lieutenant Smalls and Sergeant Lewis had been less fortunate. Spooked by the sight of an unexpected wagon his horse had reared up and deposited him on his behind in the middle of the road. The Lieutenant was even more unfortunate. He had tugged at the reins but the move was so sudden that the horse skidded and lost its footing. Down went both horse and rider. The horse quickly recovered, regained its feet and skittered back the way it had come. Its rider wasn't so lucky. As he fell the horse had fallen on him. The Lieutenant heard a snap, and as the horse regained its feet, he realised his leg was broken.

Meanwhile in front of the wagon the Commander was berating the men with the rifles. "Bloody fools, bloody stupid place to leave a wagon!"

It took a few seconds before he realised that the guns were pointing in his direction. It took Marmaduke less time to realise that no one was looking at him. In one fluid movement he dismounted and leapt in the air where he twisted and cleared the hedge at the side of the road.

One of the men with the guns suddenly gave voice. "Here where did that other one disappear to?"

The others followed the man's pointing finger which gave the Commander time to leap of his own horse and take refuge behind the wagon itself. He drew his sword and waved it under the wagon, trying to strike the men's legs. It wouldn't reach.

The men behind the wagon pointed their weapons down the road. All they could see was the stunned Sergeant still sitting in the road and the injured officer sat upright clutching his damaged leg. There was a sudden movement in the hedgerow beside them. One of the men panicked and fired his gun. All eyes looked in the direction in which the musket ball travelled. That was their mistake. As they turned a figure sprang from the hedge behind them. The first man Marmaduke hit had no idea what happened. He dropped to his knees immediately. The second turned just in time to find two large hands that seemed to have grown talons scrape down either side of his face. Instantly he dropped his gun, put his hands to his face and fell to his knees screaming. The third man had turned and was levelling his musket at Marmaduke's chest when a throwing knife suddenly appeared sticking out of the man throat. His face filled with surprise as he dropped his gun and put his hands to his throat in a vain attempt to stem the blood. He too fell to his knees. The fourth man was the man who had fired the shot and as he tried to reload his weapon he suddenly began to hop from leg to leg. The Commander had rolled under the wagon and was viciously attacking his attacker's legs with his sword. Marmaduke hit him once and the man fell.

"Jolly good show!" remarked the Commander as he rolled out from beneath the wagon.

"Not for the Lieutenant, I'm afraid." Said Marmaduke nodding beyond the wagon to where Sergeant Lewis squatted by the side of the injured Lieutenant. He seemed to be trying to fix some sort of splint to the man's leg. Judging by the yelps of pain the Lieutenant gave out he wasn't making too good a job of it.

"We need to get him back to the garrison as soon as possible." Marmaduke said.

The Commander hit the side of the wagon with his hand. "Decent of them to provide transport! The Sergeant can hitch the horses up. If he takes the main road he'll be back there in about an hour. Best thing. Any idea who these bounders are?" He added as he gave one of the unconscious men a kick.

Marmaduke examined each one, rummaging in their pockets and inside their jackets.

"Two dead and two who will wake up with very bad headaches." He said as he stood up. "None of them were carrying anything. A few coins, a twist of tobacco. That's all, nothing to give any clue as to who they are, or were!"

The Commander nodded grimly. "Probably sent here to keep the road free and dissuade any travellers. The last thing they expected was for anyone to fight back."

"They started it!" Marmaduke replied realising that the Commander seemed slightly shocked at the degree of sudden and deadly violence that he had shown.

The Commander harrumphed. "No criticism old chap, just remarking. Those chaps weren't soldiers though. Wouldn't even put them down as militia. No, they're just robbers, bandits, common footpads."

Marmaduke cocked his head. The Commander gave a shrug. "What I mean is that if this is an example of the wreckers fighting prowess, well I don't think we need to worry very much."

Marmaduke hoped he was right.

It took them the best part of half an hour to load the wagon. The two dead men were positioned at the drivers end. The two unconscious men were tied up securely with some rope found in the cart itself and finally the Lieutenant was stretched out with his damaged leg resting on some sacking and padded with bracken Marmaduke had gathered using his sword to cut great swathes of them. Dark was descending as the Commander and Marmaduke sat on their horses and watched the cart head back towards Scarborough.

Chapter Seventeen

Night had fallen, the sunset dying behind the hills that marked the start of the moors. Agnes glided over the countryside below. Everything looked calm and peaceful. Only she knew that somewhere below her were four platoons of soldiers and a gang of wreckers waiting for their prey. She felt herself being buffeted by a strong wind. She could feel the storm blowing in from the sea. She felt some drops of rain hit her feathers. Within seconds it had turned into a downpour.

Marmaduke wiped the rain out his eyes with the back of his hand and peered into the darkness. By rights a platoon of six soldiers should be hidden around her somewhere. He looked across to the Garrison Commander. He was obviously of the same opinion. He was standing up in his stirrups anxiously look to the right and left.

"Damned simple instructions. Should be here! Where the Devil have they got to?"

Marmaduke wasn't sure whether the Commander was talking to him or himself. He sniffed the air, something didn't feel right. Despite the fact that the night was now pitch black he could still make out details of the landscape in different shades of grey. His eye was drawn to a slight movement in a small copse of trees to the right of the lane. He turned his horse and went to investigate. The Commander saw him move and followed on behind.

Neither of them were prepared for what they came across. As he neared the first of the trees all of Marmaduke's body began to tingle. If he had been in his cat form his fur would have been stuck straight out. Something was very wrong. He jumped off his horse and carefully made his way through the bracken and undergrowth into the wood. He found the first soldier tied to the tree. Without having to check Marmaduke just knew the man was dead. His head hung at a strange angle to his body. Stains darkened the front of his uniform and had soaked into the earth at the base of the tree. Marmaduke looked closer. The man's throat had been cut. His face showed signs of a beating.

Marmaduke heard a rustle in the undergrowth. He spun around pistol already in his hand. It was the Commander. When he saw the body he deflated.

"Sweet Mother of all that's Holy!" he muttered.

"Unholy!" Corrected Marmaduke. He looked around him A few yards further into the woods he could see another shape tied to the side of another tree.

"I've a feeling the same fate has befallen all of your men!"

The Commander was already thrashing through the undergrowth towards another tree further away. Marmaduke winced. If anyone was still around they would hear the Commander coming from a hundred

yards. He stood still and scanned the woodland.
With the exception of the Commander nothing was
moving, nothing else was around. The Commander
was some distance away so Marmaduke took a risk.
The air shimmered around him and suddenly the
shape of the man turned into the shape of a large
cat. It stood still for a second. The rain had eased off
a little but the wind was still strong. He sniffed the
air and silently bounded through the wood. He
paused when he reached the open countryside at the
other side. He sniffed the air again, there was a
slight scent. He followed it loping along at the side
of a hedge, his black shape melting into its deep
shadows.

He had travelled half a mile, heading towards the
coast when he heard the sound of voices. He
stopped and listened. The wind made it difficult to
tell just where the voices were coming from. He
made his decision and, like a cat on a midnight
prowl, he threaded his way through hedgerows and
across open country. Suddenly he stopped dead in

his tracks. He heard someone cough, the sound was near. It had come from behind a stone wall that lined a small cart track. Marmaduke crouched low, on all fours, until he came to a gate in the wall. He peered around the opening. Through the rain he could see a track leading towards a low stone building. A barn he thought. Through its half open doors he could see lights, shadows and movement. He heard the cough again. It was nearer. Carefully he crept around the gate post. Then he saw the man. He had obviously been stationed to guard the gate but the downpour had caused him to seek what little shelter he could find behind the wall. Marmaduke watched the man who, feeling some sort of sixth sense, turned and looked directly at him. That was his mistake. Marmaduke leapt forward, claws fully outstretched. The guard stood no chance. He was bowled over in a second, hitting his head as the claws raked down his body. Marmaduke didn't even stop to look. He bounded across the open space to the barn covering the distance in a series of leaps.

When he reached the barn wall he stopped and listened. No one had come out. He edged around the corner watching as light spilled out of the partially open doorway. Very carefully he crept closer. The voices were louder now. It seemed that someone was giving a series of instructions. Voices responded. Looking through the door would be too risky. Marmaduke looked up. The roof was made of hard slabs of stone tiles. They would be strong enough. With one leap he landed on the roof and moved carefully to its apex. He stood looking closely at the tiles. Sure enough towards the middle, there was a slight chink of light. A missing tile, just what he needed. Marmaduke thanked his luck. He crawled across the roof and lay down and peered through the small gap. Below him he could see a small part of the interior of the barn. He carefully jiggled the tile and the gap grew larger. Now he could make out a large covered cart. Men moved around it. From his position above he could count eight, or was it nine, he couldn't be sure. What he was sure of was that there were more men beyond his vision. Voices suggested that another group of men were seated at the far end of the barn. From the noise and conversations he figured they were passing the time playing dice. He quickly recounted. There had to be more than a dozen men inside. Then there was a commotion at the door. He moved across the roof and looked down. A party of eight men had arrived and were walking towards the barns entrance. A voice shouted over the rest of the voices.

"I thought you had a guard on the gate?"

A second voice replied. "Course I have. Red Eyes out there."

"Well if he's there he's asleep! We walked straight through the gate, no challenge!"

The second voice growled. "If he's asleep he won't wake up!"

A figure appeared at the barns door and walked quickly towards the gate. As he walked down the track Marmaduke studied him. He must have been over six feet tall. He was wearing a long black frock coat held closed by a heavy, thick leather belt. His trousers disappeared into a pair of long sea boots. Black greasy hair fell from his tricorn hat. He had pulled his collar up against the rain and Marmaduke noticed the sword and pistol tucked into his belt. Marmaduke watched as the man reached the gate and listened as he hissed out the name of his missing companion. There was no answer. The man looked around. It didn't take long before he found the body. Without hesitation the man turned and ran back to the barn.

"This is going to be interesting!" thought Marmaduke to himself as below him, inside the barn, a whole lot of shouting and yelling broke out. A group of nine or ten men burst out of the doors led by the man in the frock coat. He led them straight to where the body of Red Eye lay. There was some shuffling, pushing and shoving as someone shone light onto their dead comrades face. Despite the wind and rain Marmaduke could distinctly hear the sharp intake of breath as they saw the injuries. Some immediately stood upright and looked anxiously to their left and right, fearing that whatever had attacked Red Eye was still lurking nearby. Marmaduke flattened himself to the roof. The last thing he needed was to be spotted. The men returned to the barn, four of them carrying the body of Red Eye between them. As they entered the building another commotion broke out. Marmaduke took the opportunity to leap from the roof and bound across the field. He made his way back through the open country to where he had left the Commander. There was nothing he could do at the barn. There were just too many men for him to take on single handed. As he bounded through the trees a worrying thought struck him. Perhaps the men he'd seen weren't all the men involved in the "enterprise". Perhaps somewhere between here and the sea there was another group of men. As he bounded through the wind and the rain he wondered just how many wreckers there were.

Agnes had been flying across the countryside when she spotted a cart below her. It was travelling down a small country lane in the direction of Scarborough. She swooped down to take a close look. What she saw shocked her. It was Sergeant Lewis driving the two horses whilst in the back lay Lieutenant Smalls together with a group of men trussed up like Christmas turkeys. There was a shimmer in the air that disturbed the falling rain. Suddenly Sergeant Lewis spotted an elderly woman standing in the middle of the road. He pulled the reins and the horses stopped. As he looked he recognised Agnes, she was looking at him with her head to one side. Without even realising it he began speaking.

"We were held up. Four men with guns. They blocked the road with this cart. Marmaduke attacked them. Got two dead and two unconscious in the back. Lieutenant Smalls fell of his horse and broke his leg. Commander told me to take the cart back to the garrison."

Agnes took it all in at the first hearing. "Don't move!" she instructed him as she walked to the back of the cart.

The first thing she did was to check on Lieutenant Smalls. He was semi-conscious, soaked to the skin. A soft moan came from him as she gently moved him to examine the break. She placed her hands either side of his leg and closed her eyes. It was a clean break. She gave a move with her head and a warm glow passed through her body, through her hands and spread through the Lieutenant's body. A second glow travelled the same route and concentrated itself in the area around the break. Just a little help to persuade the bones to knit together quicker. She looked up to the Sergeant.

"Did you fix the splint?" she asked.

He nodded.

"You did a good job!"

He nodded again.

Once she was satisfied that the Lieutenant was comfortable, or as comfortable as a man with broken leg laying in the back of a cart in the pouring rain could be, she examined the others. Whatever had hit the two unconscious men had hit them hard. They were deeply unconscious. Just to ensure they would remain that way for a good few hours yet Agnes cast a little spell. She glanced across at the two bodies. There was nothing she could do for them. Marmaduke had certainly not pulled any punches, his claw marks were very, very obvious.

She walked back to the front of the cart and looked up at the Sergeant.

"Get back to the Caste as soon as possible. The Lieutenant will be fine, but all the same, get him to the Garrison sick bay as soon as you arrive!"

The Sergeant nodded.

"Well off you go!" Said Agnes as the man sat still transfixed. She clapped her hands and he quickly snapped the reins and the horses began walking forward.

As he moved off Agnes made a move with her fingers. The cart and its occupants, dead and alive, glowed for a brief second and then disappeared from sight. Agnes knew the cloaking spell would last long enough for the cart to make it to the outskirts of Scarborough safely without being seen.

She stood at the side of the road and closed her eyes. As the rain fell and the wind grew stronger she reached out with her mind. She found the Commander standing by the edge of a wood a few miles away. What she saw behind him upset her greatly.

The air shimmered and the owl flew fast and low across the open country and landed in a tree on the outskirts of the wood. There was a second shimmer and she stood next to the Commander. He looked up without expressing any surprise.

"Don't go in there!" He said.

"I've already seen." She answered.

He nodded. "Got 'em down, had to. Couldn't leave them tied up like that."

Agnes was about to ask about Marmaduke when her senses picked up a movement at the far side of the wood. A black shape was leaping and bounding silently through the undergrowth. As it approached it began to look less like a giant cat and more like the shape of a man. He was breathing hard when he arrived at her side.

The Commander and Agnes listened in silence as Marmaduke told his story. When he had finished Agnes began to speak.

"This changes everything." She said. "We need to locate the other platoons. It's obvious that attacking six soldiers holds no qualms for them. As

Marmaduke said, we have no idea how many wreckers are actually out there. I have a feeling that the group you saw arrive were the ones responsible for this despicable carnage."

Marmaduke nodded. "They came from this direction, I think."

Agnes shrugged. "We've still no idea how many there are out there."

She looked up at Marmaduke and lowered her voice. "I've completely underestimated them haven't I?" She asked.

"This is no ordinary gang of wreckers." He said, and then added under his breath, "More like a small army!"

Agnes nodded. "Now that's interesting that you should say that." She said thoughtfully. But this wasn't the time for explanations. There were still soldiers out there whose lives could be at risk.

"Wait here!" She told them. The air shimmered and an owl flew out of the woods and across open countryside. She flew high and scanned the ground beneath her. The rain didn't make it easy and the wind buffeted her. She visualised the map in the Commanders office and flew to the place where the X marked the location. It was on an outcrop of rock. She had a feeling that, despite being told to position themselves on the rock the soldiers, being soldiers, would find somewhere to shelter. As she approached she spotted a slight movement and swooped down. She had found the first group. It was as she thought, they were sheltering from the weather under the overhanging rock.

She knew she would have to warn them, but the idea of suddenly appearing in front of six armed troopers didn't really appeal. She knew soldiers. They preferred to shoot first and ask questions later. She landed silently in the trees a few yards away. The air shimmered and an elderly woman appeared and disappeared. As she walked towards the soldiers her fingers were moving in intricate patterns keeping the cloaking spell in place.

She walked up to the soldier who she assumed was in charge. That assumption was based on the fact that he was sat in the driest place and seemed to be the one doing most of the talking. As she neared him her fingers changed their pattern. The man's eyes suddenly grew wide. His mouth opened but no sound came out of it. Around them the rest of the soldiers carried on with whatever they were doing as if nothing was happening, which as far as they could see, nothing was.

Agnes leant forward and whispered in the soldier's ear. His eyes opened even wider. When Agnes finished speaking she stood upright and simply walked back to the woods. She moved her fingers once again and suddenly the soldier shot to his feet. His face looked like he had just awoken from a very bad dream. He barked series of orders and his men leapt to attention. They picked up their weapons and held them at the ready then slowly and carefully they moved out of their sheltered position and headed towards the small road that Agnes hoped, would lead them to safety.

To say that the soldiers now walking with primed muskets and fixed bayonets were surprised at this turn of events would be an understatement. But orders are orders and at least they might get out of the rain and avoid the coming storm.

Years later an ex-soldier would be given free tankards of ale for narrating his story of how one night on patrol a vision of his mother came to him and warned him of a great danger. How also on that very night a vicious gang of smugglers, bandits and robbers had landed on the coast and were heading straight for their position, and if he wanted to escape with his life, he should order an ordered retreat. That his story must be true as another patrol, just like his, had been attacked and butchered.

As Marmaduke and the Commander waited in the wood Marmaduke thought he heard a sound. He cocked his head. It was the sound of a distant gunshot. At first it was so feint that he couldn't be sure. But there again...

His body seemed to bend and twist and blur as he raced through the wood in the direction of the noise. He heard another shot and sped up until he came to a cross roads where two small lanes intersected. He stopped and shrank back under cover of a nearby tree. On one side hiding behind a dry stone wall were six troopers. Opposite them and moving down the road towards them were a group of heavily armed men. Marmaduke counted, there were eight of them, spread out in a wide arc, advancing slowly through the rain towards the troopers. Four were carrying storm lanterns that cast small pools of light on the roadway. Marmaduke saw movement from behind the wall. It was a trooper's head that quickly popped up to see what was coming their way. It quickly disappeared again as a musket ball flew off the wall sending splinters of stone flying in all directions. Time to act. Marmaduke aimed for the men carrying the lanterns. They never knew what hit them. It was if a black, solid shadow armed with fangs and claws had swept out of the driving wind and rain. Suddenly the night was filled with the sounds of screams and shouts and breaking glass from the dropped lanterns. Curiosity got the better of the soldiers behind the wall and they risked taking a look to see what was happening. In the darkness they could just make out the shapes of their attackers. Instead of standing they were now just black shapes writhing and screaming on the roadway. Before they could lift their rifles they were aware of someone standing amongst them. In the darkness they could make out a tall man with an eye patch and missing one ear. However what made his sudden appearance so alarming was that his hands were dripping with not rain but blood. As he spoke each soldier took an involuntary step backwards.

"I wouldn't worry about them anymore. The missions abandoned. You are to return to barracks immediately."

Looks of shock, surprise, relief and panic crossed across six faces simultaneously. They looked at the man with one eye, looked at the dark shapes lying in the roadway, turned and half ran and half marched down the road until they disappeared into the rain and dark. The air next to Marmaduke shimmered.

"That was a bit reckless!" Agnes said.

"Wasn't much time to do anything else. They had them trapped behind the wall. They were just closing in for the kill, another couple of minutes...." he shrugged and left the statement hanging. Agnes nodded. She walked across to the shapes in the road, clicked her fingers and a low light glowed around her illuminating the carnage at her feet. Carefully, one at a time, she examined them. Marmaduke watched on. After she had examined the last one she stood up and turned to Marmaduke. "Four have their throats ripped out, one has a broken neck, and two seemed to have died from heart attacks."

"Eight!" Said Marmaduke. Agnes looked back at the bodies.

"There were eight of them!" He repeated looking out into the rain and darkness.

Agnes let go a small locating spell. Nothing. It seemed the man had long gone. They returned to a very anxious Commander, still sitting with the bodies of his troopers. He looked up as they approached him.

"All safely on their way back to the Castle Garrison!" Agnes said.

The Commander gave a sigh of relief. "Rather upsets our plans of catching them red handed!" he remarked.

Agnes nodded. "At least the ship will be warned and not be wrecked on the rocks. Lives have been saved there!"

Marmaduke resisted the urge to scratch his back against the tree.

The Commander grunted. "Saved at the cost of the lives of my troopers! And we've been forced to abandon the operation. "

Marmaduke nodded. "We won't capture them now, but at least we know they are actually out there. All we have to do is find them. Mark my words, when the ship sails past they'll disperse. We simply follow them!"

Agnes nodded her head in agreement, then paused. "We can but I'm not sure about the Commander here."

Before he began to splutter his indignation Marmaduke held his hand up. "She's right. We have, shall we say, certain advantages that you don't possess."

Before he spoke the Commander actually paused to think. He remembered seeing the owl just before

Agnes appeared. He remembered how he had see Marmaduke shape shift. They were right, but he still didn't fancy being left to fend for himself. When Agnes spoke it was as if she had been reading his mind. "Just ride back to the Castle. You need to catch up with your reserve force. Remember they are still out there. Get them safely back to the Garrison, oh and just in case you bump into anyone...." She made a slight move with her hand and the air around the Commander shimmered, his image faded, appeared and then disappeared.

"That's a cloaking spell. To all intent and purpose you are invisible. I'll put one on your horse as well. That should see you safe until you catch up with your reserves. Then march them back and we'll join you for breakfast! Oh and don't worry about them." She nodded at the bodies still in the wood. "I will place a spell of protection over them. You may send a troop out to collect them in the morning. They will be here."

The Commander nodded. Unused to taking orders, when Agnes spoke in her common matter of fact way he knew she was talking sense. A few minutes later an invisible military man mounted a horse that wasn't there and set off into the wind and rain. He was disappointed to discover that visible or invisible, it made no difference to the rain. He was still soaking wet.

Chapter Eighteen

A little later an owl took off from the woodland heading directly in the direction of the sea. At the same time a black shadow loped across the fields and hedgerows, almost invisible against the black night.

Agnes flew as high as she could scanning the land below her. In the distance she could see hear the sea. She drove her wings harder and made a sweeping glide over the cliffs and across a small bay below her. She scanned the beach using all her senses. Nothing. She continued flying northwards. She was almost at Ravenscar when she saw what she was looking for. Below her she could see tiny pin pricks of light. She swooped down and silently glided through trees until she landed on the upper branches of an old, weather beaten oak. She tucked her wings into her body and swivelled her head like only an owl can do. In the distance she could make out men moving along the beach. Below her in a small cleft in the cliff she could see other men holding a string of pack horse. Halfway down the cliff she could see a number of men walking along a stream that cut a small valley that ran down from the cliff onto the beach. As the rain poured down the normally quiet little stream had turned into a small river. She noticed that many of the men slipped and fell, splashing in the fast running water. "I bet they didn't account for that much rain!" she thought to herself.

The man at the head of the line of men was having the same thoughts. When he had visited the site some days previously the stream had been a small trickle, now it was a river. Another problem! So far his night had not gone very well. First of all he'd come across a platoon of troopers. What they had been doing out here in this sort of weather was anyone's guess. They had been easy to overcome. They were outnumbered and hadn't even heard his own men approaching. He had tried to find out why they were there but they claimed they didn't know. Just claimed they were on manoeuvres. Just kept saying their orders were to await a further signal. No matter how hard he had pressed them they kept to their story. Eventually he had lost his patience and ordered his men to dispatch them. He left their bodies tied to the trees. Then there had been that problem back at the old barn. He had seen the body of Red Eye himself. He had no idea what had killed him in that manner. It had spooked the rest of the men in the barn and it had taken him all his time to calm them down and to persuade them to continue with the night's enterprise. Finally there was the mystery of the shots. Both he and his men had heard them, behind them in the distance. He had no idea of who was firing and at what.

As the rain eased he could make out the men on the beach. They were standing looking out to sea, in the direction of the headland. As he watched a red light suddenly penetrated the rain. It hung in the air briefly before falling back to earth. It was the signal.

He looked down onto the beach. The signal had been seen and was being acted upon. Now a new light appeared. At first it was a feint flicker, then it grew stronger. It was on the rocks out at the very end of the reef hidden under the high tide.

Marmaduke saw the signal light as well. It seemed as if it originated from a headland a mile or so away. That would mean they would all be on the beach he thought. He wondered how many men there would be gathered there, then gave up. He simply had no idea. He changed direction and headed towards the sea.

From her perch in the tree Agnes counted twenty men on the beach and the second party that had just marched down the stream numbered the same amount. At least forty she thought. Then there were the men below her with the pack horses. As she watched them moving along the beach she realised that each man was moving with a purpose. The men with the horses were preparing saddle bags and panniers. The new arrivals were now spreading out in a large fan all along the beach. The men on the headland scurried and moved again with purpose. To Agnes it looked as if they were moving in some well drilled operation, as if they were trained, as if they were all part of a small army. That word again. Army! She let the thought settle at the back of her mind as she felt a slight tingle ruffle the feathers along her back. She sensed that Marmaduke was somewhere near. She just hoped that he wouldn't do anything rash. She had seen at close hand just how vicious he could be. She wondered if she should be worried but then remembered the way a cat would kill mice or birds.

"It was just their nature." she said to herself. All the same she knew there were far too many for even Marmaduke to think about tackling them single handed. At least she hoped he did. If an owl would have had fingers they would have been crossed.

Marmaduke carefully lowered himself down the cliff until he found a shelf of rock where he could sit and observe the comings and goings on the beach below him. He saw the light at the end of the reef. He saw the men and the horses. He saw other men fanning out across the beach. He tied to count them all and couldn't. He felt his claws extend and he let out a low growl.

"No!" he told himself. There were just too many to tackle. Anyway the object of the exercise had changed. Now it was purely a watching brief.

The man on the beach looked around. The signal had been given. That meant the ship had been seen. It should be close now. The false light on the rocks was still shining, lighting up a treacherous area of sea that crashed, bubbled and boiled on the hidden reef. He became aware of distant shouting. He cocked his head trying to make out the words but they were blown away on the wind. Then a dim shape appeared around the headland. He strained his eyes to see through the rain and darkness. It was the white sails of a ship, however it was still some distance out to sea. He held his breath. Any minute now the helmsman would see the false light and the ship would veer towards the rocks. He waited. The ship maintained its course. He watched with an open mouth as driven by the wind, it turned slightly and with breakers crashing over its bows and all sails flapping and snapping in the wind, it headed back out to sea and back towards the deeper waters of the sea lanes. In his frustration he kicked a large stone. It skittered across the beach.

Agnes let go of her breath. It had worked. Peter Potts had carried out his duties to the letter. The helmsman of "The Venture" had brought the ship close enough for it to be recognised but had then changed course, bringing her around the headland in deeper and safer waters. Sure enough he had seen the light the Rear Admiral had warned him about. He turned from the helm and pointed towards it. Peter Potts looked over the side of the ship and saw it for himself. He shook his head. In the dark and through the rain and clouds of sea spray it looked very convincing. He wasn't sure if that he was at the helm he would have suspected a trap.

"Perhaps that's why I'm still a junior officer." he thought. Suddenly the entire beach and surrounding cliffs and landscape were illuminated by a giant bolt of lightning. Peter and the helmsman watched as it cracked and crackled hanging in the air. By its light Peter could make out tiny figures on the beach. They seemed to be running. The ship suddenly bucked as it hit the tide and headed south and to safety.

Marmaduke had just happened to look to the sky as the lightning bolt turned the world into a very bright, black and white place. He closed his eyes and opened them again, then blinked. The white image was still burned onto his retina. It took a few seconds for his sight to return. When it did he smiled, and let go what could only be described as a purr. Below him was a scene of utter panic. Men were running in all directions, tripping, stumbling and falling over in their eagerness to get off the beach.

Agnes just couldn't help herself. She had seen the surprise on the faces of the wreckers as the ship loomed out of the darkness only to change course and go sailing by. Their surprise had then turned to anger as they shouted and gesticulated to each other. She thought very hard.

The bolt of lightning she conjured up was bigger than she expected. The crack nearly knocked her off her perch. She let it hang in the air long enough for her to take in the whole scene. The men in the beach were standing like statues, looking up at the lightning bolt that still hung in the air dancing and crackling above their heads. A second group of men were standing on the rocks where the false light was still shining out to an empty sea. Below her the men who had walked down the river bed stopped and looked up. The stillness was broken by one of the horses that panicked and dragged the reins from its surprised handler. It ran across the beach, skittering and slipping on the loose rocks. Its movement seemed like a cue for everyone to come alive at once. Some men tried to get out of the horses way and slipped and fell themselves. Some ran towards the stream, anything to get out of the way of the horse and the lightning that still cracked and fizzed above their heads. The crash of thunder that followed seemed as if a hundred cannons had exploded at the same time. As it rolled and echoed around the bay, men clutched their ears. Some fell and lay flat on the rocks and pebbles looking up in fear. They regained their feet and scrambled away from the beach. Agnes suddenly became aware of movement below her. The man that had led to second group of men down the stream bed had suddenly taken a horse and was forcing it up a small track that led to the nearest cliff top. Agnes decided that he was the one to follow.

The unexpected thunderclap almost deafened Marmaduke. He was sure the vibrations had made his teeth move. He shook his head to clear his ears from the ringing. He knew such thunder and lightning was definitely not a natural phenomena. He stared at the far side of the beach where a man was quickly mounting a horse. He watched as the man forced the unwilling animal up a small track leading back up to the moors. A second later his cat like vision saw an owl take off from an old oak tree and follow in the direction of the rider.

Given the darkness and the narrowness of the lanes he was travelling along the rider was making good time. He didn't notice an owl following on behind. She had trailed him for a mile when he suddenly pulled on his reins and the horse came to a abrupt stop. Agnes glided down to perch on a nearby dry stone wall. She watched as the rider dismounted and walked across to the side of the track. It was then that Agnes noticed what the rider had seen. It was a man cowering and shaking, half squatting, half crouching, trying to press himself into the wall. The rider approached him. She heard him call a name and the figure turned. Half choked words tumbled out of his mouth. Neither Agnes nor the rider could make sense of them. The man pointed with a shaking arm further up the road.

It was then that Agnes realised who the man was. Marmaduke had said there were eight men that attacked the troopers. The rider had accidently stumbled across the one who had escaped. She peered into the darkness until she could make out his features. His face was ashen grey, his hair was white. His lips moved but no intelligible words could be heard. The rider bent down and shook the man by his shoulders. He tried to communicate. The man just gibbered. The Rider shook him once more. For a brief second a look of recognition passed across the man's eyes. He gripped the Riders arms and with his other pointed up the road. The Rider stood up and drew a pistol. It was then that Agnes realised where they were. They were a hundred yards from the cross roads where Marmaduke's attack had occurred. Half carrying, half dragging the man behind him the Rider walked up the road. It took him a further five minutes before he came across the first of Marmaduke's victims. The rain had eased off, the wind was dying down. Overhead the storm had almost passed by. A feint glow of moonlight softly illuminated the scene. It showed the Rider standing, looking down at the bodies lying on the track. The man he was with dragged himself free and refused to step any nearer. The Rider ignored him as he slowly and very carefully examined each of the bodies. His face was white and stone like as he looked at the claw marks and wounds they had suffered. He stood up and quickly looked around him. He drew his pistol. He had no idea what could have killed seven of his men. The one thing he did know was that no musket, or pistol, or sword could have inflicted such wounds as those. He bent down and picked up a discarded musket. He looked at the pan and sniffed the spent gunpowder.

Those must have been the shots he heard. For the life of him he couldn't work out who or what his men had been shooting at. Taking advantage of the pale moonlight he walked around the area, peering over the stone walls. He looked over each one until he eventually found what he was looking for, a large flattened patch of grass. He bent down and saw footprint. A glint caught his eye. He bent down and picked up a lost powder flask. He turned it over in his hand. It was army issue. It told him that there had been second platoon in the area. But what had happened to them? Whatever had attacked his men had left them alone. Why was that? He shook his head. He carefully collected the spent weapons he found in the road and stuffed them into his panniers. He looked around. The survivor was still cowering behind a nearby wall. Despite his protestations the Rider dragged him out and, not too carefully, threw him across the neck of his horse. He pulled himself onto his horse, kicked it and continued his journey.

Agnes watched it all. She allowed the rider to get some way ahead before launching herself into the air and slowly followed him in a series of low swooping glides.

From his position halfway up the cliff Marmaduke watched as the figures on the beach dissolved into the surrounding woods and countryside. He thought to himself. They had succeeded in preventing the ship wreck, but the idea of capturing the wreckers had gone very, very wrong. Six troopers killed, Lieutenant Smalls with a broken leg and the wreckers scattered to all corners of the locality. He ran his fingers through his hair and whiskers. They had entirely underestimated the strength of the wrecking gang. He wondered whether he should follow any of them, then decided against it. Those men were the hired help. Agnes had spotted the leader, and had followed him as he left the scene. Marmaduke sighed. It was a long walk back to Scarborough. There was a blur and a creature half man half cat suddenly dropped from the cliff and bounded across a deserted beach.

The storm had abated and the moon was winning its battle with the clouds. Below her she saw the Rider take the main coast road and head north. After a mile or so he suddenly turned off the main road onto a small track that ran alongside a wood. Agnes almost lost him when he made a second turn into the woods. She flew higher trying to pick him out. It was then she noticed the house. It was large. Not quite a stately home or mansion, more like someone's country house. She circled in time to see the rider emerge from the woods and ride straight to the stable block at the rear of the house.

Chapter Nineteen.

The following morning saw an unhappy group of people sat in the Garrison Commanders office. Two troopers had placed a selection of silver serving dishes in the middle of the table and the party helped themselves to a selection of bacon, sausages, eggs and kedgeree. There was also toast and thick cut marmalade and pots of hot steaming tea and coffee. Marmaduke had great difficulty in choosing what to eat next. He had helped himself to the kedgeree first, obviously because it contained fish. He was now eyeing up the sausages. The Commander sat looking down at his loaded plate, but despite the tempting aroma and his normally strong appetite, he had lost the taste for food. He poked a sausage with his knife and looked across the table to where Agnes was sitting. She had done that thing with the bread and bacon again, placing three large rashers of bacon between two halves of a large bread bun. Damn strange way of eating, he thought.

At the opposite end of the table the Sergeant Lewis sat next to a pale looking Lieutenant Smalls. The Lieutenant had spent the night in the garrison's sick bay having his leg seen to. Agnes noticed that the Sergeant had made up a plateful of food for the Lieutenant and seemed to be attending to his every need.

The only person not at the table was Peter Potts. During the night he had returned the Excise Cutter to the harbour. Finding no sign of Agnes he had gone home and gone straight to bed.

Eventually the Commander gave up trying to eat and pushed his plate away from him. Marmaduke eyed up the left over sausage.

"Damned unfortunate business!" The Commander commented.

The Lieutenant nodded. "Certainly was Sir."

The Sergeant wondered if he should agree. He then remembered that his mouth was full and that there was still food on the table and returned his concentration to eating.

Agnes had finished her sandwich and, realising everyone was edging around the subject of the previous night she decided to bring the matter to a head. She put her cup and saucer down with a clatter.

"Let's face facts gentlemen. I messed up!" she said.

The Commanders eyes widened in surprise. Marmaduke stopped eating and looked up the table towards Agnes. The Lieutenant gave a nervous cough. Even the Sergeant, who was not too sure what everyone was talking about, even stopped eating.

"I completely underestimated their numbers, and their organisation."

The Commander began to say something but Agnes silenced him by putting her hand up palm forward. "My miscalculations, perhaps even my arrogance, in assuming I knew what was going on has led to the death of six troopers, and the Lieutenant here being incapacitated. For that I am most profoundly sorry. Rest assured Gentlemen, I will not make that mistake again."

No one around the table knew what to say. It was Agnes herself that broke the awkward silence.

"Those men are trained."

Marmaduke interrupted her. "Everyone on that beach was there for a reason. They all had a job to do, and they went about it with great efficiency."

Despite her dislike of being interrupted just as she was getting into her flow, especially by her own cat, Agnes nodded. "Not only that, but they had set their own patrols. They had most of the roads and tracks covered. There was that patrol you and The Commander came across. They had blocked the road. Then there was the patrol that came across your unfortunate troopers." She nodded towards the Commander. He acknowledged her empathy with a slight nod of his head.

"Eighteen!" Said the Lieutenant suddenly. They all looked at him. He coughed. "That's how many there were in the patrols! Then there were at least another twenty in the old barn. Then they were joined by others, but they could have been a returning patrol that we've already counted."

Before they all got bogged down in numbers Agnes spoke again. "I don't think the actual number is of that great importance. What is important is that there are a lot more of them than we ever anticipated. Now just for the sake of argument, let's say there are eighty of them..."

She was interrupted by the Commander. "Damned small army!" he harrumphed.

Agnes looked down the table at him. "It's funny you should say that. Marmaduke said the same thing. It's crossed my mind that is exactly what we are dealing with, a small private army. Now before anyone says anything, last night, or earlier last evening, I did some research into this "Foxy Tom". I think I know who he is."

She explained her thinking and her research.

She left out the bit about search engines and web sites. In fact she never mentioned her computer once. She did however labour her use of her scrying bowl and gave huge credit to the Garrison Commander for remembering the name of Colonel Thomas Reynard once of York Barracks. By the time she had finished praising him the Commander thought he had actually come up with the name himself.

"So we have a trained band of wreckers on one hand and a Colonel who disappeared a couple or so years ago." With that she spread her hands and slowly brought them together again, interlacing her fingers. Just for effect she added a little flash as they met.

Marmaduke broke the magic. "Why would an ex-colonel have a band of wreckers?"

The Lieutenant spoke without realising it. "Suppose the wrecking is just a means to an end?" The Colonel harrumphed. "Plain as the nose on your face. Money. The fellows greedy. Sells the stuff inland, pockets the profits. Ends up sitting on a pile of the stuff!"

Marmaduke had fully understood the depth of the Lieutenants statement.

"They are expensive operations to mount." he said.

Agnes interrupted. "That's why he needs to know exactly what ships to go for. He knows the cargo and its value. He couldn't afford to mount that size of operation just to wreck any passing ship. The man has spies in Newcastle and up and down the coast. This is both well planned and expensive."

The Garrison Commander gave a low snort. "Military precision, can't fault it. Fellah knows his business. Ex-colonel you say? Well one basic tactic is to know your enemy and gentlemen..." he nodded towards Agnes. "And lady of course, we now know our enemy!"

Agnes burst any trace of pomposity the Commander might have been guilty of. "Actually commander, we know who our enemy is but we know nothing about the man himself or his organisation."

The Commander harrumphed again and turned his attention to a bit of sausage that had somehow become attached to the front of his uniform.

Agnes stood up. "Gentlemen, after last night's events we can assume he will be more wary. Let us try to look at the situation from his position. First and most importantly, the ship wasn't wrecked. That must be a source of great puzzlement and frustration to him. Two things must be going through his mind. Did the helmsman realise he was in the wrong position and alter his course at the last minute, or was he warned. If so how? Secondly, the fact that there were military patrols around last night must also be praying on his mind. Why last night, and was it pure coincidence that the patrols appeared on the night the ship wasn't wrecked? Sooner or later he will come to the conclusion the two things are linked, and if they are linked, it tells him that someone up here knows about his antics. It has to be from here because only someone up here can order troop movements. He'll know it was an army operation and he might find that amusing. What is keeping the smile from his face is the question of how the army knows what is happening."

The Lieutenant leant forward to speak but his movement twisted his damaged leg and as he began to speak he let out a small yelp. "Sorry, what I was going to say is, does Colonel Thomas Reynard suspect that we know who he is and that he is behind the wreckers?"

They all fell silent and thought about that particular poser. .

It was the Commander that broke the silence. "Well he won't be planning another wreck. Back in his lair licking his wounds I wouldn't doubt. Wouldn't be surprised if we never hear from the fellow again."

"He won't do that. He has too much invested in it. If I were him I'd do another run, but a dummy run. He'll want to test his operation. Find out how we knew. If we turn up again he'll know he's been rumbled for sure. If there's no sign of us he'll reckon that last night he just got very unlucky!"

Everyone looked at the Sergeant in surprise, especially as most of them had forgotten he was even there. All they had been aware of was that for the last hour was someone at the far end of the table was intent on eating everything he could reach. The Sergeant looked back self consciously. "Well it takes a sneaky bastard to catch a sneaky bastard."

He looked at Agnes. "If you'll pardon my French Missus!"

Marmaduke nodded. "It makes sense. In fact it's exactly what I'd do. It's probably taken him the best part of a couple of years and a fair bit of money to build his organisation. He won't be wanting to throw that away. The Sergeant's right he'll want to find out if he has been compromised, and if so how? He'll want to test us, test the waters, as it were." He added the last couple of words realising he had inadvertently made a very bad pun.

By the time they had finished their meeting what remained of the coffee had gone cold and all that remained on the platters were puddles and rivulets of congealed fat. As he stood up to leave the table the Sergeant tried to suppress a sudden and very loud burp. He failed. Out of the four of them he was either lucky or unlucky, he couldn't decide which. He had been sent back to his unit. On the up side that meant no more risking life and limb by riding around in the middle of the night getting soaked to the skin. On the down side it meant no more free breakfasts of the like he had just enjoyed. The Commander had agreed to delaying the inevitable reports for the next few days. He also agreed to return the Garrison to normal duties. However he agreed to keep one unit on full alert.

The Lieutenant agreed to return to the sick bay at least for a couple of days. To alleviate his boredom Agnes asked him to estimate the possible number of men, the cost of the lookouts and their share of the takings and then compare that figure with the estimated profits of the stolen cargoes. She knew full well that if she really needed to she could find the appropriate programme run it through her computer and have the figure in less time it took to boil her kettle. But she knew that despite his injury the Lieutenant still needed to be involved. He had a good brain, it was a shame to waste it. Mind you she had no idea what she was going to do with the resulting figure. As for herself and Marmaduke, well they were going fox hunting.

Chapter Twenty

Both Marmaduke and Agnes agreed. There would
be no more wrecks for the time being. There well
might be a dry run, but they figured they had two or
three weeks at the very least before another wreck
would be planned. In the meanwhile instead of
waiting for him to reappear they would go looking
for him. After all Agnes had two advantages. Firstly
she knew who he was, secondly she knew where he
lived. Oh and there was a third advantage, she was a
witch. This was one of those occasions when she
admitted to herself that she wasn't a wise woman.
That it wasn't a time for just lotions and potions.
The gloves were off. This was a war the ex Colonel
Thomas Reynard declared when he killed sailors
and the troopers. Now Agnes planned to bring that
war to his own doorstep, and she was prepared to

use every weapon in her armoury and Agnes had a very large and very creative armoury.

Know your enemy. It was good advice. She hadn't and it cost men their lives, she wouldn't make that mistake again. The next day was spent in front of her computer downloading and printing every list of information she could find about the man and about his house. By the time she had finished she knew the man's family history and had a set of fully detailed drawings and plans of the house, she now knew to be called Hawkstone Grange.

Then she turned to her scrying bowl. At first she examined the grounds. The house sat in the middle of small park surrounded by trees where sheep grazed. In addition to a rather grand gatehouse there were three other entrances, each approached through woodlands that provided enough cover for visitors to come and go without being seen.

Hawkstone Grange itself had been built as a rather large country house during Elizabethan times by a merchant who supplied the Royal Court. During the English Civil Wars it was fortified, the owner being a staunch Royalist. It was said that the walls still showed signs of where Parliamentary cannon balls and musket shot had hit the building during a siege in 1645. The house had been refurbished and greatly altered at the beginning of the eighteenth century when it had passed into the hands of a tea merchant. There the history of the house grew a bit muddled. From various on-line documents Agnes pieced together a story of how the merchant supplied the Army, and had dealing with York Barracks and a certain Colonel Thomas Reynard. Within three years the merchant had gone bankrupt and, to avoid his debtors, had fled to a new life in the Americas. Somehow his house and estate passed onto the Colonel. Within months the Colonel had been dismissed from the Army and had taken up residence at Hawkstone Grange.

She peered into her bowl and looked down on the house noting that there were a number of large outbuildings. Some, like the stable blocks and what seemed to be a dairy, appeared on the plans. Others seemed to be new. She looked closer. There was movement. A group of men were walking between the buildings. She looked closer at them. They seemed to be engaged in a variety of tasks. At the rear of the building two men were chopping logs. Two others led a string of pack horses towards the stable block walking across a large square between the buildings. She altered her angle of vision so she could look a little inside the stables. She could make out at least a dozen horses, and she couldn't see to the far end. Judging by the size of the building she estimated that there could be as many as thirty or more horses in there. Another movement caught her eye and she opened up her range of vision. A man was walking past the stable door holding five muskets. He seemed to be heading for another building, a square building further back standing by itself, almost at the edge of the woodland. When he reached the double doors he placed the rifles against the wall and unlocked the door, took the rifles inside and closed the doors behind him. Agnes altered her view once again. This time she was looking down on the square building. She moved her hand over the surface of the water and the roof below her simply dissolved. Now she could see directly into the building. She let out a small gasp. The building was an armoury! Inside she could see long barrelled guns, muskets and blunderbusses stacked in racks along the inside of the walls. On the opposite wall were racks of pistols. On the floor were stacks of swords and daggers of all shapes and sizes. Finally, at the end of the building opposite the door were the objects that caused her exclamation. There were eight culverins, four demi-culverins, and two cannon. Behind then were stacked barrels of gunpowder.

She waved her hand and the image dissolved, leaving just a bowl of water with some herbs floating on its surface. She sat down and thought very hard. It slowly dawned on her what she had just seen. The outbuildings were housing a small private army. Hawkstone Grange included a stables and an armoury. This wasn't just a wrecking crew. This was more, much more. She looked up at her window. Outside it had grown dark She flicked her fingers and the room lit with a soft glow. From the street outside it seemed that the room was candlelit. Inside there were no candles just a soft flickering glow lighting up the cottage interior.

As she returned to her cellar and re-emerged into the 18th century there was a sudden noise and Marmaduke walked in from the backyard. Agnes looked up as he sat heavily in the easy chair. She watched as he tried to curl his legs up underneath him and then stopped as he realised that he wasn't in his cat form. He gave a little growl and stretched his legs out in front of him.

Agnes raised an eyebrow.

Marmaduke shook his head. "Nothing! Not a whisper. In fact the only thing that's being talked about the length and breadth of the harbour side is how First Lieutenant Peter Potts took charge of the Excise Cutter, sailed it north, then brought it back again next morning. The thing that is driving everyone crazy is how anyone persuaded the Excise men to take their ship out of the harbour during last night's storm. Evidently it's well known that they don't go out to sea if it's just raining!" He paused and scratched at his whiskers. Agnes gave a polite cough and Marmaduke continued.

"No one can get a word out of the Excise Men themselves, and they can't get hold of Peter. The moment he landed our First Lieutenant dismissed the men, and then went straight home to his mothers and went to bed. No one has seen him since."

Agnes nodded. "I must pop down to see him. We owe him a great deal of thanks. You do realise that if he hadn't managed to intercept "The Venture" we would have had a shipwreck to contend with as well."

Marmaduke began to pick at his teeth with a very long and sharp finger nail.

"He did well!" He said.

"Oh yes!" Agreed Agnes. "He'll go far. I'll make sure of that!"

Marmaduke stopped picking his teeth and raised an eyebrow. Agnes smiled.

"Oh, in a month or so an official report will land on someone's desk at the Admiralty. A report praising our First Lieutenant. He'll be noticed. You know how the Navy is always crying out for good senior officers. No, don't worry about young Peter. His future looks very bright."

As they spoke, just down the street, the subject of their conversation was tossing and turning in his bed. He was having a nightmare. In it he was facing a naval tribunal explaining why he had impersonated a Rear Admiral. Suddenly the nightmare ended and the First Lieutenant fell into a deep and untroubled sleep.

They'd moved onto the kitchen and Agnes was opening yet another tin of sardines. She piled them onto a saucer and placed it in front of Marmaduke. As he ate she told him all about Ex Colonel Thomas Reynard, and his house, barracks and armoury.

After he had finished the sardines he ran his tongue across his lips and stroked his whiskers. He tilted his head to one side.

"Why?"

Agnes shook her head. "I have no idea whatsoever."

Marmaduke looked up. Agnes shrugged. "I have some ideas, some theories but I don't really know. I'm not making any assumptions. I made a big mistake by underestimating our ex-Colonel Thomas Reynard. I do not intend making the same mistake again. We are going to keep a very close eye on Foxy Tom. We are going to examine everything he does. I want to know exactly what he is up to and exactly why he has his own private army before we make any move against him."

Marmaduke flicked out a long finger nail. "I take it you want me to go up there and have a look around?"

Agnes shook her head quickly. "The last thing I want at this stage is for you to go up there and have a look around. It would be like poking a large stick into a very angry hornet's nest. For some reason you don't understand subtly....." She suddenly stopped and thought for a minute.

"However come to think about it there is something you can do. Look....." she leant forward in her chair. "Bear with me. Right now he'll know most of the details of what happened last night. His first in charge will have told him all about the ship sailing off and the failure of his mission. We know that and, as we said, that will be his priority. However his men will also have mentioned the mutilations.

That will give him something else to think about, but his men will also be wondering how their comrades perished. Others will also have found the bodies. They too will have passed them on their way back from the beach. You know armies. They talk. They are hot beds of gossip and rumour. I would like to lay a bet on the fact that whilst Thomas Reynard is wondering about the ship he has a barracks full of men wondering what clawed their friends to death.

Rumour and speculation! Soon they'll be convinced that there's some sort of giant cat prowling the moors. That will have them looking over their shoulders. Now if there were more sightings of this giant cat they would become more and more unsettled, and the more unsettled they become, the less of a fighting force they become. I think you could undo most of our Ex-Colonel's training single handed."

Marmaduke smiled. "So you want me just to wander around the moors letting myself be seen now and again?"

Agnes gave a smile that an uncharitable person would have called wicked. "Precisely, but preferably in cat form. However, and this is serious, do not go anywhere near Hawkstone Grange or its grounds. Just keep to the roads that go up and down the coast and lead to the cliff tops. Keep to the moors. Show yourself to locals as well. Let rumours and speculations spread. Yes Marmaduke, go out and have some fun. Keep them frightened."

She rubbed her hands and her smile grew wider. "Anyway that leaves me to concentrate on Ex-Colonel Thomas Reynard."

Chapter Twenty One

Marmaduke was having fun. It was his second day out on the moors and so far he had frightened to farm labourers, a carter, and a man on a horse who was possibly heading in the direction of the big house. He knew that tongues would wag and that in the local pubs and inns rumours would start spreading.

He sat on a wall that stretched across the open moorland and was just admiring the view. He found his mind wondering whether he should change shape back into his cat mode and stalk a couple of partridges he could see scratching at the field beside him. He didn't see the traveller until he was almost alongside him. He returned quickly to the presence as he heard a voice hailing him. He turned to see a man on a horse. He was wearing a long leather coat, high riding boots and a triangular hat. He was leaning forward on his horse addressing

Marmaduke. It only took a glance for Marmaduke to notice the man's sword and two very expensive pistols tucked into a broad leather belt. Marmaduke recognised a fighting man when he saw one. He nodded an acknowledgement aware that the horseman was taking in the sight before him. He wondered if he had noticed his bandoleer and the throwing knives.

The man looked around him before speaking again.

"Have you lost your horse?" he asked as he returned his gaze to Marmaduke.

Marmaduke nodded. "Got spooked by a pheasant. Threw me and ran off."

He pointed a hand in the vague direction of the road. "Been walking, rested up on this wall."

The rider stood up in his stirrups and looked around once again. "No sign of it." He said settling back into his saddle.

"No!" replied Marmaduke rather hoping the man would ride on and leave him be. He didn't. Instead he looked down from his horse. "Do you need a ride?"

Marmaduke paused. "It all depends where you are heading." He replied.

The man leant back in his saddle "Somewhere called Hawkstone Grange. Place is meant to be round here somewhere. Damned if I can find it!"

Marmaduke kept a very straight face, he wondered what business the rider had with Thomas Reynard. He played dumb and stroked his whiskers.

"I've heard of it, and yes it's meant to be around here somewhere. Not too sure where though. Never had a reason to go there myself."

The rider nodded. "Well that's two of us. I asked for directions from that last village. Must have taken a wrong turning somewhere."

"Not from round here then?" Marmaduke asked innocently.

"Me, no I'm from the other side of York. Business hasn't been that good and when I heard some country gentleman was hiring I figured the money would come in useful."

Marmaduke picked up his ears. "Hiring? What do you do?"

The rider laughed. As his mouth opened Marmaduke noticed that the man's teeth were unbroken and almost white. The man pulled a coin out of a pocket in his waistcoat. He tossed the coin high in the air and in one swift movement pulled out a pistol and fired. The coin chinked and danced in the air before landing in front of Marmaduke. He looked down and saw that the coin now had a hole through its middle. Marmaduke was impressed. The driver slid the pistol back into his belt. Suddenly he became aware of a slight blur of movement and heard a dull thud and a short squawk. He looked in the direction of noise. Down the road he saw a dead partridge. It had a throwing knife right through its throat. It was the riders turn to be impressed. He waited whilst Marmaduke jumped off the wall and retrieved both his knife and the dead bird. As he approached the rider he held up the carcass.

"Fancy some lunch?" Marmaduke asked. The rider jumped off his horse.

The two men sat at the side of the road next to a small fire. The partridge was roasting in the ashes between the burning branches. Marmaduke felt his mouth watering. Personally he never saw the need for cooking his food, but this was an occasion where he thought it better to stick to convention. They ate in silence, enjoying the hot tasty flesh and sucking noisily at the small bones.

Eventually when they had both licked their fingers clean of juices and fat the rider sat back and looked across at Marmaduke. "So you are heading the Hawkstone Grange yourself."

It wasn't a question.

Marmaduke shrugged. "It's an option!"

The rider laughed. "The way I see it you're out here in the middle of nowhere without your horse. You don't have many options available. It's a long walk back to....well wherever you hail from."

Marmaduke could see where this conversation was heading. He was in a quandary. Agnes had virtually forbidden him from even going near Hawkstone Grange. On the other hand there was this rider. Obviously if Marmaduke refused his offer it would arouse the man's suspicions. He could hardly turn into his giant cat persona in front of him. Or could he? No fate had taken a hand. It was offering him an opportunity to have a look around at the very least. If the situation got tricky he could always pull his inner cat out of the bag. He looked up. The rider had stood up. He trampled the fire till it went out, and remounted his horse. He sat there, leant forward and held his hand out.

Marmaduke stood up gave the fire a final kick and walked towards the rider. With one swift move he took the man's hand and pulled himself up on the back of the horse sitting behind the rider who tugged on the reins and the horse continued down the road.

Chapter Twenty Two

Agnes had spent the previous day deep in her research. Using her computer she looked at plans and drawings. Using her scrying bowl she peered deep inside the house. She discerned that Hawkstone Grange had a number of staff. It had a cook and a housekeeper. She seemed to be married to the man who acted as butler, though both his manner and the way he walked around the place armed with pistols and a very nasty looking dagger would probably disqualify him from a position in the more genteel houses in the county. She also discovered that the man from the beach whom she had christened "First Lieutenant" also lived in the house. Both the front and back doors were guarded by four very large and very tough looking men. Two at each door. She also noticed that regular patrols guarded the grounds, although Agnes couldn't work out whether they were training or actually guarding the property. Probably both she thought.

She then concentrated on the spider sat in the middle of his web. She found the ex-colonel as he sat at a desk in what seemed to be a library. She watched as he leafed through various documents, making notes in a large ledger beside him. She looked closer. She was mistaken, he wasn't making notes he was writing down figures. The book was a ledger.

Of course the man had been a Colonel in supply. He would know where every barrel had gone, and the price it had fetched. They say an army marches on its stomach, Agnes reflected that this army was being built by the stomachs of others, stomachs eager for illegal contraband. Unknowingly the men and publicans who dealt in illegal liquor were paying for the establishment of a private army. The same question came back to Agnes time and time again. Why?

Later in the day, the second time she spied on Thomas Reynard, she found him in a large sitting room. He was standing over a table where a series of large maps were spread. She looked over his shoulder. They were maps of the surrounding area. They showed the coast and the roads leading to it. They were all criss-crossed with lines and markings. She noticed that Ravenscar was marked, as were the two wreck sides. There was a large cross on the site of the failed shipwreck. She also noticed a number of smaller crosses. She assumed they were the places where the troopers had been seen. So he was trying to make some sense of the nights events.

"Well good luck with that!" She said to herself.

As she watched Foxy Tom turned around. A second man had entered the room. It was the First Lieutenant. The pair had a brief conversation before the Lieutenant was led to the maps. Agnes couldn't hear the conversation. The scrying bowl wasn't wired for sound. No matter how hard Agnes tried she couldn't get the sound to travel through the water. Sometimes she managed to lip read. Not today. The two men were standing with their backs to her. By their movements Agnes could guess they were discussing just where and when things had occurred. She felt a small glow of satisfaction when the ex colonel straightened himself and shook his head.

"Good!" thought Agnes. "He still can't make any sense of it!"

Just before she wiped her scrying bowl clear of images she decided she would check on Marmaduke. She cast some fresh herbs and powders over the water. It rippled and she looked into it. An image appeared. It was of a small, green parkland surrounded by trees. Agnes realised that she was looking at Hawkstone Grange again. She shook her head in annoyance. She must have used the wrong powder. She was about to clear the image when she noticed some movement. A rider had emerged from the woodland and was heading towards the house. She let out a groan. Behind the rider, sitting astride the same horse was Marmaduke!

She cleared the waters, shook her head, and sighed again. Despite her explicit instructions the stick had been pushed into the hornet's nest!

Chapter Twenty Three.

The rider continued on his horse until he reached the front door of Hawkstone Grange where he dismounted. As he helped Marmaduke off the horse the two guards suddenly appeared. They both held pistols in front of them. The rider looked across to them and gave a low bow.

"And good afternoon to you too, boyo's. Now let's not get anxious here. Just be good lads and let your master know that two gentlemen of the road have come to answer his call."

The two guards were not impressed. "You go round the back. Ask for Quartermaster John. He'll see you right."

Now it was the turn of the rider to be unimpressed. "Now lads, let's be reasonable. I've ridden a fair few miles to answer your masters call and I'm not about to be paying lip service to any Quartermaster John."

From his position at the rear of the rider Marmaduke noticed one of the men, the one who hadn't spoken yet, had narrowed his eyes slightly. Marmaduke also noticed a slight movement of his trigger finger. There was a blur of movement and the man looked down in surprise at the small throwing knife that had suddenly appeared sticking out from the back of his hand that was holding the pistol. Only it wasn't holding the pistol anymore. It had fallen to the floor. The sudden impact with the stone step caused the powder to ignite and the pistol fired. Instantly the second guard dropped his pistol as he instinctively bent down to hold the ragged, bloody wound that had appeared in the back of his calf. He had been shot. The Rider turned to Marmaduke.

"Effective!" he said.

Before either of them could move they were aware that they were not alone. The sound of the shot had brought company. From around the corner of the house eight men had appeared and were running towards them. The newcomers were armed with a variety of swords and pistols and didn't look as if they were afraid to use them. They were brought to a quick halt by an order shouted out from the doorway of the house. Marmaduke looked up to see the man from the beach, the one that Agnes had followed. Behind him was a second figure, in the shadows stood a man dressed in full military uniform.

Between the doorway and Marmaduke and the rider the two wounded guards were both on the ground, trying to attend to their injuries.

"He shot me!" Shouted the man with the bloody leg, pointing at the rider.

The rider shrugged his shoulders. "The only discharged pistol around here is the one on the ground there. I think it may have been dropped by your mate. Him with the knife in his hand!"

Everyone looked at the second guard who in his painful attempts to get the knife out of the back of his hand seemed oblivious to the events going on around him.

The rider looked towards the doorway of the house and made a low sweeping bow.

"May I be having the pleasure of addressing Colonel Thomas Reynard himself?" He asked.

The man from the beach looked at him. He had his pistol drawn. "Who are you?" he snarled.

The rider ignored him and spoke beyond him to the man standing in the shadows. "Now here's a tale for you. But before its telling may I request something be done about those two unfortunates? I'm afraid they are distracting from my tale."

The man from the beach exploded in anger. "You cheeky..." He took a step forward and his hand went towards his sword. He was stopped by a firm hand on his shoulder.

"This is a tale I want to hear the telling of." Thomas Reynard said. He nodded in the direction of the eight armed men who were standing wondering what they should do. They took the hint and went to the assistance of their injured comrades. As Thomas Reynard waved his hand in a dismissive gesture the men helped the wounded to their feet and walked them back to the corner of the house, and Marmaduke hoped some sort of medical assistance, although he had his doubts.

Once the men turned the corner the Rider continued his story.

"My tale begins in York. A few goodly years ago now. It concerns a certain Colonel at the Barracks. In charge of procurement I think it was called. Now this fine gentleman wasn't opposed to the idea of free trade and would deal and trade with certain gentlemen of the road. Well Foxy Tom, you won't recognise me because I was in the shadows. But you know my name and my reputation. Allow me to present myself. I am the one and only Dancing Jack!"

He paused and doffed his hat giving a small bow from his waist.

Colonel Thomas Reynard took a step forward. Dancing Jack looked around him and continued speaking.

"It looks like the years have been good to you."

He turned back towards the Colonel. "When I heard a certain country gentleman was offering a profitable enterprise for gentlemen of the road I thought it could be an offer that was of interest to me. The pickings around York are sparse. There's been a lot of hangings. Times ain't as good as they used to be."

Thomas Reynard nodded towards Marmaduke "And your friend?"

Marmaduke thought he'd better speak up for himself. He copied the bow that Dancing Jack had given.

"Ginger Tom at your pleasure. I used to work the Leeds Bradford turnpikes. Like Jack here says, times got hard. I drifted to York, heard the word in a tavern there."

Thomas looked suspiciously at Marmaduke. "What happened to your horse?"

Dancing Jack took up the story. "A shame it was. A fine animal, Came to grief in a warren. What could we do, both heading in the same direction after all?"

Thomas Reynard sniffed but seemed satisfied with Jacks explanation. Marmaduke wondered why Dancing Jack, a highwayman whose acquaintance he had been for three hours at the most, had lied on his behalf. It wasn't anything to do with a highwayman's code. There wasn't such a thing. Out on the road it was every highwayman for himself.

He'd have to keep an eye on Dancing Jack he thought. He seemed too good to be true.

Thomas Reynard turned back into his house. "Come, follow me!" he said.

They dismounted and he led them through the open door and into a large hall. Marmaduke looked around him. The hall was supported by large marble pillars. A marble staircase swept its way upstairs to a balcony that ran right to left and presumably led to a series of upper rooms. Downstairs a number of doors led deeper into the house.

They followed the Colonel through a set of double doors into a drawing room. Marmaduke noticed a large map on a table over by a window. Aware the man from the beach was watching him Marmaduke extended his look so it appeared to take in the entire room.

The Colonel marched across the room and pulled a huge bell pull hanging down by the side of the fireplace. It had hardly stopped moving when a large man appeared at the doorway. Marmaduke thought he must be a contender for the ugliest man in the town competition. It looked like someone had used his head as punch bag.

Jack asked for coffee, Marmaduke indicated he would have the same. The ugly man poured and offered the steaming cups to the two highwaymen. Both of them looked ill at ease handling the small cups.

Dancing Jack looked across the room. "So am I right in my assumption that I am addressing the very same country gentleman offering the profitable enterprise?"

Thomas Reynard sat down behind a large desk, opened a drawer and pulled out a roll of paper. He slid it across the desk.

"A commission gentlemen." He said.

Dancing Jack stepped forward, picked up the paper, and read the finely worded document. Then he put it back on the desk top.

"So you are recruiting?"

Thomas Reynard shook his head. "It is a commission. Strictly a business agreement."

"A business agreement that gives you more than a fair share of the proceeds." Noted Dancing Jack.

"In exchange for food, lodgings, and a safe harbour. Are they not the very things a gentleman of the road needs? Face it, how many inns and taverns can you truly trust? Lying in bed at night, not knowing if you've paid the landlord enough not to fetch a constable or the excise men? Under my contract you'll be guaranteed a good night's rest and a decent meal."

Dancing Jack nodded his head. "To be sure it has its attractions. But....."

The ex-Colonel held up his hand. "There are regular mail coaches between York and Malton, between Pickering and Whitby. There's fair pickings, especially if you know which stagecoach to take."

Marmaduke joined in the conversation. "And how would we know which ones to take?"

Thomas Reynard looked Marmaduke straight in the face. "Because you take the ones I tell you to!"

Dancing Jack looked down on Thomas. "And how is it you know what's going where, and when?"

Thomas smiled. "I have my ways. Information is my business."

Dancing Jack looked out of the window. "And why is it that you can't use your own men?"

The Colonel shook his head. "I require experience and finesse. Professionals like yourselves. The men are good, I have trained them myself. Let us say they are my infantry. My foot soldiers. The jobs I require call for more specialised expertise."

"How do you know we have the required skills?"
Asked Marmaduke.

Thomas Reynard looked at him. "Because you're still alive, because no one has managed to hang you, yet!"

Marmaduke felt a slight threat in the man's tone. "And suppose I say no thank you and walk away?"

The man from the beach stepped forward until his face was directly in front of Marmaduke. So close that Marmaduke could smell old liquor on the man's hot breath.

"People have a habit of not saying no. Not if they know what's good for them!"

Dancing Jack moved forward towards the desk. He hadn't gone two paces before Foxy Tom pulled out a pistol aimed right at the centre of Jacks chest. "May I suggest a compromise gentlemen? Think it over. Take your time. I don't think you're going to be missed for a while. If ever."

His hand moved to the desk and lifted a small hand bell. It rang and the butler stepped back into the room followed by six of his friends. They were the same men that had appeared around the corner of the house. They were all carrying pistols.

Thomas Reynard glanced at them and then returned his gaze to Dancing Jack. "Take them away. Put them in the pinfold for the night. Let them mull over their situation until morning. Oh and let it be known they are the same men who stabbed and shot George and Old Michael."

The six men stepped forward and grabbed the two highwaymen by their arms whilst the butler deftly removed their pistols and swords and Marmaduke's bandoleer. Then they frisked him again and found a long dagger and two more throwing knives.

Dancing Jack looked on. "You don't believe in leaving anything to chance I see." His wit was rewarded by a blow across his face from the man on the beach.

The ex Colonel coughed and then spoke as if he were barking out orders. "No subordination in the ranks! Troopers, remove these men. Bring them back in the morning. Perhaps then they will have had a change of heart!"

The men manhandled Marmaduke and Dancing Jack out of the room, along the hall and through a series of corridors until they reached a wide double door. It opened onto a large courtyard. Marmaduke stopped. He could see the stables, barracks, men walking and going about their tasks in ones and twos. Suddenly he was hit over the back of the head with the butt of a pistol. It was so hard it made his knees sag and rattled his teeth.

"I didn't say you could stop!" A voice behind him said.

As the two prisoners were pushed and shoved across the courtyard the men in sight stopped what they were doing to watch. Other men appeared from between the buildings and emerged out through doors. One of them bent down and picked up a handful of horse manure. It hit Dancing Jack on the side of the head. Everyone laughed. Another man bent down and picked up a stone. As he moved to throw it Marmaduke moved his head slightly to one side. The stone zipped passed his ear and hit the man behind him fairly and squarely in the middle of his forehead. He went down as if he had been pole axed. The men around Marmaduke turned their pistols in the direction of where the stone had been thrown.

The man from the beach stepped forward keeping his pistol aimed at the men. "If anyone else as much as raises an arm he'll find himself looking at a hole in his chest. The Colonel wants these men alive, he has business with them in the morning. He'll decide if and when any stones are to thrown. Get back to your duties."

The men took one long, lasting look at the two prisoners before melting away and continuing whatever they were doing before the appearance of the escort. Marmaduke looked around. The man who had been hit was standing up rubbing a large lump that was rising at the centre of his forehead. He rubbed it and checked his hand to see if there was any sign of blood. There wasn't.

The pinfold turned out to be a round stone prison set out at the end of the stable block. Inside rotten straw was spread over the floor. A small barred window let in a little light. Along the bottom of the wall were metal fixings set deep into the walls. Attached to the fixings were lengths of rusty chains. The prisoners were pushed inside. As they entered they were each hit over the head by a pistol butt.

When they came around it was dark. Marmaduke tried to move and found a manacle around his ankle. It was attached to a chain. The chain was attached to the wall. He moved his leg and the chain rattled.

"They certainly know how to make a fellow welcome." Dancing Jack said.

Marmaduke peered into the darkness, which for him posed no problems, but he did it for effect. He didn't want Jack to know he could see in the dark, yet.

"How long have you been conscious?" he asked.

"Not long." Came the reply. "Just long enough to realise I'm chained to a wall, and wonder why?"

"I don't think Thomas Reynard took kindly to our refusal of his contract." Marmaduke replied.

"Now I've been thinking about that as well and it pains me to point out that I seem to remember it was you who refused. I never said a word so I did."

Marmaduke pulled at his chains. "So why put out the word for highwaymen when all you do with them when they turn up is to lock them up. I wonder how many have said yes?" he added.

Something skittered across the damp straw, catching Marmaduke's attention.

"Now there's a thing". Dancing Jack said. He moved his free leg out in a sharp and vicious kick. The skittering stopped. He continued talking. "I know of at least three gentlemen of the road who left to take up the offer. I heard one got himself caught the far side of York. Tried to rob the Leeds Mail. Danced his last jig at York Tyburn a couple of months ago.

Marmaduke nodded in thought. "That could be why he wants a new man, a replacement."

Dancing Jack rolled over and peered into the darkness towards Marmaduke. "That makes as good a sense as anything else around here."

Marmaduke took to thinking himself. He had remembered a conversation with Agnes where they had compared wreckers with highwaymen. Same people doing the same job. One at sea, one inland. Thomas Reynard not only employed a large gang of wreckers working the shipping lines along the coast, if he had understood the Colonel, he also had a network of highwaymen working the roads and turnpikes. No doubt he had a similar network of spies. He let out a low growl. Ex Colonel Thomas Reynard had certainly spent a very productive three years since he left the army. He now seemed to control robberies on both land and sea. His thoughts were interrupted by Dancing Jack's alarmed cry.

"What in all that's holy was that?"

Marmaduke knew exactly what it was. "Sorry, just clearing my throat." He said.

Back in her cottage Agnes watched the two prisoners as she peered into her scrying bowl. She stood up, arched her back, waved her arm and wondered whether she should intervene. She decided against it. For one thing she wasn't ready to tackle Foxy Tom just yet. A few things had to be put in place first. She was only seeing a part of the picture. She had to make sure that when she acted there was no chance of mistakes. No chance of him escaping. The other reason was a lot closer to home.

It would serve Marmaduke right to spend an uncomfortable night under lock and key. That just might teach him to listen to what she said. She went to her comfortable bed and slept a good night's sleep without any misgivings. After all she knew Marmaduke was well capable of looking after himself.

As Agnes's head touched her pillow Marmaduke was trying to find a comfortable position. He couldn't. He looked across to where Dancing Jack lay snoring. Marmaduke couldn't sleep. He was cold, damp and bored. He gave the ring on the wall a slight tug. It wouldn't move. He felt the manacle around his ankle. It was firmly locked. Only one thing for it. The air shimmered and suddenly the shape of a giant cat could be seen. Despite the inside of the jail being dark, the shape of the cat was even darker. It appeared like a black shadow. It disappeared as quickly as it appeared. Marmaduke stood up. The manacle was never intended to fit the leg of a cat, no matter how large it was. It had slipped off and lay on the floor still attached to the chain.

"A neat trick, if you can do it! Unfortunately I can't. How do you propose setting me free?"

Marmaduke froze. Dancing Jack had seen everything. He hadn't been asleep. Marmaduke felt himself redden. He had let his greatest secret slip to a highwayman who he still didn't know whether he trusted or not. However that wasn't his greatest priority, getting Jacks chain off was. He knew full well that now Jack knew his secret Marmaduke wasn't going to let him out of his sight. Wherever Marmaduke went Jack would have to go. He just had to work out how. He tried giving the chain a tug again. The metal fixture didn't move. Suddenly Jack gave a low chuckle. He reached up and removed his tricorn hat. He turned it upside down and felt inside the brim. After a second or two he looped his finger around something, gave a tug and pulled out a length of thin wire. As it revealed itself Marmaduke noticed it twinkled in the feint light.

"Almost forgot this little gem!" Jack said as he looped on end of the wire around one hand, fed the wire through one of the links in the chain, then looped the free end around his other hand. He pulled the wire tight and began moving his arms in a sawing motion. Marmaduke watched as the wire began to cut through the rusty link. It was the better part of fifteen minutes before the link broke. During that time Marmaduke had taken a turn and looked closely at the wire and its twinkling surface.

"Tiny bits of diamond would you believe." Jack commented seeing the question on Marmaduke's face.

"I got it from a man who claimed he had got it from a man who had used it to escape from The Tower of London. I kept it tucked away for a rainy day." He stood up and walked to the window. "Funny that. It looks like a fine night out there."

It took them a further thirty minutes to cut through the metal bars.

Marmaduke was the first through the window. He dropped quietly on all fours and crouched there listening intently. He signalled for jack to remain where he was and silently moved around the building and peered around him. The place seemed asleep. Some lights hung in windows of the building opposite. Men were moving around inside. He could see their shadows. He continued until he came upon the first guard. He was seated in an old rickety chair. There was a long barrelled gun placed over his knees. His eyes were open watching in the darkness. Marmaduke reversed and went around the building in the opposite direction. Sure enough a second guard was seated in a similar position with a blunderbuss across his knees. Marmaduke figured the door must be between them. Again he reversed his position and stopped under the small window. He gave a nod and Dancing Jack climbed down. Using hand gestures Marmaduke signalled the position of the guards. He was silently making the suggestion they should creep around when Jack shook his head and pointed straight ahead. In front of them were two barns; beyond the barns was a small patch of woodland. Marmaduke nodded.

Moving as quietly and carefully as they could, they made their way to the nearest barn. A sudden noise made them freeze. Behind them someone was shouting. Surely no one could have discovered their escape so quickly. A door burst open and a group of men spilled out throwing punches at each other. A fight had broken out. Dancing Jack looked at Marmaduke who gave a slight nod and the pair of them broke into a run. Once they had made it to the woods they stopped and looked behind them. The number of fighters had seemed to grow. Suddenly a shot rang out and the men stopped fighting. In the distance Marmaduke could make out the man from the beach. He was standing in the middle of the men, shouting a mixture of insults, threats and orders. He was accompanied by the butler. The man from the beach nodded and the big man stepped forward, grabbed two of the men who had been fighting by the scruff of their necks and banged their heads together. Both men dropped to the floor. As they tried to pick themselves up the rest of the men skulked back through the doorway and disappeared inside the building. The man from the beach looked across to the pinfold.

"Anything?" he shouted.

The answer must have come from one of the guards out of Marmaduke's sight. "Not a peep."

The man from the beach nodded, turned and returned to wherever he had come from.

The two fugitives entered deeper into the woodlands.

"Do you have any idea where we are?" Dancing Jack asked as a lower branch snapped back on him almost hitting him across the face.

Marmaduke shook his head. "Let's get to the other side of the woods and see how the land lies."

Dancing Jack grunted and the pair passed through the undergrowth and brambles as silently as possible. When they came to the opposite side they found themselves on the edge of a small pasture. Beyond that was a stone wall.

"Could be a road." Marmaduke said.

Dancing Jack looked up at the moon. It was low in the sky.

"There are still some precious few hours to dawn which is when someone will open the door and find us gone. There will be a mighty hue and cry. They have men and they have horses. We need to be a long way from here and as quickly as possible."

Marmaduke lifted his hand. His ears had picked up a distant sound. He cocked his head and pushed Dancing Jack onto the ground. As Jack spluttered

Marmaduke whispered in his ear. "There's someone coming!"

They wriggled deeper into the bracken and looked towards the wall. After a couple of minutes the moonlight picked out movement. A man on a horse came into vision. He was leading a group of eight or nine men marching behind him. The two men remained motionless until the party had passed. Marmaduke sat up and brushed the undergrowth from the front of his jacket.

"They have patrols out!" he said.

Dancing Jack sat up and tipped his hat back to allow himself to scratch his head. "Now why would they be after doing a thing like that?"

Marmaduke turned to him "They could be guarding Hawkstone Grange, or they could be on their way back from some mission or other. I mean to find out!"

"You want us to follow them?" asked Jack in surprise.

By the tone of his voice Marmaduke could tell his companion didn't think much of the idea.

Marmaduke shook his head. "I mean I'm going to find out. I have, shall we say, certain advantages. Wait here I won't be long!"

Dancing Jack settled back in the bracken and watched as Marmaduke took a few paces along the edge of the wood. Then the air shimmered and Marmaduke simply seemed to disappear. Dancing Jack blinked and looked again. There seemed to be a low black shape moving across the pasture. He lost the shape as it disappeared into the dark shadow created by the stone wall

He estimated that the best part of twenty minutes had passed when he heard shouting in the distance. He sat up and looked towards the wall. Then he heard the sound of a horse at full gallop. Almost instantly the rider he had seen earlier raced past.

The rider was lashing the horse with his reins trying to get more speed from the animal. As they flashed by Dancing Jack noticed that the rider's eyes were wide open with terror. The horse was foaming at the mouth. He disappeared down the road in the direction from where he had first appeared. Dancing Jack scratched his head.

"Now that's a sight you don't see every day!" he thought to himself.

He began to wonder what had happened to the rider's men when a number of running figures appeared on the road. They would have passed right by if the fellow in front had not turned to take a look behind him. The moment he turned his head was the same moment that his foot met with a large clump of mud throw up by the galloping horse. The man stumbled and tripped. The men running behind him stood no chance of stopping and ran straight into him. Although their fallen had taken them below the level of the wall, by the shouting and cursing Dancing Jack could fully imagine the scene. He smiled to himself. As the men began to stand up he became aware of a dark shadow moving quickly along the inside of the wall. The shadow stopped at the other side to where the men were still standing, pulling each other to their feet and brushing themselves down. Then Jack heard the noise. It was a cross between a snarl and growl. It was so loud that it put the fear in him and he felt an ice cold shiver run up and down his back. The effect on the men in the road was instant. With a cacophony of screams and yells and shouts the men took to flight and ran as fast as they could after the rider.

A few minutes later there was a shimmer at the edge of the wood and Marmaduke reappeared carrying a variety of weapons in his arms.

"Like I said, a nice trick if you know how!" Dancing Jack remarked as Marmaduke dropped a selection of swords, daggers and pistols at his feet.

"They're not the best quality, but the swords are sharp and the pistols loaded. Take your pick."

Dancing Jack sifted through the small armoury. As he picked his choice Marmaduke added,

"Surprising what men suddenly realise what it is they don't need to make them run faster."

Dancing Jack laughed. "That growl put the fear of God up me, and I was sitting up here."

Marmaduke ran his thumb down the edge of a long slender dagger. It was sharp enough. He tucked it into his belt. "Usually does the trick!" he said.

The feint grey light of dawn was breaking as the two heavily armed highwaymen trudged down a country road that, Marmaduke hoped, wuld lead them back to Scarborough.

Chapter Twenty Four

The same dawn light filtered through the small bedroom window and illuminated Agnes's bed. It was empty. She was downstairs holding a cup of tea to her chest as she peered into the scrying bowl. The events of the previous day and night up at Hawkstone Grange repeated themselves in fast forward mode. It ended on an image of two heavily armed men walking down a country road.

She waved her hand briefly and the image cleared.

"At least he did something he set out to do!" She said to the empty room. She placed the tea on the table, took put a pinch of herbs and potions, sprinkled them on the water in the scrying bowl, and looked down. Once again she was viewing the events of the previous night, this time it was an image of the barracks at the rear of Hawkstone Grange. The image she saw was one of panic and chaos. She was viewing the image a few moments after the rider had returned. The place was full of activity. The rider was shouting and pointing in the direction of the road. Agnes tried to make out what he was saying. So were the men standing around him. Whatever was coming out of his mouth didn't appear to be any words discernible to the listeners. Aroused from their sleep in the middle of the night they were not blessed with a great deal of patience. One of the stepped forward and took the rider by both shoulders and shook him. Impatient for a reaction another man stepped forward and gave the rider a hard slap across the face. That seemed to have had an effect. The rider suddenly pulled out his pistol and pointed it at the head of the man who had just slapped him. Everyone took a step back. Agnes continued to watch as more and more men appeared shouting out questions. The slap seemed to have galvanised the rider's brain. He suddenly fired the pistol into the air and began to shout. The men around him shut up and listened. As he told his tale the listening crowd kept taking anxious glances towards the entrance and out to the road beyond.

They were rewarded by the sight of their compatriots stumbling and falling over in their haste to get to safety. The crowd left the rider and ran forward to meet the newcomers, helping them to their feet and into safety. Eventually as they regained their breath they began to tell their story. The all mouthed words whilst looking behind them in terror as they pointed back down the road. Their story didn't take long to narrate and soon the men gathered into one large unified group and marched towards the big house.

Agnes smiled to herself. "That's going to take some calming down, a nice distraction for our Ex-Colonel to deal with. Perhaps now is the time to take a closer look at Foxy Tom whilst he's looking in the opposite direction."

Before she wiped the image away she took a close look at the pinfold. She flicked her fingers and three metal bars jumped from the ground and reset themselves into their place at the prisons window. "That will give him something else to think of." She almost felt sorry for ex Colonel Thomas Reynard.. ..almost!

The morning was clear and crisp as the seagull rose over the old town and flapped its way inland. Eventually it flew over two men walking down a small country lane. The seagull landed on the road ahead of them.

Dancing Jack had experienced a very strange night so when they rounded a corner to see an elderly lady standing at the side of the road he didn't bat an eyelid. He was however, surprised to hear a low growl from the man beside him.

"Good morning gentlemen!" Agnes said.

"Good morning to you too my lady." Dancing Jack replied, doffing his hat and giving a low bow.

He turned to Marmaduke. "I take it you two are already acquainted?"

Marmaduke nodded. "Good morning Agnes. I take it you had a profitable night?" he asked politely.

"It was certainly more comfortable!" she replied.

She turned to Dancing Jack. "Nice trick that diamond wire!"

Jack looked at Agnes in surprise. "It's not really a trick. I got it from a man who got it from...."

Agnes held up her hand for him to stop talking.

"Everything is a trick!" she said enigmatically. She had chosen to stop by a low wall. She hopped onto it and moved her hand. Beneath her a small fire set itself and blazed brightly.

"I take it you gentlemen would appreciate breakfast?" She asked.

They nodded. Her fingers moved again and a frying pan appeared complete with bacon, sausages and eggs.

Dancing Jack noticed the food was almost cooked when it appeared. Three large bread buns, freshly cooked and still warm appeared and Agnes sliced them in half and put the food between the two halves. Plates appeared and Dancing Jack found himself holding one of England's first ever all-day breakfast baps. He looked down on his plate and cocked his head.

"I'm not too sure if I've invented it." Agnes murmured as they ate.

Once the sandwiches had been consumed and fingers and plates licked clean Agnes related the events she had seen from the previous night.

"His so called army is falling apart. Right now instead of a highly trained band of brigands he has a lot of very worried, very scared men. At the moment the guard has been trebled and all patrols have been pulled back into the grounds. Suddenly our ex-colonel has found himself with a lot of stuff to deal with!"

"Objective achieved!" Said Marmaduke licking the side of his whiskers with what Jack thought was a very long tongue.

Agnes brushed some crumbs from the rest of her dress. "If the objective involved getting captured, repeatedly getting hit over the head and imprisoned in a cross between a rats nest and a pig sty for half the night – well yes, I suppose it has!"

Marmaduke let out a small petulant growl and Agnes decided she might have been a bit unfair to him. "But at least you managed to panic the entire camp, even if it was more by luck than good management!" She added under her breath.

Dancing Jack watched the interchange with interest. There was no doubt who was in charge here. "So what now?" he asked.

Agnes looked at him. He felt her eyes borrow deep into his, almost as if she was reading his very soul. "Life is full of choices." She said. "You can carry on to Scarborough, find a horse and go back to York and the live you used to live. Or ..."

The highwayman cut her off. "Ah now, there we might have a little problem!"

Marmaduke looked at Agnes. It was unusual for anyone to interrupt her. It was even more unusual for her to allow it. They both watched as Dancing Jack took off his hat and without hesitation, ripped out the inner lining. He removed a small waxed slip of paper and handed it to Agnes. She unfolded it, read it and handed it back to him. Marmaduke raised an eyebrow.

"Royal warrant!" Agnes said. "It seems our highwayman here isn't exactly the man he pretends to be."

"I have a tale for the telling!" Dancing Jack said. Marmaduke and Agnes sat back in the roadside grass and listened.

It was a tale of highwaymen, of robberies and hold-ups, of seedy inns and taverns, of secret meetings and liaisons, of treachery and betrayal and ultimately capture. However instead of a hanging a deal had been stuck. Someone in the army had decided to put into practise the old adage of "set a thief to catch a thief." Jack had been spared his life on the condition he worked for them. It seemed that a very clever junior clerk had noticed discrepancies in some purchase accounts for the York barracks. A long and very protracted investigation was started and when finished pointed an accusing finger at a now retired Colonel Thomas Reynard. Dancing Jack was the thief the army had chosen to track their man down.

As he told his story Agnes kept nodding, even when the story ended. "Who do you answer to?" she asked.

Dancing Jack smiled. "Ah now lady, that I do not know. I was, shall we say, recruited by a Colonel with no name and a Lieutenant also nameless. There is a sergeant involved, I'm meant to report my findings to him. He doesn't have a name either."

Agnes looked into Dancing Jacks eyes. "And you trusted them?" she asked.

"Given the choice between their proposal and a hangman's noose, which would you be a choosing of?"

Agnes smiled and rubbed her hands. "Well, a real army spy and a highwayman to boot. This really is getting better and better."

She turned to Jack. "And of course, if you flailed, or even of you decided to throw your lot in with Foxy Tom it wouldn't matter very much. That army plays a long game. They would simply recruit someone else. It seems to me they are seeking evidence before making their move. Whatever they know about his past misdemeanours they yet have to prove. That means they are contemplating an arrest, and that would involve army lawyers. If they get involved our Ex-Colonel will find himself tied up in legal actions until he is bankrupt. Well if they want proof, proof is what they'll get."

She looked across at Marmaduke. "We just need to get proof and let the army do their job. If I were him I'm not sure what I'd fear most, a strange giant cat roaming the country side, or a platoon of army lawyers marching across his lawns!"

Marmaduke turned to Dancing Jack. "What kind of proof were you asked to find?"

Dancing Jack scratched his head. "Ah well now, that's where it all gets just a bit vague! They said I'd know it when I see it!"

Agnes stood up and brushed her hands down her skirt ridding herself of crumbs. "Typical Army. Send someone in without really knowing what they are looking for, just on the off chance they might get lucky!"

She looked up at Dancing Jack. "No clues at all?"

He shook his head.

Marmaduke leant forward. "What does the army say about his ship wrecking activities?"

Dancing Jack turned to Marmaduke. "Shipwrecking? Nobody mentioned anything about ship wrecking to me!"

Agnes tutted. "I thought not, the army seems to be concerned with Foxy Toms past, not what he's actually up to now!"

Dancing Jack "Well to be honest I got a bit of a shock when I realised I had ridden into more than we anticipated. From the briefing I received I was expecting to find a retired country gentleman dabbling in petty crime. All the Colonel in York knew was that the man was hiring highwayman. It was assumed he was just building a small criminal network of robbers and footpads. No one back In York mentioned that our man had built himself his own private army."

Agnes looked up into the morning sky. "Well it seems I'm not the only one to underestimate Ex-Colonel Thomas Reynard."

She moved her hands and the frying pan and fire simply vanished. The only evidence of their al fresco breakfast were a few crumbs scattered among the flattened grass. "It's time I paid Hawkstone Grange a visit." She said

She looked at Marmaduke. "I think the best thing for you to do is to return to Scarborough. Visit the Garrison Commander and let him know of the recent events. I'll join you later in the day."

The two men stood up and looked down the road. "Don't worry!" Agnes said. "You'll find two horses in the next field. You'll be there in an hour."

True as her word as the two men walked down the road, two horses stood eating grass, fully harnessed, patiently waiting for the two riders.

As Dancing Jack leapt into the saddle he thought he glimpsed the shape of an owl flying off over the tree tops. It was heading towards Hawkstone Grange.

Chapter Twenty Five

Agnes waited until the two men saw the horses. As they mounted up the air shimmered and an owl flew off.

Making a series of low quick flights it eventually landed on the roof of the pinfold and shuffled and fluttered until it found a roost in some broken stonework just below the eaves. From there it had a clear view of the barracks and the rear of the house.

Men were coming and going. At first glance everything seemed as if things were operating as normal. Then she noticed that, scattered around the buildings, were a number of armed guards. The owl turned its head. Agnes wondered whether the guards were there to protect the men, or dissuade them from making any complaints. A noise from inside the pinfold distracted her thoughts. She realised the jail was occupied. Someone was being punished. Whether it was for allowing the two prisoners to escape or whether it was for inciting last night's riots she couldn't tell. Probably the safest conclusion would be for both.

There was a noise across the yard and she looked up in time to see the the back door of the house open. The man from the beach, the one she recognised as the First Lieutenant, emerged. Behind him two other men appeared. Between them they were holding up a third man by his armpits. The man's face was bruised and swollen. Dried blood covered his chin. The owl watched as the man was half led, half dragged to the pinfold. One of the two men unlocked the door and, helped by his companion, roughly bundled the third man inside and locked the door after him. She remained where she was as she watched the two men return to the house and enter, closing the door behind them.

Agnes hummed a little tune to herself. The words came into her mind. "Something is happening but you don't know what it is...." Agnes quite liked

Bob Dylan. She had to admit to herself, the twenty first century certainly had all the best tunes.

From her perch Agnes observed the house. The owl then flew from the prison and landed on the roof next to a chimney stack. Then it simply wasn't there. No one could see the rat scurry down the roof, enter a drain pipe and drop onto a window ledge on one of the upper floors where it squeezed its way through a half open window. Agnes was in the house. She tried hard to visualise the plans of the house. It wasn't easy, especially as the bit of rat that remained wanted to scurry around looking for food. She concentrated harder. She was in an end bedroom. Above her would be the servant's quarters. Below her should be the sitting room. Outside the bedroom was a corridor that led to the large staircase coming up from the hall. Everything seemed quiet so she headed out of the door towards the staircase. Suddenly there was a large explosion, a thump and a large piece of plaster almost hit her. The rat's instinct took control and it ran the length of the corridor taking refuge behind a plinth that held the bust of a man's head.

"Bloody rat!" she heard a voice say.

Downstairs a door crashed opened.

"What is going on? Who fired that shot?" A voice shouted.

Agnes peered round the corner of the plinth. Below her were two shabbily dressed men. From her position Agnes guessed they had been on guard inside the main entrance. One held a smoking pistol in her hand. He was looking down at the ground. Agnes looked towards the new arrival. He had grey hair, side whiskers and wore the full military uniform of a colonel. She looked on as the man stepped forward and quickly slapped the man holding the gun across the face.

"Fool!" he shouted.

There was more clatter as doors opened and several men appeared on the scene all holding loaded pistols. As they took in the scene before them they came to a stop and, realising there was no danger, began to slide their pistols into their belts. One stepped forward. It was the man from the beach. He looked at the colonel.

"Man here thinks that firing a pistol inside the house is a good idea!" The Colonel said with a red face.

The "first lieutenant" took one look, walked up to the man still holding the gun.

The man looked up. "I saw a rat sir!" He said in his defence.

The "first lieutenant" gave the unfortunate man another slap across the face. "Idiot!" he shouted at him. He turned to the other men who had appeared.

"Right, back to your duties! The next man who discharges a weapon without good reason will regret it!"

The Ex-Colonel stood and watched as the men disappeared back from where they had come. No one saw the rat as it disappeared from behind the plinth and reappeared downstairs. It scurried across the hall and entered the room the Colonel had just entered. It quickly ran to the far end of the room and came to rest hidden away under the large desk she had seen in her scrying bowl. There was the sound of a door closing and two sets of footsteps sounded on the wooden floor.

"Trigger happy idiot!" The Colonel exclaimed.

"Every man is jumpy! The events of last night have everyone on edge." The man from the beach answered.

"What events? Fellow sees a shadow on the road and panics!"

The first Lieutenant coughed. "The men swear they saw something. Heard it as well."

"Superstitious bumpkins!" The Colonel retorted

"Proper spooked the men, Sir. Almost had a rebellion on our hands last night. Some hot heads got them all roused up."

The Colonel grunted. "I trust that they have all been dealt with in an appropriate manner Grimes?"

"Grimes!" Agnes thought. So that was the first lieutenants name.

"Got them under lock and key, Sir!" Grimes replied.

There was a tinkle of glass and the sound of drink being poured. The colonel had poured himself a glass of something. Agnes noticed he didn't offer or pour one for his second in command. That spoke volumes, Agnes thought.

The Colonel slurped from his glass. "I hope you can actually keep these prisoners this time."

There was an awkward silence.

Then the Colonel spoke again. "I don't suppose you can explain how two men disappeared from a locked jail yet, can you?"

The last question was barked rather than spoken.

"No Colonel. It's a mystery. The door was locked, window barred, No one could have got out of there!"

"But yet it was empty this morning!"

"They must have escaped during the hullaballoo last night!"

"How Grimes, how? They simply can't have heard the commotion and simply walked out of the door."

"Had to have been then Sir. It was the only time the guard left their posts!"

The Colonel harrumphed. "I assume they have been made aware of their failings?"

"They are inside the jail now Sir!" Replied Grimes.

The Colonel grunted "Good, serve 'em right. Should have had them strung up though. Hanging offence desertion of post! Hanging offence in the army!"

Grimes shuffled his feet. "Some of the men are a bit worried about that sir!"

"About what? Speak up man. Worried about what?"

Agnes could almost hear Grimes' Adams apple wobble. She could tell the conversation, as far as he was concerned, had taken a turn for the worse.

"About being in an army Sir." Grimes almost whispered the words.

The Colonel snorted. "Of course they are in an army. My army! They didn't quibble when they took the coin. They didn't quibble when they signed their marks on their papers. And they certainly didn't quibble when they received their share of the proceeds from the cargoes!"

As he spoke the Colonels voice grew louder and angrier. Suddenly he slammed his fist onto the top of his desk. There was the sound of glass breaking. Some small shards of glass and spilt whiskey found its way under the desk to where Agnes was hiding. There was a moment's silence. Then the Colonels voice returned to normal.

"Get out!" He said. "Get out!"

Agnes heard footsteps move across the room. The door opened and then closed again. There were a few moments of silence as the small puddle of whiskey began to grow around the rats feet when there was the sound of a second door opening, a door towards the rear of the room, near to the desk. Agnes heard a new voice.

"Complications Colonel? Complications?"

Chapter Twenty Six

When Marmaduke and Dancing Jack arrived at the Castle Garrison Sergeant Lewis was in charge at the Gatehouse. He nodded at Marmaduke and waved him through the open gate.

"I take it he's with you?" he nodded towards dancing Jack.

"Oh yes, very much so!" replied Marmaduke.

The Sergeant ordered one of his men to escort then straight to the Commanders Office. As the two passed through the gates the Sergeant whispered in Marmaduke's ear.

"No chance of a late breakfast up there I suppose?"

Marmaduke smiled down at the man "Sorry Sergeant, we've already eaten!"

The Sergeant's face fell. "Pity!" he said as they passed into the Castle.

As they entered his office Marmaduke saw the Commander slide a pile of papers away from him. He looked up and tapped his hand on the top of the pile.

"Paperwork! Reports. Spend more time behind this desk shuffling papers around than there are hours in a day!" he looked up at Marmaduke "I take it you have news?"

He gestured with his head that the pair should sit down. As they settled themselves he looked the newcomer up and down.

"I assume somehow you've got yourself embroiled in these shenanigans." Without waiting for a response he answer this own question. "Of course you have, otherwise you wouldn't be here. Go on then!"

The last comment was aimed at Marmaduke.

Marmaduke nodded. He did the introductions and then narrated to the Commander the events of the last twenty four hours. The Commander listened in silence as Marmaduke told the story, deliberately omitting details of Dancing Jack and his undercover role.

The Commander harrumphed. "Highwayman you say? Dashed odd bedfellows. Then what do you expect when Agnes is involved."

He then let go a deep guffaw and laughed. "I'd liked to have seen the look on their faces when you growled at them. Probably frightened the life out of them. Serves them right!"

He looked back at Marmaduke. So what's the plan of action?"

Marmaduke shook his head. "I've no idea. Agnes said to wait here until we hear from her."

A worried look crossed the Commanders face. "I take it she'll be alright in there?"

Then he caught sight of Marmaduke's face. "Of course she will. She's Agnes."

There was really nothing else they could do and Marmaduke could tell that the Commander needed to return to his paperwork, whether he liked it or not. Anyway he was uncomfortable without his throwing knives. Also the weapons they had taken as replacements, whilst adequate, were neither the quality nor as well balanced as his own weapons that he had been forced to leave behind.

He needed to make a visit to Andrew Marks. They left the Commander to his paperwork promising to return in a couple of hours, unless they heard otherwise.

As the pair walked through the Castle Gatehouse Sergeant Lewis sidled forward. "I don't suppose there were any spare sausages up there?"

Marmaduke shook his head.

He walked Dancing Jack through the Old Town pointing out various buildings, inns, shops and local characters. As they walked along the foreshore they were unaware of the nods and nudges that passed among the women gutting fish. Well it wasn't everyday that two such men walked by. Even the dockers and the men on the harbourside looked up as they passed.

As soon as they entered the Chandlery Andrew motioned them towards his office. He followed on behind and was pleased to see that neither of the men even thought of sitting in his best office chair. After they were seated Marmaduke one again told the story of the previous twenty four hours, and the loss of his weapons. Andrew nodded and stood up. He walked across the room, took a key out of his pocket and opened a large double doored cupboard. Marmaduke blinked and Dancing Jacks eyes opened wide. Inside the cupboard was a lethal selection of swords, daggers, knives and pistols. As Andrew rummaged around selecting certain items he turned to the two men. "And yes. Agnes knows all about it!"

Marmaduke had picked up a sword and was swishing it around in a series of moves feeling its balance and weight.

"Never said a word." He commented.

Dancing Jack had selected another blade and was just about to test it when he noticed a vicious looking, long dagger. He picked it up and examined the blade and handle. He turned to Andrew

"I don't suppose you know where this came from?" he asked.

Andrew looked at the dagger. He held his hand out and Jack threw it up in the air, it spun and he caught it by the blade and handed it to Andrew handle first. Andrew made no comment but took the handle and examined the blade. He turned it over and over trying to remember. Then it came to him.

"It must have been about three months ago now. A fellow brought it in with along with a sword and a pair of pistols. Said he found them up on the moor somewhere."

Dancing Jack looked at Andrew. "I don't suppose you still have them all?"

Andrew put the dagger down and returned to the cupboard. After a few minutes piling and re-piling swords he eventually found the one he was looking for.

He turned to Dancing Jack. "Here's the sword. I fear I sold the pistols to a mariner. No idea what ship he came in on, or left on for that matter."

Dancing Jack looked at Andrew and held his hand out. "I'll take that if I may."

Marmaduke noticed the tone of Jacks voice slightly alter. He made an intuitive guess. "I take it the swords familiar to you?"

Dancing Jack looked down at the sword as if remembering. "They belonged to an acquaintance, a fellow gentleman of the road. His name was Dead Leg Johnson and he worked the Great North Road. He travelled north to answer the call of our friend The Colonel. No one heard from him again."

He turned to Andrew. "Whereabouts on the moor?"

Andrew scratched his head. "The man who found them was a carter. Said they were just lying at the side of the road."

Dancing Jack tipped his hat back and scratched his head. "Something's wrong. Dead Leg would never willingly let his pistols out of his sight!"

Marmaduke looked at Andrew. "Any idea where we can find this carter?"

Andrew shrugged and spread his hands out in a suggestion of helplessness. "Come on Marmaduke. You know carters. If they get a good load they'll travel to Cornwall if the price is right. He could be anywhere."

Marmaduke thought a second. "Do you know what he was carrying that day?"

Andrew nodded. "As it happens I do. He was carrying empty barrels. Delivered them to a fish merchant on the pier." he nodded in the direction of the harbour.

Dancing Jack clicked his fingers. "Empty barrels? Were they new by any chance?"

Andrew nodded. "As likely as not. Although we have plenty of coopers of our own out there."

Dancing Jack continued with his line of thought. "So we find the cooper and trace the quickest route across the moors. Somewhere along that route we'll find the spot where he found the weapons."

"And what will that prove?" Asked Andrew.

"We could find a clue as to what happened to Dead Leg."

Marmaduke shook his head. "We need to be here when Agnes arrives."

Dancing Jack gave a little shrug. "Put it down on our "to do" list. He was a friend. I owe him."

Marmaduke nodded. "Let's sort out our weapons. Then let's find a fish merchant with some new barrels. At least we can find out where they came from."

As they armed themselves Andrew went to his desk and slid open a drawer. He pulled out a bandoleer and placed it on the desk. Marmaduke picked it up and slung it across his chest.

"I don't suppose you've anything to put in it?" he asked

Andrew shook his head. "Sorry."

Marmaduke shrugged. He knew exactly where he could lay his hands on a set of throwing knives, in a cupboard back at his house. He planned on picking them up on his way back to the Castle.

Fully armed they began their search along the side of the harbour, looking among the dealers and fishermen and women at the fish market. After a few minutes it became very obvious that every dealer and fish merchant were using new barrels. Finally Marmaduke walked up to a fish merchant.

"If I wanted a dozen new barrels where would I go?"

The man nodded across the busy market. "There's your man. As many barrels as you want."

The pair walked across to the man who had been pointed out to them. They were unaware that as they walked between the boxes and tables and fishwives packing gutted fish into crates, all eyes were on them.

The man in the cooperage watched as the two men walked towards him. In his large calloused hand he held a large hammer he had been using to fix the iron hoops around the middle of the barrel. As they approached he gripped the hammer a little bit tighter. Marmaduke noticed the slight movement and held his hand up, palm outwards.

"Please. I just want to ask a couple of questions."

The men nodded but kept tight hold of his hammer. Marmaduke spoke. "Where can I get hold of a dozen new barrels?"

The man looked at him in amazement. "Are you having a laugh at my expense?"

Marmaduke looked puzzled. The man seeing the look on his face continued. "I make the damned things. I'm a cooper!"

Dancing Jack looked around him. "You mean you make all the barrels in this harbour?"

The man laughed and relaxed his hold on the hammer. In his mind he was obviously talking to two idiots.

"Of course not. I make a good few mind. Midas Stone and George Cooper make them as well. Then there's that new bloke up at the far end of the foreshore."

Dancing Jack scratched his head. "So, four coopers supply most of the barrels around here. Why then would anyone bring a dozen barrels across the moors to deliver them here?"

The cooper shook his head. "Can't answer that one, but I can tell you one thing. There ain't a barrel maker up on't moors. There's a couple up at t'Bay and a lot more in Whitby. Why set up a cooperage on t'moors. No one needs the things up there."

Marmaduke looked around to watch the activity in the market. The novelty of their presence had worn off and everyone had returned to whatever they had been doing before their arrival.

"What about farmers, and them up at that alum works?" he asked

"Farmers can't afford new. The buy second hand barrels. Them up at t'works have their own cooper."

Marmaduke turned to Dancing Jack. "So if the barrels weren't new ones ordered by someone here, why bring them here and where did they go?"

"More to the point," replied Jack. "What was inside them, and what happened to Dead Leg?"

Chapter Twenty Seven

At the sound of a new voice Agnes froze. She was puzzled. At no time had she felt the presence of a stranger in the house. The puddle of spilt whiskey had now gathered around her feet and was beginning to sting. She was fighting the rat's instinct to run from the pain. She looked out at the landscape from the rats eyes. Across the room was a large dresser holding a selection of pewter plates and tankards. She launched herself and ran as fast as she could across the wooden floor and squeezed herself behind the dresser. The voice spoke once more.

"My dear Colonel. You really should get yourself a couple of dogs, you have rats in the building. I just saw one run behind the dresser there."

Agnes froze. The last thing she needed was to be flushed out and chased across the room. The Colonel gave a grunt of annoyance.

"Can't stand rats. Eat the stores. Eat their own weight ten times over. Seen an entire barn emptied in a matter of days. Ruinous beasts. Dogs will be ordered!"

The stranger spoke once again. "I have a feeling there are more pressing matters at hand Colonel. It seems to me that the men are in danger of, shall we say, mutiny?"

Ex-Colonel Thomas Reynard slammed his hand on the desk once again. "There will be no mutiny under my command. If one man steps out of line they will be hung. Sets an example, keeps them on the straight and narrow don't you know."

Suddenly the stranger's voice changed its tone. Now it spoke very precisely and very emphatically. If Agnes was in any doubt of the order of command, it was made very obvious now.

"Colonel. Have you not thought it just might be your military discipline that has created this mood in the first place?"

The Colonels face turned bright red. "Military discipline. Must have discipline, otherwise we'll have anarchy."

The other man shook his head. "You are forgetting Colonel. Those men out there are not soldiers. They are thieves, robbers, ship wreckers, brigands and all the other ne'er do wells you have managed to attract to our enterprise. You should admit it. Trying to train that lot as soldiers is about as productive as trying to herd cats. They are bandits and the only reason they remain here is that you pay them."

Thomas Reynard spluttered. "They signed the papers. They enlisted damn it!"

The other man spoke once more. "Colonel, this is your mess and I'll leave you to sort it out. But do not forget. Every night that passes more ships sail right on by. That means no profits. When their profits stop coming in our friends get very twitchy. They start asking awkward questions. If they get no return on their investment they will take their investment somewhere else. At that point Colonel everything comes tumbling down. I don't think for one moment you underestimate the consequences of that happening. No money and your trained band of thugs will simply fade away into the night. Leaving you.....well leaving you exactly where you were before we ventured on this enterprise Colonel..."

Before the Ex-Colonel could comment the man continued speaking. "The day grows long and I must be off and trust me, the report I will be delivering will not make happy reading. Things need to be attended to. Attend to them Colonel!"

With that the man turned and left the room closing the door heavily behind him causing some of the pewter to shake and rattle. There was another crash and a tinkling of broken glass. She peered out from beneath the dresser. The Colonel had thrown another glass across the room.

She waited a while until she heard him scrape his chair across the wooden floor, stand up and march across the room. She heard the sound of a door opening and the Colonel shout the name of Grimes. As he slammed the door behind him the pewter shook and rattled once again. Agnes took advantage of the empty room and scuttled towards the window, where she ran up the curtain and onto the window ledge where she squeezed under the window, which was a bit strange as the window had been closed. There again, she thought, if you can't cheat with a bit of magic what can you do?

Outside on the window ledge the air shimmered and a wood pigeon took off and circled the house. Once she had gained height she spotted the stranger. He had mounted a horse and was just leaving the stables. She caught an up draught and allowed it to take her higher. The man below steered the horse towards the woodlands and the hidden exit to the road. She wondered why the man hadn't used the main gate. He emerged from the far side of the woodland and rode at a brisk pace down the narrow lane. She estimated he was heading south. She spent the next two hours following him until he pulled into a small inn on the junction with the main Pickering to Whitby Road. She perched in a tree as he dismounted and passed the reins to an ostler before entering the inn. Agnes figured he planned to stay the night there. She wanted to know more about this man. Was he in command of the Colonel or was he simply a messenger, and if he was a go-between, who was he representing?

Twenty minutes later, just as the man was spooning a mouthful of hot greasy broth towards his mouth, an old gypsy woman entered the inn. With annoyance he noticed she was walking towards him. He kept his head down and stared into his broth. Suddenly she diverted her walk and accosted two other diners negotiating the broth.

"Lucky heather Sirs?" She asked, and then lowered her voice. "Potions and lotions?"

The two travellers tried to ignore her. She leant even further forward. "Potions to charm the ladies? Potions to make your rivals impotent."

One of the diners flicked his spoon at her. "Be gone woman. Take your unholy wares away. They offend me Madam. They offend!"

With that both men lowered their heads and continued with their meal. Agnes chuckled to herself. She realised she had tried to sell her potions to two travelling preachers. Amusement over she sidled across the room to the man dining by himself.

"Lucky white heather Sir?" She lowered her voice again and gave a quick shifty glance around her then as if satisfied no one could hear her she whispered. "Potions Sir? Charms?"

The man ignored her. She continued. "Charms to confuse your enemies, Sir?"

The man paused, holding his horn spoon just above the thickening layer of grease. He looked up at the woman. "Enemies madam, why should I have enemies?"

Agnes gave the impression of a toothless smile. "Everyone has enemies Sir. Everyone has their secrets!"

The man placed his spoon carefully on the table in front of him. "Madam, you offend me too with your so called potions and lotions. Take them away and sell them to simpletons that believe such hokum. Leave me else I will look to the landlord to remove you from the premises."

Agnes decided not to labour the issue.

With a slight nod of her head she shuffled across the room to where the landlord was eyeing her suspiciously. She gave him one of her special looks and ordered a small tankard of small beer. He gave her a toothless smile as he served it. She must have given him too much of a look, she thought. Still never one to miss an opportunity she began a conversation that ranged from the weather, the price of sheep at the local market and highwaymen. Eventually she guided it towards the traveller who has just pushed his bowl away from him and as wiping the corner of his mouth with a very expensive handkerchief.

The landlord lowered his voice. "You mean Mr Parsimonious as I call him? He's a lawyer. Has a practice in York. Comes up here on business now and again. Arrives by the post coach, hires a horse, rides off, comes back, stays the night and then returns the same way the following day. He'll be on the ten o'clock Pickering to York flyer in the morning, Back at his desk by lunchtime."

Agnes thanked him for his information, finished her drink, winced at the taste, and handed the Landlord a bunch of lucky white heather freshly picked from the moor just outside his own front door and shuffled out of the door.

The ten o'clock flyer she thought. That gives me all night. The air shimmered and an owl rose into the night sky and flew off in the direction of Scarborough and its Castle.

Chapter Twenty Eight

"Why Dead Leg?" Asked Marmaduke

"He walked with limp." answered Dancing Jack.

"Oh!" said Marmaduke.

Dancing Jack looked across to him. "You sound disappointed."

"I was expecting something more exciting." Replied Marmaduke.

sezDancing Jack shook his head. "No. He just walked with a limp. Highwaymen are pretty literal when it comes to picking names."

"So you're called Dancing Jack because your names Jack and you dance?"

The Highwayman smiled. "My names Jack to be sure, but the only dancing I ever did was at Hatfield, at the end of hangman's noose."

With that he gently pulled down the scarf from around his neck to reveal a deep scar that ran under his chin and followed his jaw line to the back of his head.

He slid the scarf back up again. "I was dangling there for a goodly few minutes before I realised the hangman had made a mistake with the tying of the noose. It was a full ten minutes before they realised their mistake. They were lowering me down to have another go at things when the whole thing comes crashing down and me with it. The rope slipped in the hangman's hand."

He laughed. "Fell right through the hole where the trapdoor had been. I hit the ground and began running. The crowd thought it was good sport and blocked the way of them that were chasing me. Cheered me on my way so they did, I escaped with the rope still around my neck.

Marmaduke wondered if the man was having a joke at his expense. Then he remembered the scar and gave little shudder.

The two of them had returned to the Castle and were sat by a large patch of grass near to the parade ground. They had spent most of the afternoon and early evening asking questions around the harbour before returning to the chandlery to ask Andrew about the mysterious barrels. Andrew knew nothing, a situation that caused him to worry. He liked to think he knew all the cargoes coming in and out of the harbour, legal or illegal. It was a matter of concern to him that someone was shipping something out of the port without his knowledge. He promised Marmaduke he would make his own enquiries. Marmaduke nodded. He knew Andrew could get answers from the men in the shadows, the smugglers and their agents, the men who Marmaduke couldn't find, let alone question.

As they waited Marmaduke spent his time practicing with his replacement throwing knives. Dancing Jack watched as Marmaduke slid a knife from the bandoleer into his hand and threw it in one smooth motion, with deadly accuracy, at a target he had sketched out on the front of an old wooden door that led down to the dungeons. Eventually it began to grow dark. Dancing Jack raised an eyebrow when he realised that, despite the darkness, Marmaduke was still hitting the target on a door he could no longer see, He was about to comment on this when he became aware of a movement behind him. He turned to see Agnes walking towards them. She led them to the Commanders office, refusing to tell of her adventures until the Commander was present. Agnes was old school, she firmly believed in only telling her story once, and once only. She had no time for repetition.

"I don't boil my onions twice!" she would say.

No one ever knew what she meant.

The four of them sat at the Commanders table, the remains of a meal lay before them on various plates and platters. As they ate both Agnes and Marmaduke had narrated their stories and discoveries. Now they sat with chairs pulled back, contemplating the new developments. The Commander had pulled out a small pipe and a silver tobacco box. He had offered it to Marmaduke who had declined and to Dancing Jack, who accepted. As they filled their pipes there was a short, sharp crackling sound. They looked across the table towards Agnes. She was still seated only now she held a pipe in her hand. She exhaled a huge plume of smoke.

"Just making a point Gentlemen!" She remarked calmly.

The Commanders face reddened. Dancing Jack tipped his hat to her. "And a fair one at that!!" he acknowledged.

The Commander harrumphed and quickly changed the subject. "We seem to have raised more questions than we have answers." He grunted. He leant forward in his seat. "Now let me get this straight. Our ex-Colonel Thomas Reynard has hired himself a force that he uses to stage ship wrecks."

"Don't forget he also hires highwaymen, so he's overseeing robberies on both land and sea!" Added Jack.

The Colonel nodded. "But it seems someone else is underwriting his enterprise, and the only clue to their identity is a York lawyer who will return to the city on the ten o'clock flyer."

Agnes puffed a cloud of smoke across the table. "We also know that the Colonel has his problems. Seems that he is under the misapprehension that has recruited his own private army. His men think otherwise. From what I can gather they are not too happy about his style of discipline!" Agnes said.

The Commander gave another grunt. "Discipline, the key to all successful military operations. An undisciplined army is nothing short of a mob!"

"And a mob of thieves and killers!" Added Marmaduke.

"And thanks to your actions of last night a very frightened mob. Those men are jumping at the sight of their own shadows." Agnes nodded towards Marmaduke and Dancing Jack.

The Colonel followed her gaze. "The thought of giant cats prowling the countryside is enough to turn any mans liver!" He harrumphed again.

Uncomfortable with the sudden attention Marmaduke changed the subject. "We also have the mystery of the barrels, and a missing highwayman. I don't know why but I have a feeling they are linked to our Foxy Tom."

Agnes let out another jet of smoke, decided she had made her point, moved her hand and the pipe disappeared. "If Andrew knows nothing about goods leaving the harbour the chances are that your feelings could be right."

The Commander slapped the table with the palm of his hand making the platter and plates jump up. "Gentlemen, and lady, of course. What we need is a plan of campaign!"

They all agreed. Agnes spoke. "I think that ex-Colonel Thomas Reynard's army is unnerved. It won't take much to drive them into a state of panic. That I think is a job for you and me." She nodded towards Marmaduke, and then directed a look towards Dancing Jack. "We also need someone in York to keep an eye on our lawyer friend. Given a decent horse do you think you could be there in time to meet the Pickering post? It should arrive around midday. Don't do anything, just follow him. See if you can find out a bit more about our go-between. A name would be good, if you could find out whose interests he is working for would be even better."

Dancing Jack tipped his hat at her, and looked towards the Commander. He nodded.

"I'll write a note to the master of horse. Take any animal that catches your eye. It will be ready when you need it."

The plans were made. There was nothing left to do so Agnes suggested they should rest for some hours. Dancing Jack agreed to spend the night at the Garrison, as the Commanders guest to enable him an early start. Agnes and Marmaduke walked home. As they passed through the gatehouse Sergeant Lewis appeared from the shadows. Marmaduke slid a package out from his jacket and passed it to him. The Sergeant thanked him and shut the gate behind him. As they walked down Castlegate Agnes gave him one of her quizzical looks.

"Sausages!" Marmaduke replied.

Chapter Twenty Nine.

That night, as Dancing Jack and the Commander slept safely inside the walls of Scarborough Castle and Marmaduke slept curled up in the comfortable chair by the fireside, Agnes was pottering. She prepared a selection of herbs and potions, put them in her pockets, and filled her scrying bowl with water.

The first image she conjured up was the lawyer, sleeping in his bed in the inn on the moor.

She moved her hand and the image cleared to be replaced by an aerial image of Hawkstone Grange. At first everything seemed peaceful. The she took a closer look.

Guards were standing not only at the front and rear of the house but at the entrances to the building that she knew to be the barracks. She smiled. The Colonels guards were keeping intruders out whilst also keeping his own men in. She searched through the house. In one room she found Grimes hard asleep, snoring with one hand still tightly holding the neck of a bottle. She moved down the corridor and saw a light filter under a closed door. It was the Colonel. He was sat at a desk in front of a large window staring out into the dark night. She watched as his lips moved.

"Talking to himself!" she thought, "he's a very worried man."

She shook Marmaduke awake. "Time you were on your way." She said. He let out a small growl then realised where he was and who he was with. He nodded and smiled allowing Agnes to see a glimpse of his fangs. "I won't be far away. I'm going on ahead." She said.

In the early hours before dawn an owl flitted out of the town and headed towards Hawkstone Grange as a black shape bounded across open country. No one was abroad to see the shape as it passed by cottage, farm and village.

As Agnes perched on the roof of the stable building she noticed the light was still burning in the window of the Colonels bedroom. He had not moved from the position she had last seen him in. No time like the present she thought.

The air shimmered and the vague shape of an elderly lady could just be made out squatting by the side of a small bell tower positioned at the centre of the stable roof. She moved her hands and fingers in an intricate pattern. Below her there was a rustling sound as loose sticks and stones and mud began to move, forming a shape that could only loosely be described as humanoid. She moved her fingers once more and the shape raised itself off the ground and moved slowly upwards. As it neared the Colonels bedroom window Agnes moved her fingers and a large mouth appeared. Just for effect she added fangs and a pair of bright red eyes. She gave a final flick of her fingers and the shape moved up until it was in position outside the bedroom window. The resulting effect was better than she expected.

There was a muffled scream, a pistol shot and the sound of crashing glass. The window exploded, shards of glass and sticks and stones and mud showered to the ground outside the house. To add to the confusion she flicked another finger and the bell in the tower began to ring. The air shimmered and an owl flew from the roof to a nearby tree where it proceeded to preen itself and watch the proceedings with interest.

From a distance Marmaduke heard the bell tolling. He sped up. Agnes had started without him. He sped up and soon arrived at the woodland surrounding the house. This was no time for discretion he thought as he let out a huge growl and leapt over the stone wall into the grounds of the house. The result of his leap was spectacular. The patrol that had just stopped by the wall to take a slight rest saw the

shape as it leapt over them. At the same time the
noise of the growl turned their insides to jelly. They
dropped their weapons and turned and fled. Some
ran towards the house but others ran through the
woods. Marmaduke thought he wouldn't be seeing
them again. The way they set off they probably
wouldn't stop running till they reached
Scarborough.

From her position in the trees Agnes watched
Marmaduke's arrival with interest. She saw half the
patrol run into the woods and the other half head for
the barracks. Once there they came across the men
who had been awoken by the crash of broken
windows and the tolling of the bell and they were
not too happy about it. As their fellow bandits ran in
from patrol shouting and screaming something
about a black shadow, panic and confusion spread
among the men like wildfire. Soon the area between
the big house and the barracks was full of angry,
panicking men, all armed and none of them
knowing in which direction to point their weapons.

Then a shot rang out. It was Grimes. He stood on the step of the rear entrance to the house surrounded by his men. All of them carried muskets. At the sound of the discharged shot everyone in the square froze and turned towards the direction of the shot. Grimes shouted at them and two or three stepped forward. He asked questions, but no one seemed to be able to answer them. Instead they looked up at the broken window. The face of the Colonel could be seen looking out. It was white. The man kept pointing towards the ground.

Grimes tried to ignore him. From her position Agnes decided to add some more confusion into the mix. She closed her eyes and concentrated. Casting the spell wasn't easy as she had reverted to her owl form, but by holding out her talons and fluttering her wings she managed it. From nowhere there was a flash of lightening followed almost immediately by a clap of thunder. Then it began to rain, only instead of rain drops it rained small, black, wriggling snakes. It took a few seconds for the men in the yard to realise what was happening. By then the ground was full of snakes. They fell from the sky and landed on shoulders and heads. The men frantically tried to brush them off. Other lifted their feet and hopped around in a vain attempt to prevent the snakes from slithering over their feet and wrapping themselves around their ankles and lower legs. In the midst of this confusion a black shape slipped between the buildings. The growl was so loud that every man in the yard believed it had occurred right behind them. If an owl could have laughed this one would have. The growl had been so terrifying that it took the men's minds off the snakes, which was just as well for very slowly they began to dissolve into a black viscous slime that oozed around their feet and slid under doors and clogged up drains and gutters. Suddenly for the men involved, it seemed as if they were walking through very black and very sticky treacle. By now she could see the abject fear etched into the men's faces. Their eyes were wide open. Some were screaming, others sobbing. The hair on some men's heads had turned white. To her left she could see at least ten men sneaking through the woods away from the house. The Colonels army was getting smaller by the minute.

She looked across to the house. Grimes and his men had retreated back into the house and were busy building a barricade in front of the door. It was obvious that the men inside the house were made of much sterner stuff. Two ground floor windows opened and two musket barrels poked out.

It was then that Agnes remembered that the small isolated building at the edge of the woodland was the armoury. The air shimmered and, if anyone had been looking, they would have seen an elderly woman slip behind the trunk of a tree. They would also, if they had been very quick, seen her put her fingers to her mouth and blow what they could never have heard. It was a high pitched whistle in a frequency too high for the human ear. I did however reach the ears of Marmaduke. Within seconds he was standing by her side.

He turned towards her. "I've got black slime all over my boots!" he complained.

Agnes glanced down. They seemed to be covered in tar. She flicked a finger and the slime ran off his boots and soaked into the floor of the woodland. It disappeared.

"Don't worry!" Agnes said. "It's biodegradable!"

Across the way the scene around the barracks was still one of utter pandemonium. Men ran hither and thither, bumping into each other in their panic to be anywhere but where they were. At the rear of the house order was being restored. Grimes and his henchmen had managed to create a small area of calm. Gums were being passed out of the window.

Agnes turned to Marmaduke. "Cover your ears!"

She moved her hands and fingers in a series of patterns and took a step back. Marmaduke stepped back as well for no other reason than if Agnes took a step back, then a step back was what was needed. There was a low rumble that sounded like a heavy object being dragged across a stone floor. Agnes nodded to herself and then made another slight move of her fingers.

The explosion lit up the area as if midday had suddenly burst out. There was the sound of a roar and the far wall of the armoury disappeared as a cannon ball hurled across the space and crashed into the rear of the house taking with it an entire window, its frame and most of the surrounding stonework. Muffled screams came from the debris and destruction.

"That will give them something to worry about" Remarked Marmaduke.

Agnes smiled. "Let's take a rest and watch what happens next."

Above them a pale dawn began to break, its feint thin light illuminating a scene of destruction.

"Might as well make ourselves comfortable." Agnes commented. There was a shimmer and suddenly Marmaduke found himself floating up in the air. He came to rest in a hammock slung between the higher branches of the tree he had been standing underneath. He turned his head. Agnes was already stretched out in a hammock of her own. Marmaduke noted that hers also had the added comfort of some cushions. They both settled down.

Below them the grounds were completely free of men. Some, the braver ones, had rushed towards the house and were pulling and tugging at the rubble underneath the demolished window. Instructions were being shouted at them from inside the building. The less brave ones had disappeared into the woods, never to be seen again.

Agnes relaxed her mind and closed her eyes and visualised the scene inside the house. The cannonball had demolished most of the furniture before embedding itself in the opposite wall.

Inwardly she was pleased that there seemed to be no fatalities. That wasn't to say there were no injuries. Three men had been in the room when their world exploded around them. One had been hit by the exploding glass and was being bound up whilst his many lacerations were being attended to by a man who really didn't seem to know what he was doing. Another seemed to be affected by shock. Despite being covered in black dust and bits of wood and plaster his head had turned white. He kept shaking his head and rubbing his ears. She realised he had been deafened and wondered if it was permanent. She allowed her vision to drift through the other rooms where heavily armed men were still in position, aiming their guns towards the barracks.

Eventually she located Grimes. He was in the upstairs room with the ex Colonel. Foxy Tom was still shaking. Grimes had poured him a glass of whisky but the Colonel was unable to drink it. He tried to hold the glass but his hand shook so much that the whisky was slopping over the side of the glass. H seemed unable to raise it to his mouth. It was obvious that he was unable to make any decisions or even capable of rational thought. She watched the look on Grimes face as he realised that he was the one who would have to make the decisions, at least for now. Agnes withdrew her mind and allowed herself the luxury of a short nap. Next to her she could hear Marmaduke snoring. She flicked her finger in his direction and the snoring stopped.

It was almost ten o'clock in the morning when she opened her eyes again. Sunlight shone down and filtered through the leaves and upper branches forming a pattern of light and shade on the woodland floor. She glanced to her right. Marmaduke's hammock was empty. Obviously he was out and about somewhere. She cast her mind across the woodland and found him at the far edge, sitting between two trees. He was eating a breakfast of raw pheasant.

Over at the house everything seemed quiet. One or two men shuffled between the barracks buildings. Agnes was pleased to note that the so called army had been greatly reduced in numbers. However, although she had successfully dispersed the foot soldiers, inside the house there were at least twenty hand-picked, heavily armed thugs, the Ex-Colonel's elite force. Sooner or later she would have to deal with them.

She did consider bringing the entire operation to its inevitable conclusion there and then. However, despite her magic, she wanted ex-Colonel Thomas Reynard to face the full force of the law. She didn't care whether it was criminal or military. She owed that to the families of the victims of the shipwrecks. After all, despite being a witch, she did have a high regard for the law, unless it got in her way of course. She wanted to see Foxy Tom in a court and to get him to court she needed some sort of evidence and the key to that was in the hands of a government spy who went by the name of Dancing Jack.

Chapter Thirty

Dancing Jack was pleased with his choice of horse. He had woken early and taken a pleasant ride into York. As he approached the City he swung around to join the main road coming in from Pickering. He didn't have to wait long before he heard the Flyer thundering down the road. He let it pass and followed from a distance. It entered the City walls through Monk Bar and drew to a stop outside a large coaching inn. Dancing Jack dismounted as the door to the stage opened. He watched as the lawyer carefully stepped out of the carriage and walked down the busy road, heading towards the centre of the City. Dancing Jack followed him through a network of narrow streets and alleyways until he came to a door halfway down a particularly dark and dank passageway. He waited until the lawyer had closed the door behind him before walking down the alley. He stopped by the door. There was a small brass plate fixed to the wall next to the black door. He read it. Messer's R Pettigrew, Solicitors and Commissioners for Oaths. Now he had a name. He turned and walked to the opposite end of the alley. Across the road he saw a small coffee house. He noticed its windows looked up the alley. He had been there over an hour and had drunk a very average pot of coffee when he saw his man appear in the alleyway once more. He walked towards him. Dancing Jack left his seat and followed as the man walked down the street, across a small bridge across a river and headed towards the City centre. In the distance Jack could see the white stone of York Minster's three towers standing proud above the red roof tops of the many shops and houses and other buildings that comprised the capital of the North. He continued to follow at a distance when he was brought to an abrupt halt. The thing he felt suddenly sticking in the small of his back was definitely the wrong end of a pistol. A voice hissed in his ear.

"I have a very nervous finger, so don't think about making any sudden moves."

Dancing Jack remained still.

"Turn round where I can see you!" The voice said.

He turned slowly until he came face to face with a man of his own height. He looked at the mans face. Through the stubble he could see the skin was deeply pitted. He glanced down to see the pistol pointing straight at his stomach. All around him the people of the City, who were going about their normal business stopped to watch the mini drama being played out in front of them. Dancing Jacks immediate thought was that nobody seemed to be doing anything, just watching. Then as he glanced back at the man holding the gun he realised why. He was being arrested by a City Constable. He let out a small sigh as the man turned to the growing crowd.

"I'm a City Constable. This is the infamous highwayman Dancing Jack, wanted for horse theft and defying the hangman's noose at Hatfield."

As he spoke the man's hand reached out and ripped the scarf from around Jacks neck. The crowd gasped as the deep scar was revealed. He prodded his pistol deeper into Jack's stomach.

"Start walking. We're off to the Castle. You'll be tried first thing, just in time for a trip to the York Tyburn."

He turned back to the gathering crowd. "Get on your way. The next time you'll see the prisoner will be when he's dangling from the end of a rope!"

He turned to Jack and laughed in his face. "Time for your last dance Jack!"

He pushed the pistol deeper into Jacks stomach. Jack took the hint, turned and began walking in the direction of the Castle. As they marched down the street they were joined by other City Constables and watchmen, making sure that he had neither chance nor opportunity to escape. They followed all the way to the Castle, where, with little formalities Jack was incarcerated in a dark, damp cell with only an iron bed as furnishing.

It took Jack less than a minute to realise there was no escape from this cell. He lay on the bed and counted the hours until the following morning and his appearance in court. He allowed himself a slight smile. They had taken his weapons, but left him his hat. He was woken by the sound of a key rattling in his door. He sat up as it opened to reveal two armed constables standing there.

"Time for you to learn the error of your ways!" One said.

The other laughed. "The justice of the peace is in a bad mood. The assize is so full he's had to get up early to see you. He's not a happy man. You could be innocent as new born babe but you'll still hang!"

They stepped forward, dragged the highwayman to his feet, hauled him out of the cell and down the stone corridor that led to the courtroom.

Despite the early start the courtroom was full. Lawyers and petitioners scurried among the benches in the body of the court. A ragged jury laughed and joked with each other. Too early to take their breakfast many of them were eating pies and assortments of tarts and foodstuffs bought from the street traders outside. The public gallery was full of onlookers shouting and jeering at each other. Word had spread that an infamous highwayman was to be tried and hung that morning and the atmosphere in the court was one of a very raucous party.

The crowd fell silent as Dancing Jack was dragged into the prisoners dock. A few loud and ribald comments were shouted out in his direction. He was aware that all eyes were on him. As he straightened himself up the door to the back of the court opened up and the judge appeared to take his seat at the head of the court. The constables were right. He wasn't a happy man. His face was fat and bloated and was the same colour as the red robe. His small piggy like eyes showed little signs of sleep and his wig was askew. It was obvious that clemency and justice were the last things on the man's mind. He began proceedings by banging his gavel on his desk. The court and everyone in it fell silent. No one dared heckle or shout. One look at the judge's face told them that any interruptions would be met by a short sharp spell in a very uncomfortable cell.

Dancing Jack stood there as the prosecution outlined their case against him. It comprised a long series of robberies, hold-ups and horse thefts. Dancing Jack was impressed. If he had done even half the crimes he was accused of he would be a very rich man indeed.

The court listened as the list grew longer and longer. Eventually to the shouts and jeers of the people in the public gallery the prosecutor sat down. The judge banged his gavel again and the court fell silent. He addressed the prisoner in the dock.

"You are charged with a series of villainous, pernicious and wicked crimes. Do you have anything to say in your defence?"

It was a rhetorical question. The judge wasn't expecting Jack to answer, let alone for him to take off his hat, locate a small waxen document and hold it aloft.

"In my defence I only have this document that I implore your Lordship to read." Jack said.

A look of surprise crossed the face of the judge. He nodded to a court official who took the document from the prisoner and passed it up to the bench. The judge took it and opened it. It was the Royal Warrant. His face remained expressionless as he read the words. When he finished he crumpled it up in a tight ball and tossed it onto his desk dismissing it with a snort of derision.

"As I suspected, no defence!" he looked at the Constables. "Take the prisoner away. He will hang at midday." He banged his gavel. "Dismissed!"

The constables grabbed Dancing Jack by his shoulders and pulled him from the dock. As they pushed him down the corridor that led back to the cells Jack was too surprised at the decision to notice a Sergeant with no name slip out of the courtroom and disappear in the direction of the York Garrison.

As he lay on the iron bed Jack estimated that it must be mid morning. He probably had only an hour before he was dragged from the cell to the cart that would transport him through the City to the Tyburn. He tried to think of a way to escape. He was still thinking as the door opened and the two constables reappeared to drag him out of his cell As he was dragged down the corridor to the waiting cart the thought crossed his mind that at least he wouldn't be spending another night in the grim place.

There were four other miscreants in the cart as it pulled out of the Castle gates and wound its way through the narrow medieval streets out of the City towards the racecourse and the Tyburn. By the time the cart had reached Micklegate Bar a crowd had gathered and followed behind hurling insults, stones, rotting fruit and vegetable matter in equal measures. They had left the City Gates and the racecourse was in sight when a troop of mounted soldiers galloped towards them. Before the guards and driver could react the troops had formed a circle around the cart. The crowd behind the cart stopped throwing things and stood in expectation. One look at the troopers holding their drawn sabres told the members of the crowd that to throw anything at them would be a very big mistake.

The commander of the troopers rode up to the cage at the rear of the cart. "Which one of you is Dancing Jack?" he asked.

Immediately all four of the other prisoners leapt to their feet, each one of them loudly proclaiming that they were the person in question. Dancing Jack just smiled and walked towards where the Commander sat on his horse. As the Commander looked up at him Jack lowered his scarf to reveal his scarred neck. The commander nodded and turned to the guards.

"Release that man!"

One of the guards stepped forward. "Man's been tried, found guilty and ordered to hang. Can't go against the law!" As if to emphasis his disregard of the troopers he spat disdainfully at the feet of the Commanders horse.

The troopers pulled on their reins and formed a tighter circle around the cart. The commander looked down in the direction of the man's spittle. He then looked across to his sergeant seated on his horse at the opposite side of the cart.

"I trust you saw that Sergeant?" The Commander barked.

The sergeant nodded. "I surely did sir. Blatant disregard for army property Sir. Chargeable offence in anyone's book!"

The Commander looked back at the Sergeant. "Remind me Sergeant, who does the Army report to?"

The sergeant feigned puzzlement and then replied. "Well Sir, first and foremost the Chief of Staff, The Major General himself!"

The Commander nodded. "And who does the Major general report to Sergeant?"

The Sergeant was warming to his role in the Commander's pantomime.

"Well sir, that would be the King himself, Sir."

The Commander kept his face as straight as a poker. "So Sergeant an assault on army property would be an assault on the King himself. Am I correct?"

The Sergeant made a great pretence of scratching his head. A bead of perspiration appeared upon the forehead of the leading guard. He had a very bad feeling that he knew exactly where this conversation was leading to. He was right.

The Sergeant suddenly smiled. "Why Sir, the way I see things, I fear our man here has just committed an act of treason."

The Commander drew his sabre and pointed it at the guard who had now broken into a cold sweat. His stomach was turning to jelly.

"Arrest them all for treason!" He turned towards the driver of the cart. "Release that man, then return to the Castle. Tell them that there can't be a hanging without attendance of the appropriate officers of the law, who you may tell your masters, are all under military arrest for treason!"

The watching crowd jeered and laughed as the guards were rounded up and pushed forwards until they were surrounded by the mounted troopers. The driver unlocked the cage and Dancing Jack jumped off the cart. One of the troopers reached down and lifted Jack onto the back of his horse. As the driver tried to turn his empty cart around the troopers trotted off at a pace that forced the captive guards to break into an uncomfortable trot. The crowd watched them return towards the Garrison and began to disperse. The morning had proved even more entertaining than the expected hanging.

Once they passed through the gates of the garrison the troopers drew to a halt. They were met by a Sergeant who saluted the Commander.

"Compliments of the day Sir. His nibs is grateful for your intervention."

The Commander nodded. "Thank you Sergeant. Most enjoyable. Haven't pulled the old treason lark for a while now."

He turned to his own Sergeant. "Well played there Matthews. Almost had me convinced back there."

The Sergeant saluted. "My pleasure, Sir. Bit of fun makes a nice change. Good for moral, keeps the men cheerful Sir."

The commander looked down at the sergeant who was standing by his horse. "Well there's your man."

He watched as Dancing Jack jumped off the horse. "Rum looking cove though I must say. Still takes all sorts. Good day gentlemen."

With that he turned his horse and led his men at a trot across the parade ground and towards the distant stables. The captured guards remained where they were. As exhausted and out of breath as they were, they were surprised to find themselves forgotten. The Sergeant walked up to them.

"Shoo!" he said.

The guards looked around them. The parade ground was empty. The gates were still open and just across the open space. They turned and looked at each other and then turned and ran towards the gate and back to the safety of the city. As he watched them sprint through the gates the Sergeant turned to Dancing Jack.

"Were you born lucky?" he asked.

Dancing Jack gave the man a sheepish smile. "It appears so Sergeant. It appears so!"

Ten minutes later he was sat in an office. Seated at a desk in front of him was the Colonel with no name. Next to him stood the Lieutenant with no name.

"When the judge simply screwed up the warrant I thought I was gone." Jack was explaining.

The Colonel shook his head. "Strange behaviour for a member of the Kings Bench I must admit."

The Lieutenant gave a slight cough. The Colonel turned to look at him. The Lieutenant took that as permission to speak.

"Well Sir. If I may say, there was no risk for the judge. Only two people in that court knew what that paper was, and one of them was just about to be led out and hung. No one would think to ask after the paper and the judge would destroy it as soon as he left the bench. It's probably in pieces now."

The Colonel nodded. "I think you are right. For some reason the judge wanted out man here to hang." He turned to the man in question. "I trust you realise just how fortunate you were this morning? If my Sergeant hadn't have been in court we would have had no idea of your fate until the balladeers started selling broadsheets about your hanging!"

Jack pushed his hat back and scratched his head. "Been thinking about that Colonel. Seems they were awful keen to see me hang, sure enough. Almost as if they wanted rid of me before anyone knew I had been captured. Also the nature of my arrest rouses certain questions. How did anyone know I was in York and know who I was? I was under the impression all warrants with my name and bearing my likeness had been rescinded."

The Colonel nodded. "Indeed they were, but enough conjecture. What I would like to know is why in the name of all that's Holy, were you in York in the first place? Your orders were to travel north and enlist in our miscreant ex-colonels network of footpads and highwaymen."

Dancing Jack sat back in his chair. "Well colonel. I have a tale to tell. There have been certain developments. I'm afraid our situation has become a deal more complicated."

For the next half hour Jack regaled them with the events of the last few days. He told of his meeting with Marmaduke, their capture and their escape and his subsequent discovery of the scale and size of Colonel Thomas Reynard's dealings and operations. He told of the finding of Dead Leg Johnsons weapons, the presence of the lawyer at Hawkstone Grange and the way he followed him to York and discovered the location of his office. He did not however make any mention of Agnes and her magic. He also left out a mention of Marmaduke's transformation into something that could only be described as half man half cat. He knew the army didn't believe in magic, well at least this particular Colonel didn't.

After he had completed his story the Colonel turned to the Lieutenant. "Get someone to watch the lawyer, and make sure he's a damn sight better at keeping undercover than our man here!" he nodded in the direction of Dancing Jack who was about to protest when the Colonel held his hand up to silence him.

"The only way events could have occurred. Out lawyer friend spotted you. He has probably no idea of who you are or who you are working for, but he must have his suspicions. He got word to someone who arranged for your arrest, and subsequent hanging. No wonder the judge ignored the Royal Warrant. He was part of our lawyers plan to see you hung. It seems our lawyer has some very influential friends. Gentlemen – This situation becomes more perplexing as it goes along. We will have to act with a greater degree of caution. We can't just march in and arrest a lawyer and a Justice of the Kings Bench. Even my superiors would hesitate to follow that course without sufficient proof. We need to dig deeper Gentlemen. We need to dig deeper. Rest assured I will not rest until ex-colonel Thomas Reynard and the men behind him are brought to book. From now on this is personal. Dead Leg Johnson was one of us. I recruited him myself!"

He looked Dancing Jack straight in the face. "When we lost word of him I feared the worse. You were his replacement!"

Before Jack could express his surprise the Colonel continued talking. "It's obvious what we must do. We will take over observations here. We will watch the lawyer. Find out who he sees, who he is acting on behalf of. As for yourself..."

He gestured towards Jack. "You have been compromised, at least here in York. Best thing to do is get back to Scarborough. Second yourself to the Garrison Commander, sounds like he has the situation under control. No doubt he'll be eager to clip our ex-Colonels wings. See if you can turn up any more connections between him and our lawyer. Better send six troopers along with you. They'll keep you out of trouble and no doubt, the Scarborough Garrison could do with some experienced men." He waved his hand and Jack realised he was being dismissed. He stood up and left the room. Outside he found the Sergeant with no name standing in the corridor.

"This way Sir!" he said and marched Jack down a corridor, through a door and into a small courtyard where six mounted troopers waited. Jack wondered whether everyone he came across were mind readers. The Sergeant noticed the look on his face.

"The Colonels always one step ahead!" he said.

Dancing Jack turned to him and held out his hand. "By the way Sergeant. Thank you for your prompt action this morning."

The Sergeant shrugged. "Soon as I saw you I realised something was wrong. Figured the Colonel needed to know. Couldn't let him lose another of his spies!"

Dancing Jack walked out to the spare horse and mounted up. As he pulled on the reins he turned back to the Sergeant.

"Tell me Sergeant, why were you in the court this morning?"

The Sergeant looked up and scratched his head. "That's the odd thing about it. I've no idea."

Dancing Jack watched as the Sergeant returned into the building. As the door closed behind him he turned his horse and followed the troopers out of the courtyard and back towards Scarborough.

Chapter Thirty One

When Agnes and Marmaduke returned to their house Agnes decided to spend the night in the twenty first century leaving Marmaduke in the old house. She was slightly worried that too much or too many changes were having an effect on him, making him more vicious. There again, many times in her long life she had born witness to the antics of the Old Town cats. Vicious was their second nature. They had to be when their natural enemies were foxes and seagulls. She carried a mug of Mr Tetley's finest up to her bedroom and gazed up through the ruined ceiling. Somehow the builders had managed to locate the appropriate bricks and had started the reconstruction of her chimney stack. She wondered how they had found the bricks so quickly. She enlarged her field of vision until she was looking down on her house. Sure enough, three doors down the street another chimney was in the process of having its chimney rebuilt. She looked closely. It became obvious. Her builders had simply walked along the adjoin roof and were in the process of replacing its bricks with her inferior bricks, and using the bricks from her neighbours chimney to rebuild her own.

"Now that is taking the concept of recycling just one step too far!" she thought.

She wriggled her fingers and the bricks rearranged themselves back into their original locations.

"That will give them something to think about!" She said aloud.

She got up again and spent the next hour on the internet she didn't have, locating the specialised bricks she needed. She paid for them with a credit card she didn't have and received a reassuring e-mail that they would be delivered between eight o'clock and midday the following morning. Then she returned to bed.

The following morning she awoke refreshed. She went downstairs and amused herself by watching the looks on the builder's faces as they ran up and down the ladders checking the chimney and the bricks. With a straight face she told them she had received an e-mail telling her of the imminent arrival of a load of specialised bricks. The she told them she was going out for the day and left them to their own devices.

Back in the eighteenth century she found Marmaduke eating a plateful of raw fish. He looked up sheepishly.

"Got them from the market. I had a craving, probably brought on by that pheasant yesterday."

 Agnes prevented herself from repeating her lecture about humans usually preferring to cook their food before eating it. Anyway, she thought, whatever he was Marmaduke wasn't human. He was a cat, and cats don't cook. She made herself a cup of tea whilst describing the inadequacies of her three builders, and she didn't just mean their building skills. In fact throughout her entire diatribe, she never mentioned their building skills. She knew they didn't have any.

Whilst Marmaduke settled down to a mid-morning snooze she used her scrying bowl to examine the effects of the night before at Hawkstone Grange. The house looked a bit forlorn. A large hole in the rear of the building was being shored up by a group of men using timber to brace up the outer wall. As she watched them she realised they were far more proficient than her own builders. The work was being supervised by Grimes who seemed to have taken charge of the operations.

She moved her hand slightly and the vision shifted towards the buildings being used as barracks. Some men still remained. They were gathered in small groups, talking in hushed whispers, looking anxiously behind them.

Another set of men were examining what remained of the armoury. Despite the cannonball demolishing the far wall the majority of both weapons and gunpowder remained intact. The men seemed to be gathering the weapons and transferring them into the house. She ran her hand over the bowl and the image changed once again. Now she was looking down at the house and its surrounding grounds. She noticed that patrols still guarded the woodlands. She stood up and ran her hand across the small of her back. There was that twinge again. She decided she needed to make herself a small potion. The last thing she needed was a bad back. Despite her great age and her powers Agnes knew full well she wasn't invulnerable. She knew she could be injured, she knew she could catch a cold, or flu, but she didn't. She was a great believer in preventative medicine. That was why every November she queued up with the Old Town residents to receive her annual flu jab. She took a powder and some herbs from a shelf and gently simmered them in a small pot of water. As she waited for it to cool she rummaged in her pocket and pulled out a packet of paracetamol. She took two, washing them down with her own potion. Agnes never left anything to chance.

She knew full well that whilst she had disrupted Foxy Toms operations, it was only temporary. He still had enough men, and his network of spies, to pull off another wrecking. She hadn't even examined his use of highwaymen, and the mystery of the barrels still puzzled her. If they had emanated from Hawkstone Grange why and where did they go?

She decided she would have another word with Andrew Mark. She put on her shawl and as she passed through her living room, she prodded Marmaduke. He woke, his one eye scanning around the room. He had been dreaming he was still in a hammock and was stalking a very large and very fat wood pigeon. He shook the confusion out of his mind, strapped on his swordbelt and bandoleer and followed Agnes out of the house and down to the harbour.

As soon as the pair made an appearance on the harbourside they became aware that they were the centre of attention. The incident with the excise cutter and the soldiers was still being talked about. Agnes felt uncomfortable.   Having the respect of the Old Town was one thing, being pointed out from the opposite side of the harbour by groups of fishermen and fishwives was just too much. She pulled her shawl tighter around her shoulders and diverted her path straight through the door of the Three Mariners.

Despite it being a bright and sunny afternoon outside, inside the small inn it was still as dark and smoke filled as normal. The sunlight trying and failing to penetrate the grime and the smoke that covered the dingy windows. She looked across to the bar. It was occupied by the usual regulars. Out of the corner of her eye she spotted Salmon Martin slide out of her special chair by the fireside. She nodded an acknowledgement and picked up the drink that Whitby John had already poured for her and walked across to sit in the now vacant seat. Marmaduke stayed at the bar. He leant forward and whispered in Whitby Johns ear. The barman shook his head. Across the bar Agnes was deep in discussion with Salmon Martin. He was unhappy. The weather didn't suit him, his boat needed some attention, his wife was wanting a new dress, and all in all he seemed to be carrying the weight of the world on his shoulders.

Marmaduke lost interest and began to look around the bar. In the far corner he noticed a barrel. It was new. He nodded in its direction. "New barrels?"

Whitby John followed his gaze. "Bloke on the harbour was selling them off. Picked it up cheap. Thought it might come in useful."

Marmaduke turned his head. "You mean it was empty?"

Whitby John gave Marmaduke a look that said he thought he was talking to an idiot. He spoke slowly.

"Marmaduke, of course it was empty. That's why it was a new barrel. If it had had something inside it, it would be a used barrel!"

Marmaduke was confused. What was it with these barrels? He looked across at Agnes, she was still chatting the local gossip. He caught her eye and indicated he was going outside. He had barrels to think about.

Outside he walked towards the harbour and watched the hustle and bustle going on up and down the quayside. Smoke drifted down from the houses gathered in a huddle up the hill leading towards the Castle, filtering the sunlight. Overhead he swore he heard a seagull cough. Everywhere he looked there were barrels. At the fish market salted herring were being packed tightly in barrels. On the other side of the harbour a team of men were busy loading barrels onto the deck of a small ketch, bound for who knows where. On the foreshore road a carter shook the reins and a team of horses strained as they pulled a load of barrels towards the town. As he leant against a wall watching the comings and goings, a thought struck him. Barrels at the harbour were two a penny, old and new ones, but try as he might he couldn't remember seeing any at Hawkstone Grange. He felt a tap on his shoulder and turned to find Agnes standing behind him.

"Let's go see Andrew." she said.

Andrew Marks saw them as they entered his doorway. He turned and informed his staff he would be found in his office. This time he would make sure that when they came in he would be sat in his best office chair. It didn't go unnoticed by Agnes as she outlined the events of the previous night up at Hawkstone Grange. Andrew winced as she told her story, at one point he actually found himself feeling sorry for Foxy Tom's men. Then he remembered the ship wrecks and the lost crews. He was brought back to the present when Agnes raised the question of the barrels. None of them could come up with an explanation. Dusk was falling as they left the Chandlery and began to walk uphill through the tiny streets and alleyways of the Old Town. As they turned a corner into Tuthill they came face to face with Peter Potts, now returned to his previous naval rank. Agnes was so full of prise for his actions that the young man began to blush.

"Actually Agnes, I rather enjoyed the entire trip. That cutter is a fine ship. Those excise men certainly know how to get the best out of her. I don't think I've ever been on a faster ship."

They chatted a bit more about his adventure. She heard how a boson's chair had been rigged between the two vessels and how Peter had stood behind the helmsman as they rounded the headland and saw the false light planted by the wreckers. Marmaduke smiled. The young man seemed to grow in stature as he narrated his adventures. Agnes was right. He certainly would go far, although not immediately. Peter informed them he still hadn't been contacted by the Admiralty concerning his new posting.

Darkness had fallen by the time they reached the Castle Gatehouse. For once they were greeted by the guard who was expecting them. They were ushered straight through the gates and led directly to the Commanders office where they found Dancing Jack and Lieutenant Smalls, sitting uncomfortably with his crutches and damaged leg. They were offered coffee and sat silently as Dancing Jack narrated the events of the previous couple of days. When he had finished the Commander turned to Agnes.

"It seems that the army are going to investigate our lawyer friend. Although I find it highly unusual, a Colonel with no name, but it seems he has some influence. I'm certainly appreciative of another six troopers."

Marmaduke leant forward to Dancing Jack. "I'm sorry about Dead leg."

Dancing Jack was grateful for the gesture. "I had no idea he had been recruited."

The Commander gave a grunt. "Huh. Typical of high command! Never let the left hand know what the right hand is doing."

Dancing Jack took a deep gulp of his coffee and looked at the Commander. "It would have been nice to have known there was a left hand!"

The Commander harrumphed. Whilst he felt at liberty to criticise the army he didn't approve of the same criticism being levelled by civilians. "Ours not to question why, eh?"

Agnes shook her head. "Another wasted life!"

She turned to Dancing Jack. "And there was nothing you could have done. It happened before you had been recruited. In fact, as ironic as it may seem, if he had succeeded you would probably have hung. The army would have had no use for you. In a way his death saved your life."

That ended the conversation there and then. For a few minutes they all lost themselves in their own private thoughts of fate and mortality.

Agnes allowed them all their thoughts before leaning forward once again. "What I want to know is what Dead Leg discovered that warranted his death."

Dancing Jack shook his head. "Whatever it was no information reached York. They knew he was missing, eventually they began to fear the worse."

Agnes looked at Dancing Jack "Do you still have his dagger and sword?"

In answer Jack pulled the ornate handle that protruded from his scabbard.

Agnes smiled. "In that case may I borrow the dagger? I would like to see if I can pick up anything from it. "

She looked across to the Commander who seemed as if he was about to say something. He saw her face and thought better of it.

"Magic!" she said.

They brought Dancing Jack up to date on their attack on Hawkstone Grange. Try as he may he couldn't help but sit with his mouth open as she detailed the destruction she and Marmaduke had wreaked on Foxy Tom and his army.

The Lieutenant scratched the bindings on his damaged leg. "Of course all this bodes the question of what to do now. The army intelligence are handling the question of the lawyer, which leaves us with our original problem. We still need to find some sort of evidence to incriminate our ex Colonel. We know something must exist, because Dead Leg found it."

Dancing Jack spoke up. "Whatever it was, or is, it has to do with the highwaymen. Remember as far as he and the army are concerned, they were looking for evidence of his previous misdemeanours and his recruiting of highwaymen. When they began their investigations they knew nothing about Foxy Toms ship wrecking activities. They only know now because I told them."

Everyone around the table nodded. It was very apparent that whilst they had come across the ex-Colonel Thomas Reynard through his ship wrecking activities the army intelligence unit were chasing him for his past.

"Has anyone any idea what he is using the highwaymen for?" Agnes asked. She was met with blank faces. No one had any idea.

"Well Gentlemen, I have a suggestion." She looked towards the Commander. "For the moment the army must play a watching role. Keep the occasional patrol moving up and down the coast roads and the moorland routes around Hawkstone Grange. That will keep him on his toes, keep him aware that something is happening, but he won't know what. By now his nerves must be shredded. He cannot be far from cracking up. His second in command Grimes seem to be handling things. Let's see what they do next."

She turned to Marmaduke and Dancing Jack. "I think you two should take a leave out of the army's book. Set a thief to catch a thief. You do what you do best. Seek out the highwaymen. Find out where the Colonel has them operating, and why. Go inland, but for everyone's sake, not as far as York. Meanwhile I will do a bit of digging of my own. I think I need to spend some time with my scrying bowl." She paused. "Oh and one other thing, think

on this, who wrote the note and slipped it under
Andrew Marks door, and why?"

Chapter Thirty Two.

As there was no time like the present Marmaduke and Dancing Jack went off to find themselves some horses. They planned to ride through the night, following the major roads and turnpikes, the very places that highwaymen would haunt.

They had left Scarborough behind and were passing through the small hamlet of Seamer inside the hour. In another hour they had reached the outskirts of the small market town of Malton. There were a number of coach houses there and, despite the late hour Dancing Jack assured Marmaduke that as Malton was a stopping place for a number of different coach routes and companies, the inns would still be open and ready for business.

Sure enough the first inn they came across had a full stable. Ostlers busied themselves rushing in and out of stables carrying large bucketfuls of bran and oats to feed the heavy horses. They dismounted, handed their own horses to a passing ostler, and entered the tavern. At the far end of the room a group of travellers had finished their meal and were pushing back their chairs to enjoy their brandy and tankards of ale before retiring for the night. Other drinkers were scattered around the room seated in twos and threes. Four or five other men, that Marmaduke thought looked like locals, were stood at the bar deep in conservation with the barman. By the fireplace a fiddle player was joined by a man playing a squeezebox in playing a slow poignant tune. As the two men walked into the room everyone fell silent and all eyes turned to them. The man behind the bar interrupted his conversation and rushed towards them. "Now lads no trouble. There's decent honest folk here. This is a respectable establishment." Then in a much quieter voice urged, "It's the Unicorn you want. Ask for James!" With that he returned to his place behind the bar. The room looked on as the two men turned and walked out.

"What do you make of that?" Asked Marmaduke.

Dancing Jack looked thoughtful. "I think he took us for our quarry. It seems The Unicorn is the choice tavern for our type of gentlemen."

The two retrieved their horses.

Marmaduke shrugged his shoulder and slipped a hand inside his jacket checking his knives. "The Unicorn it is then. Which way?"

Dancing Jack shook his head as they remounted. "I've absolutely no idea!"

They eventually found it tucked away down a small side street that seemed to lead to nowhere. The inn matched the street, dark and grubby, the lights from the small windows were almost blocked out by dirt. They dismounted and secured their horses to a metal hoop fixed to the wall. Before they entered Dancing Jack slid his sword in and out of its scabbard. He repeated his action with his dagger. They moved with ease. Marmaduke checked his pistols then with a nod they pushed the door open.

At first the room seemed deserted, then in the semi darkness, they noticed a tight group of men sat at the table furthest from the door. They were hunched over their tankards, talking in hushed whispers. They fell silent as they turned and examined the two strangers. Instinctively their hands reached down to touch their weapons.

They walked across the room to the bar where a man with a sideways grin and rotted teeth stood. Marmaduke noticed his hand move under the bar. Cudgel or pistol he thought.

Dancing Jack broke the silence. "Been told to ask for James." He said quietly.

He looked at ease, almost at home in such a place. Which of course he was. He had spent most of his life in such places. They were the food and drink of the men of his profession in more ways than one.

They were the source of information. They were also the places where asking a wrong question would be answered by a knife between the ribs.

"And who you be to be asking for James?" the barman replied.

Marmaduke decided discretion was probably the best option. "Ginger Tom and he goes by the name of Dancing Jack."

The barman moved his hand from under the bar. It was holding a pistol. "Dancing Jack? He was hung at York yesterday."

Jack genuinely showed his surprise. "Whoever told you such a tale was sadly mistaken."

As he spoke he pulled his scarf down to reveal the scars around his neck.

The barman stared hard. "The way I heard it he was captured and set to hang the next day."

He looked away towards the group of men who were silently listening to the conversation as if he expected confirmation from them.

"You must have heard wrong." Said Marmaduke.

The man behind the bar shrugged. "Any road you're wasting your time around here. If I were you I'd push onto Leeds, or even further."

Dancing Jack pulled his scarf back up. "The entire post chase stopped running around here?"

"Accounted for!" replied the barman.

Marmaduke stepped forward slightly. "And how do you know?" he asked

"I'm James!" replied the barman. His hand came up from the bar holding the pistol.

"So a couple of locals tip you the wink to keep rivals off their patch."

At Dancing Jacks comment the barman seemed to relax a bit. He gave a snort. "I wish! A bigger firm moved in about a year ago. They pay no one. Control the roads between Northallerton right down to York."

Dancing Jack shook his head. "That's a big area. They can't control all of it. Not every route."

James gave another snort. "Aye well that what a lot of people thought. Landlord of the Rose and Crown up near Pickering thought that. Found him dead at the bottom of his cellar steps. Funny thing was it wasn't the fall that killed him. It was the gash across his throat."

Marmaduke noticed that the men had left their table and had walked in ones and two until they were all standing at the bar. One of them spoke up.

"There was that incident up at Goathland. A couple of local lads held up the Pickering Mail. Got away with it as well. No one ever heard of them again. If its easy picking you're after you're in the wrong place."

James looked the two strangers up and down. "They don't like competition round these parts. If I were you I'd get on my way." He paused for a seconds thought then continued. "Probably know you're here already. How did you find me?"

"We went to the Black Swan first." Marmaduke said.

A couple of the men at the bar sniggered. One laughed out loud. James smiled. "In that case gentlemen I wouldn't even stop for a drink. That place is their eyes and ears. Nothing comes and goes in or out of Malton without that place knowing who, or why. I'd sleep with a dagger in your hand and one eye open tonight."

Dancing Jack stepped forward and placed a coin on the bar. "I'll take a tankard before I go. I gets thirsty out on the road."

The barman turned a spigot in the large wooden barrel behind and allowed the ale to flow into two black leather tankards, he put them on the bar slopping and spilling the dark liquid.

"Your funeral!" he said as he slid the coin off the bar into his pinafore pocket. He looked up at the two men. "But drink up quick. I don't want them finding in you here. Don't need the aggravation. "

With that he turned his back to them and returned to the men at the bar. The drinkers moved back to their table, all of them making sure that no one could mistakenly associate then with the two strangers drinking at the opposite side of the inn.

Marmaduke turned to Dancing Jack. "I have an idea." he said.

Dancing Jacks eyes twinkled. "I'll wager it's the same as mine!"

They drank up, walked across to the bar and banged their tankards on its wooden surface and ordered two more drinks. James shook his head as he poured out the ale.

"For pity's sake drink up and get out". He hissed as he pushed the tankards back across the bar. Marmaduke glared at him and he retreated to the far end of the bar.

They had drunk their second tankard and were just about to annoy the barman even further by ordering their third when the door burst open behind them. Neither of them turned around. Out of sight Marmaduke slid his hand inside his jacket.

"What do we have here?" A rough sounding voice asked.

"Couple of coney's lost their way!" Another sneered.

"Not a place for the likes of thee." That was a third voice. There was some sniggering. That meant another to at the least. Marmaduke was counting.

The entire bar had fallen silent. James moved further away from the door. The silence was broken by the sound of a pistol being cocked. Nobody could exactly say what happened next, because no one saw. There was a blur and the man holding the pistol found himself looking down at a throwing knife that seemed to have embedded itself in the base of his throat. He fell forward as the blood began to spurt onto the tavern floor where it was soaked up by the sawdust. The action had happened so fast that everyone seemed frozen to the spot. It was the opportunity Jack needed. In one fluid movement he leapt forward with his sword in one hand and dagger in the other. He side stepped the man in front of him and slashed the man behind him. The blow struck him on the shoulder cutting deep don into his chest. The man screamed. Jack hooked out his other arm and the man that had been in front of him found himself looking down at a dagger sticking out of his side. Three down and no one inside the inn had had enough time to take a breath. Realising that things had gone badly wrong the two other men dropped their weapons as if they had turned red hot.

"Time to talk!" growled Marmaduke.

Chapter Thirty Three

Agnes sat at her computer and began by examining the note once again. As she had already discovered that the paper originated from the army she now concentrated on the ink. She scanned the document, found various on-line tests and analysis but only discovered what she feared. That the ink was a common type sold the length and breadth of the country throughout the mid seventeen hundreds. She rubbed her temple. Whilst her continued use of the computer might find information that could prove invaluable, the harsh light from the computer screen still made her eyes ache. She closed her eyes. The image of the words "Foxy Tom" floated in front of her. She concentrated and other visions appeared. Images from the many documents she had searched flashed through her mind. Letters, ledgers, lists, receipts came and went. One floated to the front and stayed there. Agnes read it. It was a receipt she had first seen during her search engine exploration of documents from the York Barracks. She looked closer and waved her hand in the direction of the computer. Silently it pulsed into life and within seconds the document in her mind now appeared on the screen. She rubbed her eyes and looked closer at the image. It was of a document that pronounced Colonel Thomas Reynard had been dismissed from the army. She called up the note again and compared the writing. It was the same. Just because she could, and to ensure she hadn't made a mistake, she compared the two samples of handwriting in a computer program she had found. The fact she had no such program and that in order to locate it her computer had hacked into a secure network operated by the forensic department of the North Yorkshire Police didn't even cross her mind. The two samples were identical, written by the same hand.

"Now that's magic!" Agnes said as she closed the program with a click of her fingers. She sat back in her chair. So the note had been written by someone in the army. Someone who knew Thomas Reynard's past. Someone who knew what he was doing, but for the life of her she couldn't understand why it had been delivered to Andrew Mark. It had however, been delivered after the ship wrecks. Did the writer know of Foxy Toms involvement in the wrecking? Of course they must have, otherwise why write a note in the first place? Then why Andrew Mark? Because Andrew knew everything that happened in the Harbour. He would know all about the wrecks. Why so cryptic? There were so many questions and no obvious answers, but at least she now knew that the note had been written by someone in the army who knew of ex Colonel Thomas Reynard's past and present. But why send the note to Andrew?

She sighed and walked across to her kitchen. The kettle boiled instantly and she poured the hot water over one of Mr Tetley's little white bags. As she was poking the bag with her spoon, watching it bob up and down until the tea looked just the right colour, it dawned on her that whoever had sent the note either couldn't or wouldn't report his suspicions to his superior officers, and if he felt like that it meant he didn't trust anyone in the army. Now that was interesting.

She finished her tea and returned to her scrying bowl. In order to do that she had to return to the eighteenth century. Before she descended into her cellar she checked on the progress of her chimney stack. To her surprise it was half completed and with the correct bricks. She was so pleased almost forgave the large blobs of cement dropped all over her roof tiles. As she walked down to her cellar she wondered if she was being uncharitable when she realised they must have brought in someone else to finish the job.

Once she was in the eighteenth century she carefully placed Dead Legs dagger in the centre of her scrying bowl and poured water over it. When it was full she sprinkled herbs and potions over the surface and bent down to observe the image that began to appear.

The first image was one of flame and molten metal. She was seeing the birth of the dagger, seeing it being forged and cooled. She saw money change hands. She saw it in a sheath, tucked into a belt. She saw it flash in a dark back room. She saw blood flow. Saw it replaced in a belt and a man walk away. He had a limp. So that's how Dead Leg came by the dagger, a fight in an inn. She followed the daggers journey as it travelled with Dead Leg. Sometimes it was used to threaten, sometimes it was used to stab and cut. As she watched the story unfold she came to the conclusion that Dead Leg wasn't a particularly nice man. Eventually the images in the water shifted and changed and she began to see what she had waited for. She was looking at a moonlit road across the moors. A stage coach was pulling strongly towards a distant town. Dead Leg was sitting on his horse, hidden from sight of the road by a small group of trees. As the coach neared he pushed his horse into the centre of the road holding his two pistols out in front of him. As it drew nearer Dead Leg suddenly slumped in his saddle. Agnes realised with a shock that she had just seen the man being shot. As his horse veered off the road throwing its rider, the coach continued on its journey. It ran over the body of Dead Leg leaving what looked like a battered and ragged collection of old clothes in the middle of the road. She continued to watch as the coach came to a halt and two men jumped out. They ran to the body and unceremoniously picked it up and dumped it over a wall. As they ran back towards the coach a third man joined them. He held a long barrelled gun in his hand. He joined the others and climbed into the coach as it set off , leaving a sword and dagger in the long grass at the side of the road.

Agnes stood up and rubbed the centre of her back. It had been an ambush, a very elaborate ambush, more of an assassination. Someone in the organisation wanted Dead Leg dead and had gone to great lengths to make sure it happened. Something clicked in the back of her mind, and despite her aching back, she leant forward again. She moved her hands across the surface of the water and the scene repeated itself. She watched closely. As the third man with the gun ran towards the coach she looked closely at his face. She thought it looked familiar. It was Grimes, the Ex Colonel's right hand man.

Chapter Thirty Four.

After witnessing the fate of their three friends the two men still standing were only too willing to talk. Marmaduke led them to a table at the far end of the dingy inn. As they moved down the room everyone else moved away, giving them a very wide berth. Dancing Jack walked across to the bar. James had already poured out two tankards of ale and slid them across the grimy wooden surface.

"On the house!" he said.

Dancing Jack picked up the tankards and glanced down at the pistol still lying on the bar. James followed his look.

"No offence!" He said hurriedly, and his face reddened.

"None taken!" Jack replied as he took the drinks to the far table where Marmaduke was already seated.

He listened as he pulled out a battered stool and sat down. The two men had already begun talking. In fact they were talking so fast and at the same time that they were unintelligible. He glanced down to where Marmaduke was resting his hands on the table top. He was doing that thing where his finger nails appeared as very sharp claws again.

"May I suggest, friends that we begin again? One at a time, and slowly!" He caught Marmaduke's eye and glanced at the table once again. The claws returned to finger nails.

The man who began talking was thin, with a face that remained Jack of a weasel. It was scarred and pox marked. His hands bent and calloused. Something about him told Jack that he was probably an ex-soldier. He listened as the man told his story. He told how he had been through hard times after being discharged from the army, how he had taken to thievery. Then he heard of a man who was hiring men such as him. He told how he travelled to a

York inn and met with two men who claimed to represent a military man, and how they were interested in his past. Eventually the men offered him a purse in exchange for his services.

When Marmaduke enquired about the nature of the services the second man spoke up. His story was different he was wanted in London for horse theft. He claimed it was a case of mistaken identity. Marmaduke and Dancing Jack didn't believe him. He too claimed to have heard the word about someone hiring. He too had met with two men, only this time the meeting took place here in Malton. He too had accepted the offer. The services he agreed to provide were mainly that of a strong arm, a hired thug, to travel the countryside dissuading the local footpads and thieves from carrying out their normal business. To either join them or move on. They knew others went about the same commission. They believed they were a part of a much larger network, but the only contact they had with the command was a dead letter drop, a secret place where they would find written orders and the purse of money.

Despite repeated questioning it soon became apparent that there was no more relevant information to be gleaned from the men.

Marmaduke asked about the three dead men whose bodies were now being moved from the doorway and dragged unceremoniously outside to be dumped in the shabby alleyway outside. Their stories were very similar to the stories of the two men left alive. Petty thieves recruited by the same two men. Then the second man added a bit of information. The gang of five were responsible for a wide area of roads and trackways spreading out from Malton for ten miles, and yes they had been told to help and assist any highwaymen who carried a certain emblem, a small token that held the image of a crudely drawn fox. Dancing Jacks eyes glittered, a large piece of the jigsaw had just dropped into place, his first piece of evidence. He wondered if Dead Leg had carried one of the tokens.

As the second man finished his story Marmaduke turned to Jack.

"Do we need them anymore?" he asked.

Dancing Jack stroked his chin as if he were deep in thought. "Well it seems we have a number of choices." He flicked a finger out as if in the act of counting. "One, we kill them now. Two..." another finger flicked out. "We get them to clear up the mess, dispose of their dead, and then kill them. Three we let them go to explain to their paymasters why three of their men are dead and how they were forced to compromise their operation. In which case their paymasters will probably kill them."

He looked across the table to the two men. "Unfortunately none of the three options appear to have good outcomes for yourselves, mind you!"

The two men seemed to shrink in their seats. When Marmaduke flicked a finger nail that turned to a claw one of the men wet himself. The weasel faced man's face turned white. Dancing Jack smiled. "Of course there is a fourth option, and one that just might have a happier outcome for you both."

The men looked into his face wondering whether this was a ray of hope or just another aspect of the sick joke and bad luck that had brought them to this point in their lives.

Dancing Jack reached into his pocket and produced a small leather bound notebook and pencil. He scribbled something down, ripped the page out of the book, read it, and folded it into four. He held it out between his two outstretched fingers and waved it in front of the two men.

"Here's the plan. You ride to York tonight. No stopping. You take this to the Garrison. At the gatehouse ask for the Colonel with no name. When you are seen hand over the paper with these words

"Dancing Jacks compliments!" He leant even further forward until he was almost nose to nose with the man. "Do not make the mistake of thinking you can escape. If I do not receive the answer I am expecting my friend here will hunt you down, but only after we have put the word abroad that you have informed. It will be an interesting race to see who kills you first, and where and how."

The weasel faced man almost snatched the paper out of Jacks hand.

"Decent horses, be there in an hour, two at the most." He said.

The other man nodded his head frantically.

"Have you got decent horses?" Marmaduke asked, picking at his fang like tooth with a small claw.

The first man nodded nervously. "We will have!" he said.

As the two men tripped over themselves to get out of the inn Marmaduke turned to Dancing Jack. "Receive the answer?" he questioned.

Dancing Jack grinned. "They need to think we'll know if they abscond. A man has got to have an incentive!"

As they walked out into the grim alleyway they looked to their left, and then quickly turned to their right. Their horses had gone.

Chapter Thirty Five

Despite her discoveries Agnes's still hadn't made a link between ex Colonel Thomas Reynard and whoever his backers could be. There was a niggle at the back of her mind. She closed her eyes and visualised her observations of him. Then the penny dropped. Paperwork! Every time she had viewed the ex Colonel through her scrying bowl he had been surrounded by paperwork. After all, for his entire military career all he had done was to sign orders, check receipts and keep ledgers. Paperwork. The ex Colonel would have had to have kept records, transactions of goods outward, costs of supplies, monies to the recruits and other outgoings and incomings. Paperwork, the answer had to be in the paperwork. She let out a deep sigh. She hated paperwork.

After another mug of Mr Tetley's finest brew she set to work. More water, more herbs and potions and she was viewing the upstairs rooms of Hawkstone Grange. The first thing she noticed was that a relative calm had fallen over the house. In the shattered room some men were clearing away the debris. Men still guarded the windows, but they were much more relaxed. The guards inside the front door were unable to stop their heads dropping onto their chests. She travelled into what might have been described as a drawing room where a number of men slept fitfully slumped in chairs and settees. One man had even stretched out on a chaise longue. At the far end of the room, seated behind a desk was Grimes. He was leant back in his chair with his feet resting on the top of the desk. Two pistols rested on his lap and a long barrelled gun was at his side. Agnes noticed that he dozed with one eye open.

She allowed the vision to drift upstairs. She drifted through the room where injured men slept fitfully, moaning and groaning in their sleep. Other rooms held more sleeping men. Eventually, at the far end of a long corridor she found Ex Colonel Thomas Reynard. He was bent over his desk still seated in front of the broken window. Agnes flicked her finger and a gust of wind blew in through the window sending papers flying and swooping across the room. The ex Colonel tried to ignore the breeze and placed his hand firmly on the pile of papers. She noticed he was writing a note. She looked closer. It was not a note, it seemed to be a report. Of course it was a report; the man still believed he was in the army. She looked over his shoulder to see who it was addressed to. It was certainly a long report, there again the last couple of days had been very eventful.

Despite her best efforts she could see no name or address on the document, she scanned the room. Papers were scattered everywhere, receipts, pages of figures, accounts. She closed her eyes and tried to hold the images in her mind. Bit by bit she covered the room and took in the contents of every bit of paper she could see. The she stood up and cast her hand over her scrying bowl. The image faded and she left the room to return to the twenty first century where she sat in front of her computer and waved it into life. Even she wasn't sure how it worked. All she knew was that she moved her fingers, closed her eyes and thought very, very hard. One by one the images floated on the computer screen. It took all of the night and some of the next morning before she opened her eyes again. She looked at the computer. On the screen was a file. She opened it up. There locked in a series of single images was every piece of paper she had seen in the ex Colonels office. She smiled, moved her finger and her printer kicked into life. She sat back as the pages piled up in the printer tray.

She was woken by the sound of her front door opening. Cheery voices echoed down her hallway. The printer had stopped. She flicked a finger at the screen and a game of football manager popped up. Her side was still languishing at the bottom end of a lower division. The cheery voice was now in the room.

"Ah good morning Agnes. A fine morning to be up and around I'm sure. Playing a hand of patience is it? Or are you one of those Candy Crush people?"

She had no idea what he was talking about, but she knew she was being patronised. She gave him a terse good morning and informed him that the building inspector needed the receipt for the special bricks. That wiped the smile from the builders face. All of a sudden, faced with the prospect of finding a receipt for a load of special bricks that had arrived from nowhere, it didn't seem such a fine morning anymore.

As he left the room Agnes tutted. The one thing, well one of the many things actually, that annoyed Agnes was being patronised. In her vexation she flicked a finger at the computer screen. Within seconds she had sold Wayne Rooney and bought Harry Kane.

She gathered up the pile of papers, tucked them under her arm and without a backwards glance at the builders who were gathered in a small huddle at the bottom of her stairs deeply involved in a series of urgent whispers and much arm waving, she headed towards her cellar. As she left she flicked a finger in the direction of the kitchen. Her back door opened and shut. The builders heard it and assumed she had gone out. Their voices changed from whispers to loud to shouting. She smiled as she headed for the eighteenth century.

The morning was bright as she made her way down to the harbourside. Neighbours nodded in her direction as she strolled down the cobbled street. A couple of ragged children followed her. She turned quickly and pulled two very large sweets out of her pocket. She gave them to the children and they ran off down the street whooping and shouting with glee. She smiled to herself and wondered what it must be like to see the world through the eyes of a child. She must have been a child herself sometime, somewhere, but try as she may she could never conjure up and memories. She stopped herself from thinking along those lines. She had a job to do.

Andrew looked up from his best office chair as Agnes entered. Without saying a word she deposited the pile of paper onto his desk. He looked at them, blinked and looked back at Agnes.

"I suppose there's a reason behind it?" he asked, although deep down he had already developed a sinking feeling.

"Of course!" Agnes replied. "I would greatly appreciate it if you could go through them."

Andrew looked back at the pile. "And what would I be looking for?" he shifted the papers around and took a quick glance at those on the top of the pile, "They look like receipts, ledgers and accounts!"

Agnes gave him one of those looks. "They are."

She went on to explain what they were and where they came from. She then went into great detail about what she wanted him to look for.

"Somewhere in those papers is a clue. A link to whoever is funding the ex Colonels enterprise. Somewhere he must have a record of monies and goods passed on. Despite being a Colonel the man was basically a clerk. He knows how to do magic with figures."

She leant forward and spoke in a low voice. "Andrew, somewhere he will have notated every transaction, accounted for every penny piece that has passed through his hands and hopefully that will lead us to his masters. They are the people we need to find."

Andrew nodded. Against his better judgement he agreed to undertake the task.

After Agnes had left his office he wondered why. As he pulled the pile of papers in front of him the penny dropped. Agnes knew full well he made his living buying and selling. She knew that just like the ex Colonel his business depended on keeping accurate records and ledger. She also knew of Andrews dealings in contraband. She knew he would keep records but that they would be hidden away within the documents and ledgers. He smiled as the phrase "set a thief to catch a thief" came into his mind. He took the first document off the pile and began examining the paperwork.

Agnes returned to her house. Word about free sweets had obviously got around for, as she entered her street, there were about a dozen or so children hanging around her door. She reached into her seemingly bottomless pocket and handed out a sweet to every child there. She never bothered with wondering where the sweets came from. She just knew that when children were about she had sweets in her pockets and no matter how many children she saw, there was always enough to go around.

As soon as she entered her front room she consulted her scrying bowl and paid a visit to Hawkstone Grange. Apart from the rubble the place and conspicuous lack of men the place looked normal. Guards still patrolled the perimeter by the woodlands. Other men were at work repairing the window and stonework. At the front of the house a man was leading a horse towards the front door. As he approached a guard opened the door and shouted something down the corridor. After a few moments a man appeared. It was ex Colonel Thomas Reynard himself. He looked like he'd spent a sleepless night. His hair was unkempt, he was unshaven. He epitomised the meaning of the word dishevelled. As she watched he produced small leather satchel from under his arm. As he handed it to the rider Agnes noticed it was sealed. The rider took the satchel and carefully placed it in one of his saddle bags. He saluted the ex Colonel, turned, mounted his horse and trotted it off in the direction of the woodands. Agnes stepped back from the scrying bowl. That must be the report she thought. It might prove to be interesting reading.

An hour later a lone rider travelling on the main road to York pulled his horse to a halt. Standing in the middle of the road was an elderly lady. She was almost bent double and hobbled along the road with the aid of a large staff. He tried to steer his horse around her but for some reason the horse wouldn't pass her. Each time he pulled alongside her his horse simply stopped and allowed the woman to walk on. The strange thing about it was that the woman never turned around. After four or five failed passes the rider grew tired. He dismounted and walked up to her. She turned to face him. Her eyes seemed to burn into him.

The next thing he knew was that he was seated on his horse trotting towards York. He shook his head in confusion. Perhaps he had imagined the whole thing. After a few minutes he had forgotten all about the strange meeting.

Agnes watched as the horse and rider disappear down the road. She wondered what the reaction of the York solicitor would be when he broke the ex Colonels seal to unpack a wad of blank paper. As she settled back in her comfortable chair she smiled to herself as she remembered an old saying.

"Confusion to the enemy". Give it a few more days and Foxy Tom will be so confused he'll be doubting his own sanity and when that happens he'll make his mistake." She said to the empty room.

Chapter Thirty Six

Dancing Jack and Marmaduke spent an uncomfortable night under a hedge just outside Malton. They couldn't afford lodgings as buying replacement horses had cost them every penny they could muster between them, and the horse weren't even that good. Not a patch on the ones they had been given by the army. At least that brought a smile to their faces, the thought that when the two men rode into the garrison to deliver their message someone just might recognise the fact that they had ridden in on two army horses. Now that would take a bit of explaining, as the army were very particular who rode their horses.

"Isn't horse stealing a hanging offence?" Asked Marmaduke

Dancing Jack thought for a moment "I do believe it is. Now that's unfortunate. I never even considered that option."

"Neither did they!" murmured Marmaduke as he tried to find a comfortable spot in the heather.

The following morning they decided to travel north towards Pickering. The Malton arm of the ex colonels network was destroyed. For obvious reasons travelling near to York was not a good idea, so north it was. The morning was fine, a breeze scurried the clouds across the landscape. In the distance they could see the start f the moors. They had travelled for most of the morning and were looking out for a place where they could refresh their horses and themselves. They could see smoke rising from the chimney of a building further down the road and were busy trying to work out whether it was an inn or not when they heard the cocking of a pistol behind them.

"I've two pistols, both aimed at your backs. Now slowly dismount and walk very carefully to the side of the road."

They did what was asked of them. As they turned they saw their attacker. He was wearing long boots, a leather waistcoat under a long black frock coat. As he said he held two pistols in front of him. There was a rustle in the hedgerow and three men appeared. They were not as well dressed as the man holding the pistols. It was very obvious who the foot soldiers were in this small group. Marmaduke listened and sniffed the air. He was sure there was another man still hiding behind the hedge. This attacker was no amateur. He spoke again.

"Now very slowly I would like you to remove your pistols and give them to Peggity there."

One of the men shuffled forward grinning. He wore a ragged beard through which a mouth opened to reveal a set of very black and rotten teeth. The man holding the pistols continued giving instructions.

"Now be careful. Handles first if you please. We wouldn't want to be having any accidents now, would we?"

They did as instructed. One of the horses skittered and Dancing Jack turned around to see them being led off by one of the men.

"Now that's an annoyance!" he said.

The man holding the pistols smiled. "Oh I've only just begun. Now unbuckle your swords and throw them down there."

Dancing Jack continued speaking as if he hadn't heard. "You see that's the second horse I've had stolen from me in the last two days, which is, as I'm sure you'll agree, very annoying."

The man holding the pistols turned his full attention to Jack, that was his mistake. Realising the subtly of Dancing Jacks plan Marmaduke took his opportunity.

There was a blur of motion and the man with the blackened teeth fell to the ground holding the handle of a throwing knife protruding from his stomach. On the opposite side of the road the other foot soldier didn't notice. He was too preoccupied by another throwing knife that was sticking out from his chest. The man with the pistols turned and fired both at Marmaduke. The deadly balls crashed into the hedge. Marmaduke just wasn't there. Even Dancing Jack blinked in surprise. Then he lowered his shoulder and charged. The man now holding two empty guns was utterly taken by surprise, especially when he found himself flat on his back with Jacks booted foot on his throat.

Dancing Jack looked up as something crashed through the hedge and landed in the road in front of him. It was the fourth member of the gang. His cloths were ripped and torn, long scratches down his back were bleeding. There was another blur and Marmaduke was standing in the road near to the man in the road who looked up, held his arms and hands in front of his face and whimpered.

Dancing Jack looked at Marmaduke. "Now you really must teach me how to do that!" he said.

Making sure the man in the road posed no further threat Marmaduke walked up to Dancing Jack and looked down at the attacker turned prisoner.

"You have to channel your inner cat!" He said. He looked down "Is his face meant to go that shade of blue?" he asked.

Dancing Jack glanced down and removed his foot. The failed robber tried to sit up, held his throat and began to cough. Jack prodded him with the toe of his boot.

"Now, what do we have here?"

The man on the floor continued coughing. When he stopped he looked up.

"You have made a bad mistake!" he sneered.

Dancing Jack burst out laughing. "If any mistake has been made this morning I think the man sitting on the road is the prime choice here!"

The man on the floor attempted to rise. Marmaduke stepped forward and trod on his hand. The man gave out a small yelp.

"Why are we making a mistake?" he growled.

The man on the floor reached into his waistcoat pocket with his free hand and drew out a small round token. He held it up to Marmaduke. It had a crude carving of a fox on it.

"I'm protected." He said.

Dancing Jack looked at Marmaduke. "Well now, that's what I call interesting. We seem to have found ourselves one of Foxy Tom's pet highwaymen."

Marmaduke gave the man a sharp kick. The man groaned. "What is his cut?" He asked.

Dancing Jack walked across the road and picked up their weapons. "I'll say this for you Marmaduke. You get straight to the point. No beating about the bush with you."

Marmaduke shrugged. "Saves time." He said.

He gave the man on the floor another kick. The man grunted. Marmaduke reached into his jacket. Instantly one of his throwing knives was in his hand. He gave it a flick and the man on the floor looked down to see the knife sticking into his boot.

"Sixty forty." The man said.

"But effective!" Said Dancing Jack.

It took them the best part of an hour to extract the full story from the man. Mainly because of Jacks insistence that Marmaduke hunt down the fourth robber and their missing horses.

"Two horses in two days. That is very annoying!" Explained Jack.

It turned out that the robber went by the name of Dammit Johnson wanted for horse theft in Kent. He had worked for Foxy Tom for the best part of a year robbing the main road between Malton and Pickering. In a very similar story to the one they had been told the previous night he had been recruited in a York inn and told to patrol this area. He received his instructions on who and what to rob by a message left in a tavern on the far side of Pickering. His agreement allowed him the freedom to "freelance" between assignments to top up his retainer provided the proceeds were split sixty forty as Foxy Tom and his organisation kept the roads free of any local competition for those that held the token.

"And that will be the pattern we'll find between here to Northallerton!" Dancing Jack added.

Marmaduke nodded took the token and put it in his pocket. "What shall we do with these?" he asked.

The two men looked around them. Two men lay dead, one was still writhing in the road moaning and holding his face. The man who had led the horses away was nursing a deep gash across his arm and Dammit Johnson was feeling very sorry for himself. On the up side he had stopped coughing.

"Leave them. Let them tidy up their own mess!"
Said Marmaduke. They remounted their horses and
continued towards Pickering.

They arrived uneventfully and stopped their horses
by an inn called The Rose where they handed their
horses to an ostler. They were just entering the
establishment when Jack stopped.

"We've no coin!" He said.

Marmaduke reached into his pocket and pulled out
the token. He tossed it up in the air, caught it, and
replaced it in his pocket. "I think this might assure
us a meal and a bed for the night. We just have to
find the right inn."

It wasn't difficult. It was the place they were
standing outside. They simply walked up to the
large, thick set man polishing tankards with a dirty
cloth, showed him the token and he nodded them
through to a small private room at the rear. He
followed them in.

"A meal and a bed!" Said Marmaduke. It wasn't a question.

The man looked anxious. "You passing through?"

Dancing Jack sat on a table and rocked his legs back and forth.

The man wiped his hands on the cloth. "There are arrangements. Ever hear of a man called Dammit Johnson? He's the cock around these parts if you take my meaning."

"Just passing through!" remarked Dancing Jack

The man looked relieved; he nodded and went off to place an order for the preparation of beds and hot food.

"He'll find out about Dammit Johnson in due course." Jack said.

The meal arrived and to both men's surprise it was both edible and tasty, although neither of them could guess what meat had been used. Apart from that it was an uneventful night and the pair of them spent a night in a comfortable bed with full stomachs.

Marmaduke woke sensing someone was outside the door. He lay where he was as his door slowly opened. The figure crept across the room to where Marmaduke's jacket hung on the back of a chair. As the figure stretched out a hand to reach into the inside pocket he suddenly found his hand was pinned to the seat of the chair by a very sharp throwing knife. Before he had time to scream out there was a large hand across his mouth. He shivered as he felt long finger nails gently dig into his cheeks. A voice purred into his ear.

"You have one choice. Talk or die. It's really up to you."

The man nodded quickly and Marmaduke lifted his hand from his mouth then pushed the man further away from the door. He tapped on the door and within seconds Dancing Jack was standing in the room with his pistol drawn.

"A party is it?" he asked innocently.

He shut the door behind him, walked across the room and lit a candle. Marmaduke ignored him and pushed the interloper in the chest. The man fell backwards towards the bed dragging the chair behind him. He placed his good hand ion the chair and wondered if he could pull the knife out of his hand. Marmaduke made the decision for him. He held the man's hand down and pulled the knife out with one quick jerk. Blood spurted out from a vein and began to stain the bed sheets. Dancing Jack stepped forward and lifted the man's hand above his head. He took a large handkerchief out of his pocket and adapted it as a tourniquet tying it tightly around the man's wrist.

"I'd leave it up there if I were you. That way you just might not bleed to death, now start talking and if I hear the name of Dammit Johnson I will get very annoyed."

The man shuffled into a sitting position and held his hand up high in the air.

"Dammit Johnsons had it round here. He's finished!"

Marmaduke cocked his head to one side. "Keep talking!" he growled.

As he spoke he wiped the blood from his knife and slid it back into his bandoleer. The gesture wasn't lost on the man.

"Word came that him and his men been done over pretty good. Word said it were two strangers. Then two strangers turn up here claiming bed and board with his token."

"So you came to find out? Who sent you?"

The man shrugged. "I just got word."

Marmaduke pulled out another knife and idly tossed it up and down in the air.

The man took the hint. "Usual way. Rider comes and delivers a letter. The letter has my instructions."

"I don't suppose it's any use asking who the rider was sent by?" asked Dancing Jack, although he had a feeling that he already knew the answer to his question. He was right. The man just shook his head.

Marmaduke threw the knife even higher. "There's a name isn't there?"

The man watched the knife as it spun up and down in the air. There was a blur and he found himself looking down at the knife that was embedded in the wooden frame of the bed, right between his legs. He tried to move backwards and brought his arm down to steady himself. That started the blood flowing again.

"I'd be careful of getting blood on my handkerchief!" Jack remarked.

The man quickly put his hand up again and began speaking.

"The rider said there'd been some trouble in Malton yesterday. Then word came about Dammit Johnson. Them up at the big house are talking about two escaped prisoners. From the descriptions it were the same two men."

Dancing Jack tutted. "If I were you I'd have a word with your man. It seems to me a foolish act indeed to send a man into the room of someone who's suspected of besting the Malton men and Dammit Johnsons gang. A foolish act, or you're not by yourself!"

As he spoke Marmaduke looked out of the small window. Across the road, under the shelter of a group of trees he could make out three men sitting on horses. Marmaduke quickly ducked back from the window.

"Three of them!" he said.

"They sent a sneak thief in first!" he turned to the man. "What were you looking for?"

"I was sent to find the token. That would prove things either way. Then I was told to take it to them out there."

"And what happens then?" Asked Dancing Jack

"They comes up to kill you."

As he spoke the man leapt to his feet catching Jack off balance. He made it to the door. As he tugged at the handle his eyes opened wide with horror and a flash of pain caused him to almost pass out. He looked down to see his other hand pinned to the door by a throwing knife.

"Some people never learn." Marmaduke said as the man fainted and slumped down behind the door.

"Better not leave him like that, he'll bleed to death." Observed Jack

Marmaduke stepped forward, lifted the mans other arm above his head, took out a knife and pinned the arm upright by sticking the knife through the arm of the man's sleeve into the door.

The door opened inwards so they had to move the man and the door to squeeze out. As they descended the stairs they found themselves in a passageway. One direction led to the front of the building. The other towards a kitchen. They chose the kitchen route. Sure enough at the rear of the kitchen was a door that led onto a courtyard at the rear of the building. Once outside they split up. Marmaduke turned left as Dancing Jack turned right. They crept around the building until they reached the front where the three men were still waiting under the trees. One of them was looking up at the light in the window. They all turned their heads at the sound of a voice speaking in the darkness.

"Good evening gentlemen, or is it morning? Indeed can it even be called morning before the rising of the dawn?"

Dancing Jacks words confused them just enough for Marmaduke to make his move. In one quick leap he seemed to change his shape into that of a very large and very angry cat. He landed on the back of one of the horses, swiped the man sitting on it to the ground, and before the horse could rear in fright, he had accounted for the men either side of him.

Dancing Jack blinked as the air shimmered and Marmaduke stood there rubbing one of his hands. "Bejeesus, that's a fine trick you have there. Scares the living daylights out of me I don't mind saying, but it's a fine trick!"

Marmaduke looked down at the three men. They were all lying on the ground, holding their faces where claw marks scarred their cheeks. Blood was seeping through their fingers. Marmaduke had been very careful not to use too much force. The men would live.

They dragged the three men into the inn where they were met by the landlord wringing his hands. Dancing Jack looked him straight in the face.

"See where telling tales leads to. Who did you send word to?"

The landlord took a step back and raised both hands.

"Wasn't me honest. There was a man who left just after you arrived. Must have been him. Spies everywhere. Don't know who's who half the time."

Dancing Jack smiled and took a step forward. Suddenly he lashed out his hand and slapped the landlord across the face.

"Never play Dancing Jack for the fool. You sent someone as soon as you saw the token. You'd seen it before. You knew it belonged to Dammit Johnson."

The man began to protest is innocence when a knife flashed past his ear and embedded itself into the barrel behind him.

"Please don't lie!" Marmaduke purred.

The landlord nodded. "You have the measure of it. As soon as I sees the token I knew something had happened to Dammit. Sent one of the stable lads to Jack Barrow with a note. I know nothing about that lot." He looked to the three men who were trying to rise but, realising that Jack and Marmaduke had their pistols trained on them, decided they should stay where they were on the floor. The landlord looked around the room.

"Where is Jack by the way?"

"If you're asking the whereabouts of our would be sneak thief I suggest you go upstairs, but be careful how you open the door." Dancing Jack made a movement with his pistol and the landlord scurried upstairs.

"Seems like they're well organised." Observed Marmaduke

"And well informed. They knew about events at Malton the next morning."

"How?"

Dancing Jack moved his head in the direction of the staircase. "Landlords. I'll wager a large purse on the fact that every landlord is a part of Foxy Toms spy network. How else could they find out about Malton so soon? It makes sense when you think about it. Foxy Tom makes a very profitable trade. He has kegs of liquor, they have the information. Add to that the eyes and ears of his robber bands and their network of informers and well, the man has half the entire county under surveillance."

Marmaduke nodded. "And the robber bands know exactly which coach or wagon to pillage. Just as he knows which ships to attack."

"Knowledge!" Exclaimed Dancing Jack.

"Knowledge, it certainly is powerful stuff!"

Chapter Thirty Seven

Sergeant Lewis wasn't happy. He'd been sent to York with despatches from the York Garrison. He'd been waiting for the return documents when a Lieutenant appeared and led him down a corridor into a room where a Colonel sat behind a desk. Before he could salute the Colonel indicated that the Sergeant should sit down. Now the Sergeant knew he was in trouble. The Colonel stood up and looked down at the Sergeant.

"I have a report here. It says you're good in a crisis."

Sergeant Lewis racked his brains to remember an incident in his entire military career where that could have been said about him, he couldn't think of one. Now he was very worried. The army never flatter unless they want something.

That had been yesterday, and that was how he came to be dressed in a shabby set of civilian clothes loitering halfway down a tiny, shabby, York alleyway. He had been instructed on whom to look for. A tall, well dressed solicitor. As he stood looking down the alleyway he ran through the Colonels explanation once again in his head.

"Chappie probably knows every face of every soldier in the Garrison. Can't trust a civilian, this is army business. New face was just what we wanted."

He was brought back to the present by the clatter of a carriage passing the end of the alleyway. As he turned his head he saw a door open and the man described by the Colonel step out into the alleyway. He looked up and down before setting off at a brisk walk towards the far end.

Sergeant Lewis followed him.

He was led along a network of streets, passed churches, shops and houses until the man turned up a street that was more gentrified. At its far end,

positioned on the corner was a coffee house. The
man he was following entered. Sergeant Lewis
walked up to a large window that looked out onto a
small square. He peered inside. Sure enough he
could see his man walking across the room to a
table set inside a recess. Three men were already
seated. They looked up as he arrived at their table
and bid him to be seated. As soon as he sat down
the solicitor produced a small leather pouch and
withdrew a sealed package of papers and slid it
across the table. One of the men took it up and
broke the seal. He examined the papers. Then he
turned the page over, and the next and the next,
quicker and quicker until he came to the end. Then
he slammed the papers down on the table and spoke
to the solicitor. The solicitor grabbed the papers
from the table and flicked through them. He shook
his head. The other men at the table looked
increasingly unhappy at this turn of events. The man
who had opened the package slammed his hand on
the table. Although he couldn't hear the noise

Sergeant Lewis knew it had been loud as half the customers had turned around to stare at the men in the alcove.

One of the men tried to pass the incident off and appeared to break out into a very loud and unconvincing laugh. Then the four men lowered their heads and held an urgent whispered conversation. After some minutes the solicitor stood up and walked quickly out of the building. Sergeant Lewis remained where he was. He realised it was pointless following the solicitor. He knew where he was going, back to his office with a flea in his ear. It was the other men he knew the Colonel would be interested in. Suddenly he felt his pocket being picked. He spun around and was about to deliver a punch to someone's jaw when he realised there was no one there. Then he looked down. A small scruffy boy, who could easily be mistaken for an urchin was hopping about in front of him. He was hopping because he had his hand caught in the Sergeants pocket, and his hand was caught because the

Sergeant was holding it there. The boy looked very frightened.

"Right!" Said the Sergeant. "Let's get you down to the constable, see what he has to say." He dragged at the boy's hand. The boy burst into tears. A number of passers-by paused to look at the confrontation. The Sergeant met their stares. "Lad's a bit upset. Toothache you know."

The passers-by knew and passed by. The Sergeant looked back through the coffee house window. The three men were just finishing their coffee. He bent down and put his face close to that of the young boys.

"Stop snivelling, otherwise you'll really have something to snivel about!"

The boy stopped crying and wiped his running nose with the back of his sleeve. "Don't take me to no constable, mister." He said and added a few sobs for good effect.

The Sergeant lent down to him. "On one condition. You do a little job for me and I'll give you a florin!"

The boy's eyes grew wide and his mouth dropped open. He'd never seen a florin before, let alone earned one. He quickly sniffed and nodded his head.

The Sergeant looked him in the eye. "You got a mate?"

He boy nodded and pointed across the road. The Sergeant looked in the direction the grubby finger was pointing in. Standing on the opposite side of the rod watching on anxiously was another, younger boy.

"He's my brother." The boy said.

The Sergeant smiled. "Good in that case you can both earn a florin each!"

The boys eyes opened even wider and his mouth dropped even more open. For a brief second the Sergeant wondered whether the boy was changing into a frog. He signalled for the boy's brother to come across the road. He didn't need telling twice.

Sergeant Lewis then put his arm around both boys' shoulders and whispered conspiratorially. He pointed out the three men still sat at their table. The two boys nodded. The Sergeant them took out of his pocket a bright florin and waved it in front of their faces. The boys nodded harder.

Eventually the three men stood up and walked towards the door. The Sergeant pulled the boys back behind the corner. As he suspected as soon as the three men walked onto the street they split up. One of them went off to the left and disappeared round the next corner. Sergeant Lewis tapped the youngest of the boys on the shoulder. He gave a nod and set off down the road and disappeared around the corner. The other two men turned right and continued to walk together, right past the Sergeant and the boy without giving them a glance. They gave them a few paces start and then set off after them. They followed them across the road and down a small alleyway that seemed to lead towards the river. They made a sudden sharp turn and passed through a small stone archway that led to the entrance of an old stone building. The Sergeant was about to follow them when he felt a sharp tugging at the sleeve of his jacket. He looked down. The boy was shaking his head.

"Can't go in there Mister." He said.

The Sergeant looked around him. "And whys that then?" He asked.

"Cos it's the Guildhall. Only Mayor and councillors go in there. You go in there and the Constable will get you and you'll be up a'for the beak in the morning before you know it."

Sergeant Lewis nodded. "Wait here." He said and turned and ran into the building.

The boy was right. He'd hardly got a few feet inside when he was stopped by a constable. Before the man could say anything the sergeant blurted out. "I'm after Mr Pilkington and Mr Kirk. I just saw them enter through here."

He had read the names on a notice board fastened to the wall behind the constables back. The constable looked confused. "Sorry friend. Pilkington and Kirk aren't here. You're mistaken!"

The Sergeant put on his best exasperated expression. "I could have sworn I just saw then walk down there with my own eyes!" he pointed down the corridor.

The Constable shook his head and looked down the corridor to where the Sergeant had pointed. "That weren't Pilkington and Kirk. That were Councillor Cobbitt and Councillor James!" he shook his head "Don't look a bit like the Pilkington and Kirk!" he turned around to discover that he was talking to himself. The man had vanished. He shook his head and returned to guarding the entrance to the corridor.

As the Sergeant left the building he found the young boy in the alleyway waiting for him. He gave the lad a wink and the two walked down the alleyway to find the younger brother. They found him standing at the corner of the coffee house anxiously looking up and down the street. When he saw his brother he ran across the road. "I did what you asked mister, I followed him into that big house behind the Assembly Rooms. He went in there."

The Sergeant leant down to the boy. "Can you show me?"

The boy nodded and led them down the street, then he stopped and looked up at the Sergeant. "As he went into the house a pretty lady said hello to him. She said Hello Mr van der Vlies."

The Sergeants face broke into a wide grin. He had the names. He reached into his pocket and brought out two large shiny coins. With great ceremony he handed one to each of the boys, ruffled their hair and sent them on their way. He watched as they ran down the street laughing and joking clutching their precious coins tightly in their dirty hands.

Chapter Thirty Eight

Two days had passed whilst Agnes waited to hear from Andrew. She spent most of the time checking on events at Hawkstone Grange. Other than patrols and mending the damage, nothing much seemed to happening so she decided to check on Marmaduke. She changed the water in her scrying bowl, added some more herbs and potions and an added pinch of essence of sardine.

The waters cleared and an image of Marmaduke and Dancing Jack appeared. They were mounted, just preparing to leave an inn. She checked their position and was surprised to find they were on the outskirts of Pickering. She moved her hand and an image if the interior of the inn appeared. Three men lay on the floor. They were tightly bound and gagged. By the look of things they had spent a most uncomfortable night. She took a look upstairs and was met by the unusual sight of a man sat pinned to the door of a bedroom by his hands giving the strange appearance that he was surrendering. By the look of him Agnes guessed he had passed out. He was having his wounds bandaged by a second man. By the dirty apron he was wearing Agnes assumed he was the landlord. She shook her head. It was the usual scene of devastation that Marmaduke left behind. Time to bring him in, she thought. In fact it was time to bring everyone together. Whether Andrew had found something or not it was time to start planning the end game. Ex Colonel Thomas Reynard was on the edge. It was time to push him over. Even if there wasn't enough proof in the paperwork she didn't want to give him time to regroup. At least with him out of the way the ship wrecking would be ended. She decided that she could wing it from here on in. She could always make it up as she went long. She usually did.

An hour later two riders stopped as an elderly woman stood at the side of the road. Once again Agnes conjured up a full breakfast. As they ate

Marmaduke and Dancing Jack told their stories. They told of the destruction of Foxy Tom's operations in Malton and Pickering. They told how each highwayman and robber carried a token unique to himself. They told how most inns and coach routes were spied upon by a network of landlords, low level criminals and inn keepers. She remained silent until they finished their tale.

She stood up and moved her hands. All trace of the alfresco breakfast disappeared. "Right! Time for a final campaign meeting, as the Commander would say. We'll meet up at the Castle. I'll go see Andrew. The man has had two days now, he must have found something. You two go straight back to the Garrison, you'll make it if you travel fast, and don't allow yourselves to be distracted." The last comment seemed to be aimed directly at Marmaduke.

The two men mounted their horses and set off in the direction of Scarborough. Agnes stood at the side of

the road watching them go. As they disappeared
into the distance she moved her hand slightly.

For a brief second Dancing Jack felt the air around
him shiver. He looked to one side. The countryside
was passing by in a blur. His eyes widened, no
horse could travel at this speed. He held on tight and
gave out a joyous whoop. If he could only ride a
horse like this at the races he would be a very rich
man indeed.

It was lunch time when Agnes walked into the
Chandlery. An assistant working behind the counter
nodded towards the office door.

"Hasn't left the office since your last visit." He said.

Agnes walked straight in.

Andrew was sitting behind his desk in his best
office chair. In front of him were piles of papers and
documents. He looked up as Agnes entered the
room. She could see he hadn't had much sleep. His
face was grey and his eyes red, his hair was

dishevelled and he was unshaven. His fingers were stained with ink.

"I think I've found something!" he said.

Agnes sat down as Andrew began a long and very detailed breakdown of the accounts and profits and losses of ex Colonel Thomas Reynard. A few minutes into the explanation her mind glazed over. She wanted to tell Andrew to cut to the chase but the poor man had spent two days and nights unravelling the Colonels finances and he shouldn't be denied the pleasure of relating every twist and turn.

"It's here!" he finally said.

Agnes refocused and looked at the paper Andrew was holding in front of her. She looked at the columns of figures. Nothing made any sense.

"What am I looking at exactly?" She finally asked.

Andrew sighed. "It's a list of transactions. It begins with a loan. See here."

He pointed to a figure at the head of a column of figures. "These are repayments. There you can see the money has been paid back, but the payments continue. It seems that most of the money our Colonel has gained through his wrecking ventures has filtered back through this account. To me it seems as if the original lender has financed Foxy Tom's enterprise and is now sitting back raking in the profits. That makes perfect sense. It's good business. However...." He picked up another piece of paper and dropped it in front of Agnes. "Here's another list of accounts. What makes this one interesting is that if we look closely, at the purchases that pass through the account relate to the purchase of weapons. See here, cannon, here powder, here semi-culvines, and here....."

He dropped another sheet of paper in front of her. "This is a list of payments to men. It's his wages bill. See the lender is paying for the ex Colonels not only to equip his enterprise, they are also paying for its upkeep and maintenance."

Agnes placed the paper carefully back onto Andrews's desk and sat back. The sight of all the columns and numbers were making her head spin. "I suppose the question I should really be asking is who is this lender?"

Andrew sat back as well and rubbed his eyes making them even more redder. "It's a company." He said and then added. "A company owned by very respectable Dutch Bank."

"How on earth did you find that out?" Agnes asked. She was impressed with Andrews work.

He simply shrugged. "Paperwork! One document appeared to be details of a company's formation. It listed the owners. Three men. A certain Mr Cobbett, Mr James and Mr Van de Vlies. The company was underwritten by the Dutch Bank."

"Have you any idea who these men are?" She asked hopefully.

"Not a clue!" Was Andrews reply.

As if the explanation was the final act in a very long two days Andrew slumped in his chair. Agnes nodded. She told Andrew to freshen himself up and meet with the rest of them in the Commanders Office as soon as possible. As she opened his office door she looked behind her. Andrew was resting his head on his arms that in turn were resting on the top of his desk. He was fast asleep. She closed the door quietly behind her.

After leaving the Chandlery Agnes went straight home and straight back to the twenty first century and her computer. As she entered she heard the builders still arguing about something or other. She ignored them and moved her hands and the front room shimmered. It was a cloaking spell. If anyone should look into the room they would see it empty, just as it was five minutes before she got there. No one would see the elderly woman sitting in front of her computer moving her hands and her fingers, selecting a series of documents and records. She began by checking Dutch banks in the 1700's, there were a lot but not many who operated in England, leastways outside London. There was one though, it was called the Amsterdamsche Wisselbank and it had a small office in York. She smiled. It had to be the one. Although she dredged the records she couldn't find anything else. She did find a very learned treatise on Dutch Banking, and great mention of Amsterdamsche Wisselbank but couldn't find any details of the company's York branch. She waved her hand and the computer closed down.

The late afternoon sun shone down into the Garrison Commanders office. The remains of high tea lay on the table. Agnes was impressed with the quality of the scones. She had three and before they began their business she enquired about the cook and the recipe. The Commander harrumphed; to him a scone was a scone.

Probably due to the scones and tea the mood of the meeting was a deal more positive, especially when

Dancing Jack and Marmaduke reported their destruction of both the Malton and Pickering arms of the Ex-Colonels operations.

Then Andrew took over and explained the money trail. Despite trying hard, everyone around the table got lost as soon as Andrew passed around sheets of papers covered in figures. Andrew looked up and could tell he was losing his audience. He sat back and summed up the situation in words everyone could understand.

"Ex Colonel Thomas Reynard's entire operation is financed by this company, who in turn are underwritten by of Amsterdamsche Wisselbank, a Dutch Bank."

The Commander interrupted with a harrumph. "I suppose that means we'll have to inform the York Garrison!"

It was obvious that he wasn't too happy about sharing the operation with the bigger command. He knew the army. Before long the big wigs at York would take over the entire operation and take all the credit.

Agnes could read the expression on the man's face. She looked across the table and smiled. "I dare say you should report the findings, although how you came about this knowledge will make interesting reading. I'm not sure the high command at York will accept the words "a witch told me" as cast iron evidence for taking any action whatsoever."

Dancing Jack gave a polite cough. "However if a message from myself was delivered to a certain Colonel with no name, the outcome might be, shall we say, different!"

Before he could stop himself Marmaduke asked the question that had popped into everybody's mind, but no one asked for fear of looking foolish. "If the Colonel has no name, how do you get a message to him?"

Jack smiled. "We have a code. I simply address the message to the office of the Garrison Commander, marked for the attention of Colonel George Thackery."

The Commander scratched his chin. "Can't say I recall a chappie by the name of Thackery, one of the Shropshire Thackery's is he? There's a lieutenant...."

Dancing Jack cut him off. He spoke slowly and quietly. "Commander, there isn't one. That's the whole point. It's code!"

Aware he had made a faux pas the Commander harrumphed. "Too many secret chaps for my liking. Action! That's what's needed, action. The bounder has got an army of ruffians out there. I've got a fully trained and armed Garrison of troops. I think it's time we tested the man's metal!"

Agnes surprised everyone by agreeing with him.

They pulled out the map of Hawkstone Grange and studied both the layout of the house and the land surrounding it. Marmaduke and Dancing Jack pointed out the lanes and roads where Foxy Toms spies would be seen. They were doubtful if the Commanders troops could march a troop of soldiers a hundred yards before word would reach the Foxy Tom.

"How many men would you be needing?" Agnes asked.

The Colonel referred to the map, and then looked up at Agnes. "How many do you think he can still muster?"

She closed her eyes and tried to visualise the house and buildings. "Probably thirty, forty at the most!"

The Commander looked at the map once more. "In which case I would suggest we use three units of twenty five per unit. If I could position them, here, here, and here we could have the house surrounded. Once the groups are in position we could form a circle around the house and stage a three pronged attack via the entrances here, here and here." He jabbed at the map with his finger.

Dancing Jack shook his head. "Seventy five troopers in bright red uniforms marching around the countryside is still shall I say a bit obvious. The man will know you're coming as soon as you walk out of the Castle."

The conversation we interrupted by loud snore emanating from Andrew who had fallen asleep leaning back in his chair.

Agnes smiled and turned to Jack. "Don't worry about that. I think I might be able to arrange some suitable camouflage. Ex-Colonel Thomas Reynard won't know of the trooper's presence until they are in position, and by that time it will be too late for him to do anything about it."

She looked up at the Commander. "Yes, camouflage."

It was agreed that the troops would muster just after eight on the following morning, and that they would be led by the Commander himself.

"Just a pity Lieutenant Smalls can't be with us!" he said

"How is the Lieutenant?" Agnes asked feeling a bit ashamed that she had forgotten to enquire about the injured man before now.

"Keeping his pecker up. Not a lot else to do really." The Commander replied.

Across the table Dancing Jack had finished writing his message. He looked across to the Commander, who shouted out at the closed door. Within seconds a soldier had opened it and entered the room saluting the Commander as he came to a halt in front of the table.

As he made his salute the soldier brought his boot down heavily onto the wooden floor. The noise woke Andrew with a start. He quickly realised where he was and leant forward hoping no one had noticed.

"Get Sergeant Lewis. Tell him I have a job for him. A dispatch to be taken to York Barracks."

The soldier looked confused. "Begging your pardon, Sir." The Commander looked up at him. "Yes?"

The soldier reddened. "Sergeant Lewis Sir. He delivered a dispatch to the York Garrison four days ago now!"

Everyone around the table looked at the soldier which had the effect of making him even more nervous. There was a pause eventually broken by Dancing Jack.

"And?"

The soldier looked at the highwayman. "Well Sir, he hasn't returned yet!"

The Commander coughed. "Bit rum, what! Should have been back two days ago. Sergeants huh! Give them an inch and they'll take whatever liberties they can get away with. Better get me another rider then."

The soldier stood where he was. The Commander looked up at him. "Go on then Chop Chop!"

The soldier saluted and left the office as quickly as he could. At the back of his mind was the thought that he hadn't exactly covered himself in glory. He realised just how much he hadn't when he got half-way down the steps and realised he hadn't taken the message. He went back and knocked on the Commanders door. He heard the Commander acknowledge his knock, opened the door and peered around the corner. He was met by the sight of four people watching him. One of them was the highwayman who was holding the message out in his hand. Without saying a word he took the message, saluted and left the room.

Agnes turned to the Commander. "He'll learn!"

The Commander just stared at the closed door. "He'd better!" he replied.

Agnes pulled her chair back and stood up. "Right, there's nothing to be done here. I will be here when you muster your troops Commander." She smiled. "I rather fancy riding out at the head of an army!"

The Commander was about to say something and then caught the look in Agnes's eye and thought better of it.

She turned to Andrew. "Paperwork. It was all in the paperwork." She let out a small laugh. "It takes a book keeper to catch a book keeper. Thank you Andrew! Now for goodness sake go and get some rest."

She put her hand in her pocket and pulled out a small white sachet. She handed it across the table to Andrew.

"Take this in a warm drink, preferably when you are in bed. It's powerful, you'll get a good night's sleep. Oh, and you'd better not make any plans for the morning." She added as an afterthought.

She turned to Dancing Jack and Marmaduke. "As for you two, I think we have a busy night ahead of us."

They said their farewells to Andrew at the top of her street. Once they were inside the house Agnes led then to the kitchen. She turned to Dancing Jack.

"Here we have a choice young man. As you have probably noticed we are an unusual house with unusual talents. Soon we will have finished with Foxy Tom, The noose is tightening."

She suddenly realised what she said. "I'm sorry about that, it was insensitive given your experience."

Dancing Jack nodded. Agnes continued. No doubt when this is all over your Colonel with no name will be wanting some sort of report. Now whilst I'm fully aware that the army, in the person of the Garrison Commander knows of our talents he chooses to make certain omissions in his reports. I would be grateful if you could do the same. The last thing I need is...."

Before she could finish Dancing Jack held up his hand. "There will be reports, verbal of course. The Colonel with no name never asks for anything in writing, and at times, well I can be a bit forgetful. Our man wants facts and names and so is probably one of the very few who see the whole picture. Now a man like that can't be bogged down in details, if you take my meaning."

Agnes nodded. "I think we understand each other."

He never even noticed where the tea came from. All he knew was that he was now holding a steaming cup in front of him.

Later that night, as the moon played hide and seek behind streaky clouds, three figures stood in the woodlands at the rear of the buildings behind Hawkstone Grange. Dancing Jack had no idea how he had arrived. All he remembered was the world speeding by and the sound of a bird flapping its wings. Next to him Marmaduke was breathing heavily.

Agnes turned towards them. "Right, you know what we've to do. Tonight we are just laying traps. Do not pick any fights with anyone. Do not get captured. In fact if you see anyone or even hear anyone, lie low. Do not be seen."

The first task involved Marmaduke gaining the roof of the nearest of the barrack buildings. He made it up there in one bound and then ran along the apex of the roof until he reached the chimney stack where he fixed a small metal plate between the chimney pots. There was a noise from below. He froze. A guard appeared around the corner. He looked one way and then the other and after a quick fumble at his leggings, quickly urinated on the wall of the building. Marmaduke considered giving out a growl when he became aware of an owl perched next to him. The owl slowly shook its head. Marmaduke remained silent. The man finished what he was doing, fastened his leggings, turned and returned in the direction he had appeared from. The owl flew off and perched on the bell tower. There was a shimmer, the bell glowed for a second and then returned to normal.

Meanwhile Dancing Jack went about his tasks with quiet and steady efficiency. He had no idea of what or why he was doing what Agnes had asked. Whatever Agnes wanted was just fine by him, though he admitted to himself that planting dead branches from the nearby trees all along the edge of the forest seemed a strange thing to be doing at the best of times.

There was a slight thud behind him and he turned to see Marmaduke brushing dirt and moss from his clothing. Jack stuck the last branch in the ground and silently made his way to Marmaduke's side.

Agnes had now transferred her attention to the roof of the house where she perched behind the central chimney stack. After a deal of head swivelling and movement of its wings it flew off and landed in the branches of a tree behind Dancing Jack. Before he could turn she had returned to normal.

"Right you two. I know it's not the most comfortable of lodgings but I need you two here when the army arrives."

Marmaduke was about to say something. He had a bad feeling. Agnes saw it coming. "Look I've seventy five troopers to look after. That's going to take a lot of concentration and there's only a certain amount I can do. When you get the signal all you have to do is to come out and cause as much pandemonium as possible. Now neither of you should find that too difficult! Anyway I've redecorated the place. The doors open by the way. Close it after you."

Without much enthusiasm Dancing Jack and Marmaduke crept though the night and let themselves into the pinfold. They closed the door behind them.

Once inside the small stone building they stopped and looked wide-eyed around them. Agnes had excelled herself. Inside the prison she had recreated her own living room. There was Marmaduke's favourite chair, right next to the fire that was blazing away. Next to the fire was a pot of steaming hot coffee, and one of tea. There were freshly made scones, a bottle of port and Marmaduke's favourite brand of sardines. At the edges of the room were two beds with mattresses and feather down pillows. As they made themselves comfortable Dancing Jack wondered how Agnes had managed to get a square room into a round building. Then he wondered why the smoke from the fire couldn't be seen or smelt outside. The he wondered why there was no light escaping from the building. Then he wondered why he was bothering to wonder when there was a bottle of port and a batch of the same scones he had enjoyed earlier to be dealt with. He sat down and opened the port.

Chapter Thirty Nine

The Colonel with no name was used to his orders being obeyed, and he was used to making his own decisions, right or wrong. His role in the secret department meant that he answered only to the Chief Of Staff, who in turn only answered to the Office of Prime Minister, who had the ear of the King himself. It was said that his original branch of internal security originated in Elizabethan England by the great spymaster Wallsingham himself. The Colonel with no name had been in charge for the last four years, and for the last four years he had never come across a situation like the one that presented itself to him. He sifted the facts in front of him.

Ex-Colonel Thomas Reynard had been dismissed from the army for financial irregularities and misdemeanours. Later investigations showed that his crime was much more than it was originally thought. The Colonel with no name sniffed, this is where it got complicated. The man hadn't just swindled the army. He had forged some business agreement with a consortium that financed him, allowing him to build an army of wreckers and robbers. That rag tag army would be dealt with in due course. That wasn't the Colonel with no names priority. What was his priority was the information gathered by the shifty looking Sergeant Lewis. He made a mental note. The man didn't just look shifty, he was shifty. He was just the man his unit needed. He scribbled out a brief note. The Sergeant would find himself under the command of a new Colonel in the morning.

The information the Sergeant had brought was more worrying and more far-reaching than anyone had suspected. The Colonel with no name played out the scenario in his head. Three men made up the consortium, two of them local counsellors. They would know of Colonel Thomas Reynard from his army days. No doubt they were a party to his crooked deals then, and it would be the profits they made back then that enabled them to become counsellors. They were in it for purely financial gain, after all they had made their fortunes with Colonel Reynard, why spoil a good thing. The third man however, he was a very different man. He was not only a banker but he represented a foreign bank, and a Dutch bank at that.

The fact that the Dutch were involved made the Colonel with no name very wary indeed. He knew his history. He knew of the three English Dutch Wars of the previous century and how they had their roots in the English Civil War. He knew how back in 1667, a hundred years ago now, the Dutch had humiliated the English by sailing a fleet up the Thames, destroying part of the English fleet and towing away the flagship of the English navy. This was a severe blow to the English King who was already struggling with the aftermath of the Great Fire of London and the ravages of the plague. Money was running out and a war would not prove popular among the population. In London there was a hint of revolution in the air and Charles II was forced to sign a peace treaty.

Later a treaty with the French forced Charles II to assist Louis XIV in another war against the Dutch but after a series of naval failures Charles was once again forced to sue for peace. Conflict between the two countries was ended with the advent of the Glorious Revolution which saw William of Orange and his wife Mary ascend to the English throne. One of William's objectives was to ally England alongside the Dutch against the French, and the Dutch began to use London as an operational base and banking centre. However the English economy had begun to outgrow that of the Dutch and a certain amount of resentment had broken out. In addition the Dutch support for the American colonies had annoyed many leading English politicians. Alongside his superiors the Colonel with no name felt that it was only a matter of time before a war between the two countries would break out again. In fact he felt it was inevitable. This was the bigger picture.

The Colonel with no name hastily crafted out another note. He rang a bell and the Lieutenant with no name entered, took the note and left again.

Whichever way he looked at the events, one dim background shape began to take shape. Dutch influence was at work. They were creating an army that would have the potential to cause havoc. Why? Perhaps they were to spearhead an invasion. A chilling thought struck him. Perhaps there were other Thomas Reynard's with their own private armies scattered up and down the country. It was audacious planning. There was only one way of knowing for sure and he would have the answer when the reply to his message was received. It had only been a simple question. He had requested assistance in discovering whether the Amsterdamsche Wisselbank handled monies on behalf of the Dutch Government. If it did and the monies could be traced to the York branch and the ex Colonel Thomas Reynard it was an action of war. If there was no link it could be put down to private enterprise, in which case Foxy Tom was unique, a one off. The Colonel with no name knew which of the scenarios he preferred. If the Dutch Government was implicated that would mean politics and once politicians got involved things usually got very messy.

He pushed the papers way from him and lent back in his chair. Whilst he was waiting for his answer he would get Sergeant Lewis to keep a very close watch on the Dutch banker. He knew full well he couldn't just haul him in and question him. If the Dutch Government were behind it all he knew such an action would cause a diplomatic incident. It could even provide the catalyst that would start the war that he and his superiors felt was inevitable. He was determined that he would not allow that to happen. He sighed, his job as spymaster was difficult enough without having to worry about diplomacy and politics.

Sergeant Lewis was back in position halfway down the street that housed the offices of the Dutch bank. Today he wore a different disguise. Today he held a tray around his neck selling bootlaces, combs, brushes, and a selection of cheap items no self respecting gentleman could be seen without. At least that's what his sales patter claimed. In the back of his mind he wondered if the army claimed the proceeds of his selling powers. As he jingled the coin in his pocket he saw a man turn off the street and walk down the short side street to knock on the door of the banks office. It was opened by a smartly dressed servant. The man presented a card and the servant admitted him. He reappeared some forty five minutes later. The sergeant was curious. He walked across the street and accosted him.

"Laces sir? Hairbrush, fine linen handkerchief?"

The man tried to avoid the salesman but whichever way he stepped the man with the tray was in front of him. Begrudgingly the man looked down at the tray that was blocking his way. The Sergeant went into his sales patter.

"Best laces in the North Sir. Won't let you down! Fine handkerchiefs, everything to help you create a good impression." He held out a comb. "You need a smart head in business, inside and out!"

The man looked the seller in the eye. "And what do you know of my business?" he asked.

The Sergeant held his gaze. "Well Sir, from your manner of dress I would hazard a guess that you are a man of the professions. A lawyer maybe."

The man snorted. "If I was a lawyer I wouldn't be buying boot laces from the likes of you"

The Sergeant simply smiled. "Ah sir, you would be surprised that men of quality like to make use of good value when they see it!"

He looked down the small side street and decided to take a risk. He lowered his voice.

"Even his nibs down the road has been known to grace my small emporium!"

Te man looked down the street. "His nibs? You mean that haughty taughty Dutch feller. Well he would like a bargain. Watches every penny that one."

The Sergeant looked offended. "Sir, I hope you are not implying that only spendthrifts and tightwads are my customers!"

The man grunted. "Tightwad describes him perfectly."

The Sergeant made a calculated guess. "I take it he bested you in a business transaction."

The man turned from looking down the alley to looking at the man with the tray. His eyes narrowed a he spoke. "No one bests me. I can make on the deal if I shaved costs."

The Sergeant smiled. "Shaving costs is the key to all good business. Look at me. No overheads, no rent, no upkeep. May I be so bold as to enquire as to the nature of your business?"

The man grunted. "I'm a carter!"

The Sergeant showed genuine surprise. "A carter? Your overheads must be high, horses, men, not to mention wagons and their upkeep."

The man sighed. "Pray do not labour the point. Six teams between here and wherever. Do you know the price of feed? Not to mention the wages the drivers are demanding!"

The Sergeant showed a sympathetic smile. "The old problem. Costs rise and customers want to pay less."

The carter turned and spat into the street. "Told him what he could do with his offer. Can't do it for that price, cheaper to keep everyone at home. Mind you he'll find some idiot to do it for the price he's offering. I'll take these."

The fact that the man was actually going to buy something took the Sergeant completely by surprise. He looked at the laces the man was holding out to him.

"On the house Sir!" On the house!" With that the Sergeant turned and walked off down the street, leaving the carter holding his new laces wondering if there was some sort of catch. He looked around him to see if he was being robbed by some assistant, but the street was quiet. He shrugged, put the laces in his pocket and walked on his way.

The Colonel with no name read the report. Either Sergeant Lewis was a skilled operator or just plain lucky, he couldn't tell. Whatever he was he had delivered another vital piece of information. The Dutch were moving on.

He considered the possibilities. Either they had finished their business here and were moving on to newer pastures, or their operations had somehow become compromised and they were making a tactical withdrawal. He shook his head. Of course, officially, if required to answer questions the bank would always claim it was purely a business decision. Well at least it will leave Colonel Thomas Reynard high and dry he thought. He sketched out a new order. It simply read "Find out where he's going."

The one thing the Sergeant didn't lack was enterprise. No sooner had he received the order than he had changed clothes and identity once again and was knocking on the door of the Dutch Bank.

It was opened by the same servant he had seen earlier. Before the servant could speak the Sergeant stepped forward.

"Eli Fraser. Carter. A little bird told me you have a load to shift."

The servant disappeared for a few minutes leaving the Sergeant standing at the doorstep. He returned and showed the visitor into a small outer office where a clerk looked up from a desk covered in papers and ledgers. The clerk indicated that the Sergeant should sit down.

Eventually after a deal of haggling the Sergeant was shown out of the office and back into the street. In the breast pocket of his jacket was a document. A contract to move office furniture, and crates of documents from York to Hull.

As he walked back to the barracks he did some quick mental calculations. If he could find the carter, and get the army to make up the difference, he might be able to do business. And make himself a bit of a profit on the side. He smiled, he was liking his new posting.

Chapter Forty

As the troopers gathered inside the gatehouse of Scarborough Castle, Agnes sat on the horse that had been specially picked for her by the Commander himself. She didn't doubt the man's skill and knowledge of horses, but Agnes was a great believer in insurance and didn't believe in surprises. She moved her fingers slightly and her horses suddenly flicked its ears. For the briefest of seconds its eyes shone. Agnes smiled. There would be no trouble from this, whatever happened. Now it was time for her to concentrate. At her suggestion the troops had been lined up four abreast. At her nod they were given their marching orders by the Commander himself.

Lieutenant Smalls had managed with his crutches to get down the stairs and see them depart. He watched as the gates opened and seventy five men lined up in fours, marched out of the gate, and simply disappeared. He blinked. He was still blinking when the gates shut behind them.

As they left the town and entered open country Agnes smiled. She was actually riding a horse at the head of an army. Mind you, the effect was rather lessoned as it was an invisible army. To the occasional person working in a field, or watching from a nearby cottage it simply appeared as an old lady riding a horse down a country lane.

They stopped a few miles from Hawkstone Grange to allow the men a break. Agnes led them to a large stone barn. The men piled in and sat down among bales of hay. Snap tins and field rations were opened. Once they had eaten Agnes waved a hand over the troopers and they all fell into a deep and refreshing sleep.

"Could do with a snooze myself!" The Commander remarked looking down at his sleeping men.

Agnes smiled. "I thought the Garrison Commander never slept." She said.

The Commander harrumphed. "Don't believe everything we tell the new recruits."

It was late afternoon when the troops were finally in position. They completely encircled the house and its grounds from positions inside the woods and behind the walls where the woods ended.

From the air Agnes could see that the formation was tight. The soldiers stood almost shoulder to shoulder. She was satisfied that there was no chance of anyone passing through them.

She landed and looked around her. The sun was just going down creating deep shadows in the woods and behind the walls. Night was falling. In the house lights had been lit. A slight mist crept across the grounds.

Dancing Jack and Marmaduke had enjoyed a restful night and day inside the pinfold. They had spent most of the day attending to their weapons, sharpening and re-sharpening a variety of swords and knives. As the evening drew on a small bird appeared at the window and chirruped. Marmaduke nodded and the two slipped out of the door to the place where Agnes and The Commander stood.

Agnes looked across at them.

"The object of the exercise is to hurt as few as possible. Leave the foot soldiers alone. By the time I've finished they will run willingly into the arms of the army."

Dancing Jack looked up at Agnes. "And the thugs in the house?"

A cloud passed across Agnes's face. "No holds barred." She said.

"Just make sure nothing happens to Foxy Tom. If he's not delivered to the York Garrison I'll be out of a job." Said Jack, as he slipped the pistol into his belt.

She looked across to where the Commander stood waiting. She gave a nod. The Commander returned it. Agnes raised her hand towards the sky. From nowhere a giant thunderclap crashed overhead. It echoed and rumbled down between the buildings shaking the wall and rattling the doors. The crash was so loud that it shattered windows in the big house. A fight of rooks rose from the woodlands flapping and squawking. The men appeared from the buildings just as the flash of lightening screamed out of the sky. It danced and crackled along the roofs of the buildings until it hit the metal plates that Marmaduke had attached to the chimneys. Then they exploded. Soot and brick and roof tiles flew up in the air only to crash down breaking the roofs beneath them. A fire broke out and spread quickly through the out buildings. The occupants, deafened by the thunder and blinded by the lightening, bruised and battered by falling debris and in grave danger of burning to death , took the only option available to them They ran.

At the same time seventy five troopers armed with muskets and fixed bayonets appeared out of nowhere. The foot soldiers of ex-Colonel Thomas

Reynard surrendered without a single shot being fired.

Suddenly a voice could be heard shouting through the chaos. They looked towards the house. The Ex-Colonel had opened a window and was shouting orders and threats at his retreating men. Below him a door opened and a group of men ran out in pursuit of the fleeing men. One of them fired a pistol in the air.

A second group of men emerged from the door holding a variety of pistols, muskets and ran to opposite corners of the house. They aimed their weapons towards the surrounding woods and the outbuildings. Agnes waved her hand in the air and there was movement at the edge of the woods. From nowhere a row of ghostly figures appeared and began shuffling forward. Behind them a second row appeared, then a third. Their movements were jerky and the clothes they wore hung like wet rags wrapped around their bony bodies. Their faces were skull like, in fact many of them were just skulls, with moving eyes and swinging jaw bones. Some moved their skeletal arms and pointed long fingers that once held flesh in the direction of the house and the armed men.

Dancing Jack gave a little shudder. "Bejeesus, I planted dead people!"

Agnes looked across to him. "The men who drowned as a result of the men's wrecking. A nice touch I though!" She added as she turned back to watch.

The thugs from the house froze where they stood when they saw the apparition in front of them. Then they turned and ran back to the house. Two stopped and turned to fire their guns at the creatures jerking their way towards them. Then, as they saw their balls and bullets pass right through their targets, they turned and ran even faster. The two groups of men met at the entrance to the house. As they tried to open the door their world suddenly turned to water. It was as if a giant tidal wave had broken over the house and sent a deluge of water crashing down its walls. It swept the men off their feet and dragged them along the ground like a lot of bobbing corks. More and more water crashed to the ground and the men disappeared from sight under the bubbling and foaming flood. As the water reached the dead mariners it simply vanished washing away the dead as it went. Soon the area was dry leaving some wrecked, ragged and drowned bodies lying on the ground.

"I thought fatalities were to a be avoided?" said Marmaduke.

Agnes turned. Her face was set to grim. "I said no holds barred when it came to them. Poetic justice I call it." She turned away. "Right lets go find our Colonel Reynard."

"Ex-Colonel!" The Commander reminded her. The four of them walked towards the house.

Dancing Jack and Marmaduke stepped ahead to check the front of the house. It was unguarded. They nodded and the Commander marched up to the front door and knocked very loudly with the handle of his sword. It was opened by the butler. The Commander saluted and requested the pleasure of the Master of the House. The butler quickly looked around and seeing no guards, nodded his head and asked the Commander to wait where he was whilst he informed the Master of the House of the Commanders presence. He turned and had only taken a few steps when Marmaduke leapt forward and knocked the Commander onto his back. Before he could register his surprise at this turn of events, a musket ball passed over his head. There was a second shot and a figure fell out of the shadows at the far end of the hall. It dropped to the ground motionless. Dancing Jack slid his pistol back into his belt whilst he held the second in the direction of the butler.

"One at a time or all together. It makes no difference."

The Command stood up. Agnes moved her hands once more. She looked into the house. In her head she travelled through the hall. Two men with guns were hiding behind a plinth at the bottom of the staircase. She travelled upstairs and down a corridor. There was a barricade manned by Grimes and four other men. She floated above their heads and through the closed door behind them. Ex-Colonel Thomas Reynard was sat behind his desk.

As usual he wore his full dress uniform. In front of his was a decanter of whiskey and a half empty glass. Agnes smiled to herself. Of course, it could be half full. It just depended on your point of view. Next to the glass was a loaded pistol.

She lifted a finger and the firing pin of the pistol very quietly became detached. Just to make sure she moved her finger again and the ball rolled out of the barrel and silently dropped to the floor.

She returned to the present and passed on her information to the three men. Marmaduke tilted his head and with one bound leapt down the hall and halfway up the stairs. The two men behind the plinth realised something was wrong. By then it was too late. Something dropped behind them. Something that snarled and growled. Something that ripped and tore at their clothing and flesh. They screamed and ran towards the doorway where they met the swinging fists of Dancing Jack.

The duo surveyed the situation from the bottom of the stairs. There was no way that could make a forward assault down the corridor. Even in his cat form Marmaduke couldn't avoid four guns pointed at him. Then he had an idea. He whispered into Jacks ear. Jack nodded his understanding and Marmaduke returned outside. Within seconds he had climbed up the front of the building and had let himself in through an upstairs window. A he dropped to the floor a small glowing light appeared on the floor in front of him.

"Agnes." He thought. He followed the light through a series of rooms and corridors until it came to a door and stopped. Without pausing Marmaduke leant back to gain momentum and launched himself forward. The door collapsed inwards as the shape of a giant cat leapt into the room. In one bound it was on the other side and standing on its hind legs, began to tear at the double doors in front if him.

As it ripped apart there was the sound of gun fire from the other side. When it fell there were five men on the other side. Two were dead with bullet holes through the centre of their foreheads. The other two were nursing cuts to their arms. Dancing Jack was standing over them holding his sword and dagger at their throats.

"I thought you'd be wanting Grimes alive!" he said.

Marmaduke looked behind him back into the room. Ex Colonel Thomas Reynard was still sitting at his desk His eyes looked distant and glazed as the man lifted his tumbler of whiskey and drained it. There was the sound of someone coming up the stairs. Marmaduke drew a knife as he and Dancing Jack looked down the corridor. The Commander appeared and marched towards them. Instead of stopped he marched straight into the room not even pausing as he flashed a smart salute at them as he passed. They turned and watched as the Commander marched towards the ex Colonel. The Commander stopped at the man's desk.

"Attention!" he shouted.

The Ex-Colonel leapt to his feet and snapped a smart salute.

"Colonel Thomas Reynard. I am putting you under arrest for certain misdemeanours relating to..."

Before he could speak the charges Foxy Tom's hand snapped down. He grabbed his pistol, put it to his head, closed his eyes and pulled the trigger. There was silence broken only by the sound of a small bit of metal hitting the floor. He opened his eyes and starred in confusion at the pistol he was still holding.

"Oh come on man!" Said the Commander and led the ex Colonel out from behind his desk and out of the shattered door.

As they left the house they saw Agnes. With the aid of a Sergeant, who seemed to find the situation amusing, she was ordering troops here and there. One group had rounding up the remainders of Foxy Tom's army and was standing guard over them. Not many of them seemed as if they wanted to escape. They were thoroughly and utterly defeated and lay in small silent groups. Occasionally one or two of them would break out in a fit of shaking.

At the doorway to the house a small number of soldiers were holding the butler and his wife and who Marmaduke assumed were other members of the household.

Agnes had set another group of soldiers the grim task of recovering the bodies and loading them onto wagons to be taken back to Scarborough. No doubt the military would arrange a suitable burial for them.

Other troops were going though what remained of the outbuildings seeking out anyone who thought hiding might be a good idea. Finally some soldiers led string after string of horses out of the stables building.

"Looks like the army will gain enough horses to form a cavalry regiment." Marmaduke observed.

"I like to leave a place nice and tidy!" she remarked as she ordered even more troops to empty the armoury building.

It was quite a procession that travelled along the roads leading back to Scarborough. In fact it was such a procession that people came out of villages, houses and inns to watch as it passed by. What they saw was a troop of soldiers marching along. In their midst and under heavy guard, stumbling and half running to keep up with the pace, were a group of very anxious and very dishevelled men. Some seemed to be mumbling to themselves incoherently. The same thought passed through the minds of everyone who looked at them. That they didn't want to have experienced what those men had experienced. Behind the troops came a series of heavy covered wagons, followed by a string of horses. In the back of one wagon was a large wooden cage. Inside the cage, heavily chained and bound, were two men. One was dressed in full military dress uniform. The other sat snarling at the people they passed.

Finally following on behind the parade were four people on horseback. The mix of the people looked odd, an elderly lady, a military Commander and two highwaymen. As they passed the people thought they looked just like four friends out on a leisurely ride. As they passed by the observers could hear them laughing and chatting with each other. They seemed completely at ease, their horses seeming to know exactly where they were going without any direction.

As the procession passed into the distance another question came to mind in the minds of the observers. Whatever was a senior officer doing riding with two highway men and a little elderly lady and why did the elderly lady keep waving to them as she rode by.

Chapter Forty One.

The following morning a full breakfast was spread out inside a grand room in Scarborough Castle. Troops came and went carrying steaming platters of chops, sausages, fried and scrambled eggs. Pots of freshly brewed tea and coffee passed up and down the table, and it was the finest tea and coffee, Andrew had made sure of that. He had also solved the mystery of the barrels.

The question of why a carter was hauling empty barrels to the harbour side had puzzled him. He discovered the answer earlier in the day when he spotted the same carter standing at the side of the harbour. Before the man could make a run for it he felt Andrews hand on his shoulder. He turned and almost fell into the water, but Andrew held him firmly and pulled him away from the quayside and dragged him to the side of the fish market where he pushed him against the wall.

"Barrels!" he said.

The man tried to face it out. "What about barrels?" he asked. The he felt a prodding in his stomach. He looked down to see Andrew holding a long dagger to his abdomen. He quickly decided he was at a disadvantage and began to talk.

"How did you know?" the carter asked.

Andrew brought his face close to the mans. "As you know my name is Andrew Marks and I run the chandlery. I gave you a fair price for those weapons. As you might have figured nothing comes and goes in this harbour without my knowing about it."

The carter shrugged. "Pity it was a nice little earner."

Andrew poked his blade a little more into the man stomach. The man pulled his stomach in.

"What was?" Andrew asked.

The carter shrugged. "Them barrels!"

"Where did they come from?" Andrew asked.

"The cooperage up at the Alum works, you know up at Ravenscar." Andrew nodded. The man continued. "Well it backs up onto the road. Easy pickings."

Andrew withdrew the blade slightly. "You mean you stole them from the Alum works?"

The carter shook his head "They were just laying there. Helped myself. Sold 'em down here. Like I said a nice little earner."

Andrew shook his head. "You didn't think you'd be caught?"

Despite the dagger in his stomach the carter laughed. "That was the beauty of it. Who's going to stop a carter carrying empty barrels? Easiest thing in the world."

Andrew withdrew his dagger and the man let out a breath. Andrew laughed. "Isn't there anything you people won't steal?"

The carter looked offended. "Fair play, it's a rough old game out there. You've got to make it where you find it. Like those weapons I sold you. Just laying there they were. I call it perks of the trade."

Andrew slid the dagger back into his belt. "The next time you want to sell barrels you come to me.Like I said nothing comes or goes in this harbour without me knowing about it." He turned on his heel and walked back to his office.

As he told his tale over the breakfast both Agnes and Marmaduke looked at each other.

"Sometimes we overlook the obvious." Agnes commented.

Next to her Lieutenant Smalls spread some butter over a large slice of toast. His crutches were propped up beside him on the side of his chair.

Opposite him sat Peter Potts who, despite eating a hearty breakfast was feeling well out of his depth and slightly in awe of the people around him. Agnes smiled down the table at him.

"You did your share Peter, you saved lives."

Peter smiled and speared another sausage.

As usual Marmaduke had started with kedgeree and was licking his lips at the thought of another helping. Next to him Dancing Jack was experimenting with placing three sausages inside a warm bread bun.

"You just might have something there." Remarked the Lieutenant looking on.

At the head of the table, sat next to the Garrison Commander was the Colonel with no name. He had left York the previous day with a set of written orders requiring the assistance of the Scarborough Garrison in the apprehension of a certain ex-Colonel Thomas Reynard. He was pleasantly surprised to find him already under lock and key and his army dispersed.

The two senior military men had spent most of the night locked away in the Commanders office. Eventually they had agreed between them what should and what shouldn't be written in the official reports. No one but the two men knew what had been said and discussed. However the people around the table had been told that, even as they ate, a number of arrests were underway in York. Warrants had been drawn up for the arrest of two City Counsellors, a constable, a lawyer and the City's leading Justice of the Peace. The Colonel assured the group that he had a team of army legal experts drawing up charges of robbery, theft and treason against them all. Only time would tell if they would be successful, but for the guilty the prospect of hanging or a very long time to be spent in the gaol they were so fond of putting people in, was becoming a reality.

As he spoke Agnes couldn't help but notice that the Colonel with no name kept looking across the table at her. She could read his mind without even trying, it wasn't difficult it was written all over his face.

"No!" She thought, "The last thing I want to be is a spy."

She twitched her nose and the idea of recruiting the elderly lady completely slipped from the Colonel with no name's mind. Instead he placed three rashers of bacon between two halves of a warm bread bun.

The Commander harrumphed. He told them that the two military men had agreed that there was no reason to mention any strange meteorological events in their report. Neither would the thorny question of how seventy five troopers could march through a countryside full of spies and informers without being seen. However the skills of Andrew Marks and the bravery of First Lieutenant Peter Potts had been noted and mentioned in despatches, although the question of how the Excise men were persuaded to assist was also glossed over.

Finally the order transferring Sergeant Lewis to the commander of the Colonel with no name had been ratified, along with a note that he should be commended for his enterprise and that receipts and paperwork for the transportation of goods from York to Hull docks should be scrutinised by an army bookkeeper.

This would prove to be a nasty surprise for the Sergeant who currently was heading a group of wagons through the open countryside between York and Hull. His orders stated he should remain there whilst the goods and chattels were loaded on board, along with Mr van der Vlies and to return to York only when he had seen the ship sail out of Hull docks with his own eyes. The Dutch spy and his mission had been compromised. An uncomfortable debrief awaited him in Amsterdam.

It only remained for the question of the note. It was Andrew who asked the question. The Colonel with no name harrumphed. Everyone found themselves wondering whether all senior army officers began their sentences with a harrumph.

"I have no firm evidence, but a suspicion. I have a feeling that it was a member of the York Garrison who had tried to raise the issue with his own Commanding Officer, and that the Commanding Officer was either stupid or a friend of the ex-colonel."

"But why me?" Asked Andrew

The answer sent a chill down his spine.

"Perhaps your fame has travelled further than Scarborough harbour." The Colonel said and he wasn't smiling when he said it.

At the end of the meeting, when all plates and platters were emptied and the tea and coffee had run out, the party began to divide up. Peter Potts shook hands with everyone gave a brisk salute to the senior officers and along with Andrew left to walk back to the old town. They were followed by Marmaduke and Agnes. They both went to where Dancing Jack was sitting. Agnes gave him a look and he stood up. She gave him a huge hug that embarrassed him. Marmaduke shook his hand put an arm on his shoulder and pulled him towards him. He wasn't used to giving hugs but if it was okay with Agnes it was okay with him.

As the farewells were been said the Colonel with no name remained seated at the head of the table. He remained quiet and looked thoughtful. His mind was elsewhere. This plot had failed, but the larger picture still remained. This wasn't a case of private enterprise and now war with Holland seemed inevitable. How many more private armies were being formed up and down the country? How many more Mr van der Vlies had been let loose in the country? He looked up at Dancing Jack as he made his farewells.

"I think I'll be keeping you very busy in the weeks and months to come!" he thought.

The End.

ABOUT THE AUTHOR

Graham Rhodes has over 40 years experience in writing scripts, plays, books, articles, and creative outlines. He has created concepts and scripts for broadcast television, audio-visual presentations, computer games, film & video productions, web sites, audio-tape, interactive laser-disc, CD-ROM, animations, conferences, multi-media presentations and theatres. He has created specialised scripts for major corporate clients such as Coca Cola, British Aerospace, British Rail, The Co-operative Bank, Bass, Yorkshire Water, York City Council, Provident Finance, Yorkshire Forward, among many others. His knowledge of history helped in the creation of heritage based programs seen in museums and visitor centres throughout the country. They include The Merseyside Museum, The Jorvik Viking Centre, The Scottish Museum of Antiquities, & The Bar Convent Museum of Church History.

He has written scripts for two broadcast television documentaries, a Yorkshire Television religious series and a Beatrix Potter Documentary for Chameleon Films and has written three film scripts, The Rebel Buccaneer, William and Harold 1066, and Rescue (A story of the Whitby Lifeboat) all currently looking for an interested party.

His stage plays have performed in small venues and pubs throughout Yorkshire. "Rambling Boy" was staged at Newcastle's Live Theatre in 2003, starring Newcastle musician Martin Stephenson, whilst "Chasing the Hard-Backed, Black Beetle." won the best drama award at the Northern Stage of the All England Theatre Festival and was performed at the Ilkley Literature Festival. Other work has received staged readings at The West Yorkshire Playhouse, been short listed at the Drama Association of Wales, and at the Liverpool Lesbian and Gay Film Festival.

He also wrote dialogue and story lines for THQ, one of America's biggest games companies, for "X-Beyond the Frontier" and "Yager" both winners of European Game of the Year Awards, and wrote the dialogue for Alan Hanson's Football Game (Codemasters) and many others.

.

OTHER BOOKS BY GRAHAM RHODES

"Footprints in the Mud of Time, The Alternative Story of York"

"More Poems about Sex 'n Drugs & Rock 'n Roll & Some Other Stuff

"The York Sketch Book." (a book of his drawings)

"The Jazz Detective."

The Agnes the Witch Series

"A Witch, Her Cat and a Pirate."

"A Witch, Her Cat and the Ship Wreckers."

"A Witch, Her Cat and the Demon Dogs"

Photographic Books

"A Visual History of York." (Book of photographs)

"Leeds Visible History" (A Book of Photographs)

"Harbourside - Scarborough Harbour."
(A book of photographs available via Blurb)

"Lost Bicycles."
(A book of photographs of deserted and lost bicycles available via Blurb)

"Trains of The North Yorkshire Moors."
(A Book of photographs of the engines of the NYMR available via Blurb)

Printed in Great Britain
by Amazon